Armand Cabasson was born in 1970. He is a psychiatrist working in the North of France. *Memory of Flames* is the third in the Quentin Margont series of thrillers set in the Napoleonic Wars. Armand Cabasson is a member of the Souvenir Napoléonien and has used his extensive research to create a vivid portrait of the Napoleonic campaigns.

Isabel Reid studied History and French at Oxford University and has lived in France and Geneva.

Praise for Armand Cabasson

'A vivid portrayal of the Grande Armée . . . worth reading'
Literary Review

'With vivid scenes of battle and military life . . . Cabasson's atmospheric novel makes a splendid war epic . . .'
Sunday Telegraph

'Cabasson skilfully weaves an intriguing mystery into a rich historical background.'
Mail on Sunday

MEMORY OF FLAMES

Also by Armand Cabasson

The Officer's Prey
Wolf Hunt

MEMORY OF FLAMES

ARMAND CABASSON

Translated from the French by Isabel Reid

GALLIC BOOKS
London

First published in France as *La Mémoire des flames*

Copyright © Éditions 10/18, Département d'Univers Poche 2006
English translation copyright © Gallic Books 2009

First published in Great Britain in 2009 by Gallic Books,
134 Lots Road, London SW10 0RJ
This edition published in 2011 by Gallic Books

A CIP record for this book is available from the British Library

ISBN 978-1-906040-84-0

Typeset in Fournier MT by SX Composing DTP, Rayleigh, Essex
Printed and bound by CPI Bookmarque, Croydon, CR0 4TD

2 4 6 8 10 9 7 5 3 1

CHAPTER 1

As he advanced along the corridor an image rose before him. It was as if each of his steps was the ratchet of a cog setting in train other movements. He had prepared his plan with the precision of a watchmaker. That night he was finally starting up the complex mechanism. He heard a noise on the stairs. Someone was coming up. He had orientated himself in the dark by feeling along the wall and had already counted four doors. Now he went back, opened the third door and hid in the bedroom that had previously belonged to the colonel's only daughter. The room had been unoccupied since she had married. The yellowish-orange light of a candle filtered under the door before moving away. A heavy footstep, slow and uneven: Mejun, the oldest of the colonel's servants, a retired sergeant whose leg had been shattered by an Austrian cannonball at the Battle of Marengo. He was on his way to light the fire in the study as he did every evening; but he was half an hour early. The colonel must have hurried through his supper. Leaning against the door, the intruder steadied his nerves – he knew the layout and habits of the house inside out. Mejun went back along the corridor with no inkling that anything was amiss.

The intruder slipped out of the bedroom and finally reached the study, where he hid behind the long velvet curtains. All he had to do now was wait.

But almost immediately he was drawn out of his hiding

place. The hearth. The fire. The flames, like golden tongues licking the air, seemed to call to him. It was as if they recognised him and wanted to show him something. The way they bent and leapt, weaving themselves together and then separating, the dark interstices they created . . . Faces with flaming skin and sooty eyes appeared in the dancing tapestry. Pain contorted their features; their mouths opened wide in silent screams. They disappeared, to be replaced by others, coming towards him. In vain they shouted for help, until their unbearable suffering robbed them of consciousness. The presences were so real . . . the logs crackled and one of them split and burst into a shower of sparks. The frenzy of the victims increased. He saw nothing but the fire. It filled his thoughts; he was reduced to a human husk burning inside. The door creaked, bringing him back to reality, leaving him barely time to hide again.

Footsteps. The exhausted trudge of someone determined to work for a little longer before strength failed. The wood of the desk chair groaned. Only the colonel was allowed to sit there. A pen began to scratch hastily across the paper. The old officer did not notice the intruder coming up behind him.

CHAPTER 2

LIEUTENANT-COLONEL Quentin Margont stood to attention. He was wearing his uniform of the infantry of the line. Although he had been promoted two months ago to field officer of the National Guard of Paris, he had not yet received his new uniform. He had been summoned to the magnificent office in the Tuileries Palace where he now confronted two of the most celebrated figures of the Empire. Unfortunately he disliked the first and was suspicious of the second.

Joseph Bonaparte, elder brother of Napoleon, had accumulated a dizzying array of titles: King of Spain (or, even more impressively King of Spain and the Indies), Lieutenant-General of the Empire, Commander of the Army and the National Guard of Paris. The Emperor had entrusted him with the defence of the capital whilst he himself fought in the north-east of France. It was astonishing to think that in 1812, just before Napoleon had launched his Russian campaign at the head of an army of four hundred thousand men, the Empire had been at its zenith. Yet today, 16 March 1814, less than two years later, he was fighting in France with only seventy thousand soldiers, trying to halt the invasion of three hundred and fifty million Austrians, Hungarians, Russians, Prussians, Swedes, Hanoverians and Bavarians, split into the Army of Bohemia, the Army of Silesia, the Army of the North (part of which operated in Holland, the other part in Belgium). To say nothing of the sixty-five thousand English, Spanish and Portuguese under the Marquess of Wellington, who had just seized Bordeaux and whom Marshal Soult was trying to contain. Or of the Austrians based in Italy, who were fighting Prince Eugène de Beauharnais. How the mighty were fallen! The thought of it made Margont quite dizzy.

Would it still be possible to save the ideals embodied by the Revolution? Perhaps Napoleon would be victorious against all odds. After all he had just pulled off some stupefying victories: against the Russians under Olssufiev at Champaubert on 10 February, and under Sacken at Montmirail on the 11th. On the 12th he had defeated Yorck's Prussians at Château-Thierry, on the 14th the Prussians and the Russians under the indefatigable Blücher at Vauchamps, on the 17th both Wittgenstein's Russians at Mormant and then an Austro-Bavarian force under Wrede at Nangis. And the Allies had been even more astounded when Napoleon routed the Austrians, Hungarians and Wurtembergers under the wily generalissimo Schwarzenberg.

The astonishing thing was that Joseph – whom Margont judged, perhaps a little harshly, to be incompetent – resembled the Emperor, with his round puffy face, brown eyes, high forehead and sparse black hair. He considered himself very intelligent, but he was like a mediocre copy of a painting pretending to be the original.

Charles-Maurice de Talleyrand-Périgord, Prince de Bénévent, known as 'The Limping Devil' was in every way, whether considering his qualities or his faults, the polar opposite. Brilliant, far-sighted, witty, manipulative, charming, affable, obsequious, deceitful and unpredictable, he had the gift of the gab. It was rumoured that he had dared to say, after the cataclysmic outcome of the Russian campaign, 'It's the beginning of the end.' The Emperor suspected him of having betrayed him on several occasions and of now plotting for the return of the Bourbons. Relations between them were so confrontational that Napoleon had referred to him to his face as 'shit in silk stockings'.

But Talleyrand knew how to make himself indispensable. As a dignitary he was always involved in diplomatic manoeuvring, either officially or unofficially. Margont considered him an astute weathervane, adept at anticipating the changes in the wind. But it was not impossible that this devious man did, in his own way, love his country. Perhaps he was sincerely trying to help France and not just working for his own advancement, but he was doing it with the arrogance of someone who believes that only his way will work.

The sixty-year-old, in his powdered wig, was observing Margont with an intensity that belied his relaxed posture and his world-weary air.

'At ease,' barked Joseph. 'Lieutenant-Colonel Margont, we have summoned you because we need you for a secret mission.'

He was studying papers spread out on the desk as he spoke and did not look at Margont, who felt certain that he knew what those papers said about him and longed to seize them and hurl them into the fire that was inadequately heating the vast room.

'His Highness Prince Eugène charged you with a confidential mission during the Russian campaign. That you know. What you perhaps don't know is how he characterised you afterwards. Eulogies and encomiums!'

He brandished a sheet of paper and read from it.

'You are, and I quote, "an admirable man"—'

He had to break off as Talleyrand snorted with laughter. The Prince de Bénévent had long ceased believing that men could be admirable . . .

'You succeeded brilliantly in your mission, et cetera, et cetera, et cetera. In view of all this praise and of your experience, Monsieur de Talleyrand and I consider that you are the man we need.'

Margont was a confirmed republican. At a time when Paris was threatened, he wanted to play his part in protecting the capital, not to be 'the man we need', whatever mission Joseph was about to reveal.

The latter settled back in his chair and stared at Margont.

'Yesterday evening, Colonel Berle was assassinated at home, here in Paris. We have reason to believe that the crime was committed by one or more royalists—'

'But perhaps we're barking up the wrong tree,' Talleyrand suddenly interrupted.

'Berle was a military genius, and although now sixty, he had agreed to be pressed back into service because of the situation we are facing. He was one of the officers I had asked to consider the best ways of defending Paris. We are preparing for the worst, as a precaution, even though, of course, the enemy will never succeed in reaching Paris!'

'But they already have, Your Excellency—' objected Margont.

'What insolence! Yet another revolutionary who believes in freedom of expression! And he dares to call me "Your

Excellency" instead of "Your Majesty"! I am King of Spain!'

Imperial Spain barely existed any more; it was reduced to Barcelona and part of Catalonia. Joseph was the only one to think his crown still meant anything. Margont made an effort to rein himself in. His candour and his love of the witty retort had already got him into trouble in the past. But the terms 'Your Highness' or 'Your Majesty' stuck in his throat. His expression was impassive but inside he was boiling. They should have started reinforcing the capital's defences months ago! But not a single entrenchment had been built and not a single ditch dug! No one had drawn up instructions in case of an attack! Such inaction was criminal. Was Joseph afraid of worrying people? Did he think that ostrich tactics would work? The lieutenant-general paused a moment, hesitating to entrust Margont with the inquiry. Then he launched in.

'The file we have on you, Lieutenant-Colonel, dwells at length on your revolutionary ardour. But so much the better. Nothing like a republican to hunt down a royalist. The victim was tortured. No doubt his tormentor was trying to force information from him. I don't know whether poor Berle talked ... He was writing a proposal for me to transform the mound at Montmartre into an impregnable redoubt guarded by large-calibre cannons to protect the approaches to Paris ... He was also working on plans for entrenchments to guard the residential areas of the city and on what to do about the bridges: how to fortify them, and equip them with landing stages ...'

Margont was shaken. Montmartre, the bridges ... Of course it was necessary to do all that to protect Parisians. But he found

7

it disturbing to think of the places he loved covered with retrenchments and artillery.

'The murderer left behind a royalist emblem. A white rosette with a medallion in the middle decorated with a fleur-de-lis in the shape of an arrowhead crossed with a sword. It was pinned to the colonel's shirt. The murderer also stole some documents. Fortunately, most of them were coded, as I had instructed. Our theory is that a small group of royalists is planning to try to disrupt the defence of Paris.'

Royalist plotters! Everyone was talking about them as if there were tens of thousands of them, when in fact there could have been only a few thousand scattered amongst several different organisations. Since the catastrophic imperial defeats in 1812 and 1813 they had regained credibility and energy. They were stirring up as much trouble as possible, fearing that Napoleon would come to a compromise with the Allies and hold on to his imperial crown. They advocated all-out war against the Emperor and some of them favoured extreme methods: murder and uprising.

'We think the murderer left the emblem to create a climate of fear. Our enemies within are only a handful – they want to appear more numerous and dangerous than they really are. We won't play their game! I demand that every detail of the crime remain secret. Neither you nor the servant who discovered the colonel's body must divulge that aspect of the affair. As for the police, they won't even know about it. It so happens that we have an advantage and you are going to exploit it for us.'

Joseph let the last few words sink in.

'The murderer thinks he can hide in the anonymity of the myriad monarchist organisations: the Knights of the Faith, the Congregation, the Aa, the Societies of the Sacred Heart . . . But he underestimates the reach of our police services. We have an informer in one of their groups, the Swords of the King. Charles de Varencourt is the son of a noble Norman family. A committed royalist, but with an Achilles heel: he's an inveterate gambler, and so he's always short of money. A few weeks ago he began to sell us information.'

Margont, who was an idealist, had no time for that kind of person. 'I see . . .' he said. 'When he runs out of money he betrays his companions.'

'Exactly. We haven't arrested them yet for three reasons. First, in this kind of operation we must avoid haste. The longer we wait the more information we'll gather, and the more members of the group we'll be able to identify. We haven't yet managed to find out 'where the members live. Secondly, the plotters can't agree on what action to take, so they don't represent any immediate danger. And thirdly, thanks to them, we will be able to hook a much larger fish, Count Boris Kevlokine. But more about him later. In the meantime Charles de Varencourt has been providing us with information. Some of the plotters plan to wage a murderous campaign against the key members of the team charged with defending Paris.'

Although Joseph tried to hide it, his voice trembled. He was afraid. Did he think that he might be targeted? Margont abstained from assuring him that he was perfectly safe since his enemies would have no interest in eliminating such a hopeless incompetent. In any case, the security of the top brass was assured. Joseph cleared his throat and tried once more to master himself, which only served to make his anxiety more obvious.

'Colonel Berle was on the list of people they plan to assassinate. I had taken steps to protect the people on the list, discreetly so as not to make it obvious to our enemies that we knew what they were up to. But I have to admit we hadn't seen this coming. Even in the Swords of the King there aren't many royalists willing to commit to murder in this way. Murder as a tactic is under discussion but hasn't been agreed. Some members would like to foment a popular uprising by printing posters; others want to raise arms; and some are just planning to wait until everything is sorted out whilst looking as if they're taking action . . . The group had gathered information about potential victims – names, addresses, places of work, regular routes, interests, friends and family, the number of armed guards each had. Colonel Berle's murderer would have known all these things. At the time of the murder there were fifteen people in the house! There were sentries, his private secretary, two valets, three household servants, the cook, the kitchen maid, the coachman . . . So the man must have got in through a window and made his way through the house, in spite of all the comings and goings, to the study on the second floor. That proves he knew the habits of his victim. And the symbol he left behind is the secret emblem of the Swords of the King.'

Margont thought of Paris. Could a few crimes like that really put the defence of the capital in jeopardy? Unfortunately, yes. And what about Talleyrand? The Prince de Bénévent had not said a word, although he was paying close attention to what Margont and Joseph were saying, and to their demeanour. Margont was curious to hear what he would have to say.

'So, Lieutenant-Colonel, what do you conclude from what I have just told you?' demanded Joseph.

'Nothing, Your Excellency.'

The lieutenant-general raised his eyes to the ceiling, then let his head fall back. He studied the ceiling with its elegant oval stucco and enormous chandelier whose candles barely illuminated the wintry gloom. But his attitude was unconvincing. Joseph seemed to have struck a pose, like an actor trying to intimidate an audience that was not delivering the correct response. He was a bit-part player who had been made a king because he was the Emperor's brother. But instead of becoming a Henry V he was nothing but a mediocre King Lear, responsible in part for his own difficulties. He rose.

'I demand a response, Lieutenant-Colonel.'

'Perhaps one of the members of the group decided unilaterally to put into operation the plan to destabilise the Empire by committing murder. By leaving the emblem, apart from making it clear that the Empire's enemies are here in the heart of Paris, he hoped to draw the other conspirators into the plan whether they liked it or not. He was setting in train a process: the crime would force you to step up your efforts against the Swords of the King, which would alarm them and push them to commit increasingly violent acts.'

Joseph was delighted and the smile he gave Margont was supposed to be a reward.

'That's what we think too.'

'Or else . . .'

The lieutenant-general raised his eyebrows. He had not anticipated an 'or else'.

'We also have to entertain the frightening possibility that our informant is the perpetrator,' continued Margont. 'The crime increases the value of what he has to sell. I'm sure you will have increased his pay after this.'

Talleyrand tapped his cane on the ground – his way of applauding. He began to speak and his voice was full of warmth, making Margont feel he was someone important.

'Monsieur Lieutenant-Colonel Margont, do your utmost to arrest the murderer. Help Paris and defend your ideals!'

Talleyrand's wily reputation was well merited. While Joseph persisted in believing that Margont would obey him simply because he was Joseph I, Talleyrand had immediately hit the nail on the head. His few words were like a finger pointing at the wound in Margont's soul. The coming days would be crucial. If Napoleon were defeated, France would have to endure an occupation by the powers allied against it. And they all had either monarchs or emperors. The gains of the Revolution, the Republic and the Empire would all be crushed like cockroaches under the boots of the incoming monarchs.

'There is a third possibility: that the perpetrator is someone close to the colonel,' Margont stated, 'and he's trying to throw the investigators off the scent.'

Joseph shook his head. 'Our informant was categorical: the Swords of the King have an obsessive fear of spies. They distrust everyone and everything. They protect their secrets. So only the members of their committee know what their emblem is – and Savary, the Minister of Civilian Police, and I.

No, it's clear that one or several of them were responsible for the crime.'

Margont was interested in the way that Joseph disposed the pieces on the chessboard – Napoleon, the Grande Armée much reduced yet still redoubtable, Louis XVIII, the royalists, the numerous pawns formed by the Allied armies, an assassinated colonel, one or more murderers, an untrustworthy spy, Paris . . . But where did he hope to place Margont?

'It seems to me that the civilian police would be more than capable of conducting this inquiry,' he commented circumspectly.

'And they will do, Lieutenant-Colonel. Whilst you – you will become a member of the Swords of the King.'

'What?' yelled Margont. 'You want me dead? I refuse to—'

'You will refuse nothing! The decision is already taken.'

'But I would never succeed! I could never pass myself off as an aristocrat, and as soon as I slipped up, I would be—'

'On the contrary! You are precisely the man for this mission. You spent several years of your childhood in the Abbey of Saint-Guilhem-le-Désert, because your uncle, against your will, wanted you to become a monk. Draw on that experience! The same thing happened to many of the younger sons of the aristocracy, whose fathers wished to leave all their inheritance to their oldest sons. You read and write well, you know Latin . . . You are going to pass yourself off as Chevalier Quentin de Langès. The Langès family did actually exist – we haven't chosen a name at random. They were part of the nobility of Languedoc and were all massacred during the Revolution. You can read their story in the documents we will furnish you with.

So if the Swords of the King send someone to investigate your past, they will find evidence of the family: a name here or there, a castle burnt down with no remains . . . And by the time they've travelled the three hundred leagues there and back . . . You're an officer, are you not? Tens of thousands of aristocrats who emigrated have come back to France to take advantage of the amnesties generously accorded by the Emperor. And a good many of them have chosen military careers. So you won't have many lies to add to your own history to make yourself into a believable royalist, and the less you lie, the more credible you will be.'

'I'll be unmasked and you'll find my body floating in the Seine. You already have an informer . . .'

'We have no faith in Varencourt. We need someone loyal. The affair is of the utmost importance, we can't leave it to a mercenary.'

'When he's lost all your money at the gaming tables, it's my life he'll gamble on! He's already sold his friends; he'll be able to redeem himself with them by denouncing me, then he'll sell you the names of the men who have stabbed me to death!'

Joseph raised his voice, gesticulating and red in the face. He looked like a glass of red wine, shaken and spilt by an angry hand. 'Be quiet! Those are my orders! Do you think anyone here gives a damn what you think? If you say any more I shall have you sent to be trampled by the Cossacks. Silence!'

There was a jumble of paper, books and other objects on the desk, and Joseph pushed it all towards Margont with both hands.

'Here is everything you need: Chevalier Quentin de

Langès's biography, an up-to-date passport stating that you returned to France in 1802 to take advantage of the amnesty of 6 Floréal, year 10, a signet ring with the Langès coat of arms – don't wear it, keep it at home – the key to your lodgings, a little money, fake letters from your former mistress, who lives in Scotland, some works describing Edinburgh, where you lived in destitution, which is what forced you to return, some details of the regiments you served in – the 18th and 84th, which you know well – a list of favourite royalist sayings, a summary of the information supplied to us by Varencourt . . . Learn it all by heart, then destroy anything that would give you away.'

'Your Excellency, why don't you use our own agents? They are accustomed to these kinds of exploits.'

'It's too risky. Paris has become the meeting point for plotters and traitors. I am under no illusions: because of our difficulties, there are imperial officials and soldiers and dignitaries willing to betray us. I am certain that the names of many of our agents have been divulged to our enemies. We need new blood!'

'New blood that you are prepared to spill—'

'That's enough!'

Talleyrand, on the other hand, seemed to approve. He said jovially, 'Good! Repartee! I advise you to behave like that with the Swords of the King. Be proud and arrogant. Adopt an aristocratic superciliousness and you will fit right in!'

'Yes, that's true . . .' Joseph immediately agreed.

Margont tried to see how Talleyrand had pulled the puppet's strings. Joseph continued as if nothing untoward had occurred.

He was so accustomed to his own changes of tack that he no longer noticed them.

'The civilian police will conduct the investigation. They must not know about you – there are leaks on their side as well. They will submit regular reports to me, which I will copy and pass to a trustworthy man whom you will choose to assist you. Whoever that is will read them and then burn them.'

'Perhaps he should eat the ashes . . .' joked Talleyrand.

'Then he will relay to you the contents of the reports. I strongly advise you not to handle the reports yourself! Proceed as I have instructed. Your man should make himself known to my police by presenting himself at 9 Rue de la Fraternité, under the name of "Monsieur Gage". He should ask to speak to Monsieur Natai, who will be the intermediary between you and me, and who will give copies of various documents to your man. You must never meet Monsieur Natai! Apart from that, you may act as you see fit. The only thing that matters is the result. Keep me informed by giving oral reports to your assistant, who should write them out and hand them to Monsieur Natai.'

Talleyrand put both hands on the pommel of his cane. He leant on it yet did not rise. His movements were like his words – it was hard to make out exactly what they meant.

'Everyone in this inquiry must play their part: you will handle the royalists, the civilian police will handle other avenues and it will all be supervised by the personal police of His Majesty Joseph I. That sums up your first mission.'

'Oh, so there's a second one?' Margont demanded crossly.

There was a noticeable heightening of tension. Joseph's

forehead creased in worry and the Prince de Bénévent tightened his grip on his cane. Both waited for the other to speak but, of course, it was Joseph who gave in first.

'I referred just now to a bigger fish, Count Boris Kevlokine. He's the Tsar's main secret agent. For several months he has been hiding here in Paris and we absolutely *must* lay our hands on him.'

'But no violence, no violence!' intervened Talleyrand, emphasising each word by tapping his cane on the parquet.

'That man is spying on us and assessing our forces. He's trying to find out if the French people are ready to fight to the last man for the Emperor or if they would accept another government . . . He runs Russian agents, forges relationships with the royalists, tries to work out whether the return of a king to France would precipitate a second revolution, attempts to guess what the English, Prussian and Austrian spies milling about Paris are up to . . . He's capable, has access to unlimited funds and knows Paris inside out. The Tsar depends on him to help him formulate his policy towards us. And Count Kevlokine thinks that all-out war against us runs the risk of provoking a national uprising. So he's in favour of a compromise. He's a moderate!'

Joseph clasped his hands together as if he were imploring God to come to his aid.

'Do you understand what is at stake, Lieutenant-Colonel? Our hope of victory lies in the dissolution of the coalition! The Saxons, Bavarians and Wurtembergers fear the dominating aspirations of the Prussians. The Prussians hate the Austrians because they also want to control the Germanic people, by reviving the Holy Roman Empire, but under their leadership. The Austrians hate the Russians, whose power rivals theirs. The Russians are in dispute with the Swedes over control of Finland. The Spanish rival the Portuguese, particularly in South America. And most of these countries distrust the English. They have almost all fought against each other over something and they can't agree on anything because of their opposing interests. Hatred for the Emperor and for republican ideals is the only thing holding their ludicrous alliance together. Each camp has its own ideas about the future of France. The Russians want to defeat Emperor Napoleon I but don't know what regime to replace him with; the royalist émigrés will only countenance Louis XVIII; the English also favour the Bourbons; Crown Prince Bernadotte of Sweden agrees that the monarchy should be restored but believes he should be crowned King of France; Austria would like a regency until the Aiglon is old enough to become Napoleon II, but of course it wants the regency to be controlled by Empress Marie-Louise because our emperor's wife is also their emperor's daughter; other camps want there to be a regency but on no account do they want it to be controlled by Marie-Louise . . .'

Joseph paused. He was trying to gather his thoughts, which Talleyrand did for him.

'At the moment the Tsar is our most implacable enemy and we haven't been able to win him over. His only thought is to seek revenge for Austerlitz, for the Battle of Borodino, for the loss of Moscow . . . Unfortunately, each time negotiations start – which they do continually – our envoy, General Caulaincourt, the Minister of Foreign Affairs, is received by all the Allies at the same time. Of course the Allies want to prevent us from profiting from their lack of unity. So it's impossible to meet just the Russians, or just the Austrians. What we need is the ear of the Tsar in private! Once we have that, we know exactly what to say: if the Emperor retains his throne, France will remain a strong country and that will diminish the margin for manoeuvre of Austria, Prussia and England – to the great benefit of Russia! We think this Count Kevlokine has the Tsar's ear. If we arrest him, we can persuade him of the advantages of our approach; then we will free him and he will plead our cause with the Tsar, who will listen carefully because they have been friends since childhood and he holds the count in high esteem. And once Alexander stops thinking obsessively about revenge and starts to consider Russia's long-term interests instead, then we're in business – anything is possible! Since the Emperor's recent victories the negotiations have gained some momentum. England, Austria and Prussia are now willing to consider the possibility that the Emperor will keep his throne, but with France reduced to its 1789 frontiers. We have to seize the moment. The Tsar is now the only one of our enemies who persists in resisting that solution. If we succeed in changing his mind, we will be able to achieve peace through diplomacy.'

Russia, Austria, Sweden, England, Prussia . . . Margont was not accustomed to thinking on such a grand scale. He considered the world in terms of individuals. But he was aware of Talleyrand's reputation and knew that he was an extremely skilled negotiator who really might be able to persuade the Tsar. He was one of the very few people left who could help Napoleon avoid disaster and prevent France from being invaded.

Joseph spoke again, irritated to hear Talleyrand expressing himself clearly and convincingly whilst he himself had rambled and hesitated. It often happened that they would be walking side by side through the labyrinth of the politico-military situation. Then the Prince de Bénévent would let Joseph hurry down a cul-de-sac or fling himself against a closed door before saying mellifluously, 'Let's try this direction . . .' And they would be on their way again. Nevertheless, if his path was leading somewhere, only he knew exactly where.

'Our best investigators are on Kevlokine's trail: policemen, spies, traitors of every hue, diplomats who've rubbed elbows with him . . . All the royalist groups in the capital are trying to make contact with him, seeking financial backing, information or goodness knows what. They also want to convince him to persuade the Tsar of the benefits of a restoration. And Kevlokine, for his part, is keen to meet the leaders of these groups, to help them stir up trouble and to evaluate whether Louis XVIII would be prepared to support the Tsar if he were crowned king. If the Swords of the King do succeed in getting in contact with him, you must tell us immediately! Your priority must be to learn as much as possible about Kevlokine to help us to arrest him.'

'I thought my priority was to investigate Colonel Berle's murder?' Margont fumed.

Joseph closed his eyes briefly. He was truly becoming irritated by this man's refusal to lie down like a doormat in front of him. He would have liked to choose someone else of the 'Yes, Your Majesty' variety. But there wasn't such a person – all he had was Margont.

'Lieutenant-Colonel, you will have to manage both tasks at the same time! All our bloodhounds are looking for Kevlokine, whilst you will concentrate on your inquiry. However, if you come across the Tsar's agent, you must not let him get away! Monsieur le Prince de Bénévent . . .'

Talleyrand nodded. 'I've already met Kevlokine during the period when I was Minister for External Relations and when we were on better terms with the Russians . . . He's forty-five, very stout, with a fleshy face and red lips. His hair is silver and he has pale blue eyes with perpetual circles under them. He's usually pale in contrast to his rosy cheeks – a sign of his fondness for drink – he gesticulates when he speaks . . . He knows how to make himself charming. He speaks with a slight accent, which is particularly noticeable when he rolls his "r"s. He's a brilliant mind. All that should be enough for you to recognise him should you happen to cross his path. Monsieur de Varencourt has never mentioned the name Kevlokine and you mustn't ask him about him. We don't want to run the risk of drawing his attention to Count Kevlokine. Where Monsieur de Varencourt is concerned, we prefer to let him come to us rather than to reveal our exact intentions by asking blundering questions.'

The interview was drawing to its close. Joseph told himself that Margont had had enough stick and now it was time to throw him a carrot.

'What reward will you ask us for when you have successfully fulfilled your mission?'

Margont was surprised by the question but immediately rose to the occasion.

'I would like permission to launch a newspaper, Your Excellency.'

A rebellion! Joseph looked like a parish priest whose penitent had just invoked the devil right there in the church.

Even Talleyrand could not hide his astonishment, but he recovered himself and said, 'Are you sure you wouldn't prefer money, like everyone else? So much less dangerous . . .'

'No, permit me to insist. I would like to become a journalist. I have always loved words, ideas, debate, art and culture . . . The—'

Joseph cut him off. 'It's impossible!'

The Prince de Bénévent added: 'The best newspapers are those with blank pages. That way they don't hurt anyone. Must I remind you of the principles of journalism under the Empire? The Emperor says something, that something becomes fact, and the journalists report it. Now you clearly lack the ability to repeat things like an echo, whilst passing them off as your own thoughts . . .'

Joseph returned to safe territory. 'You will receive five thousand francs! Double, if you enable us to lay our hands on Count Kevlokine.'

'That will allow you to finance your newspaper, Lieutenant-Colonel. In Louisiana or Siam . . . Freedom of expression is a beautiful thing as long as you express what you are told to, or you do it a long way away.'

They were haggling over his reward. Undoubtedly these people spoke a different language from Margont. Joseph took a sheet of paper from his drawer and signed it. He applied his seal and held it out to Margont.

'When one acts a part it is important to be able to prove who one really is . . .'

The letter confirmed Margont's real identity, his rank and the fact that Joseph had given him a confidential mission.

'Lieutenant-Colonel, this document may save your life, or it may get you killed. It's up to you to hide it and to make good use of it. Now you must hurry. I have arranged it so that the civilian police will not be notified until midday. You will just have time to return to your barracks, change into civilian clothes and then go to 10 Rue de Provence – not far from the Madeleine Church – to see the victim's home with your own eyes.'

'Colonel Berle is expecting you . . .' added Talleyrand without any hint of irony.

'Go to the back door, the servants' entrance,' Joseph went on. 'One of the servants, Mejun, will let you in. He's waiting for you. You'll recognise him by his limp. Don't speak to anyone but him. And don't give anything away to the other servants!'

'I'll do my best, Your Excellency. But if the murderer was so well informed it must be because he had spoken to the servants . . .'

'But not Mejun, who has been in the colonel's service for twenty years, first as a soldier, then as his valet. I order you to remove the emblem of the Swords of the King and give it to Mejun. Agents from my personal police force will then collect it from him. And they will be responsible for seeing if it can give us any clues.'

'With all due respect, Your Excellency, I would prefer to keep—'

'The only thing you should prefer is to obey me! My police will deal with the emblem. They are accustomed to that sort of task. If they discover anything at all about it you will be informed via the intermediary you choose to help you in your investigation. The less you are in possession of anything that could compromise you, the safer you will be.'

He paused to enjoy the sight of Margont biting his tongue to stop himself from voicing another objection, then went on: 'That symbol must remain secret. If it was one of the murderer's aims to make sure that the civilian police discovered the emblem, then we must ensure that we don't give him what he wants. Your next task will be to go and meet Charles de Varencourt at the Chez Camille café at Palais-Royal, arcade 54, this evening at nine o'clock. He will be the one to recognise you – we told him you had a scar on your left cheek, as mentioned in your file. We also told him you would be reading *Le Moniteur* and *Le Journal de Paris* both at the same time. He will give you various pieces of information and you will organise with him how you are to be admitted to the Swords of the King.'

'Good luck, Lieutenant-Colonel Margont . . .' said Talleyrand, concluding the audience.

His words had the ring of an epitaph.

CHAPTER 3

O N the streets of Paris people expressed all sorts of different views. Some were so confident of Napoleon's military genius that they were going about their business without a care in the world, amused that others were worried. These people reacted to the rumours with cheerful optimism. The Prussians were on the way? Let them come! The two victories of 14 October 1806, the Emperor's at Jena, and Davout's at Auerstadt, had consigned the sparkling Prussian army to oblivion. Napoleon would be able to annihilate them in a few hours, with the ease of a magician performing a practised trick. The English? Far too few of them! And they were only interested in their own survival. At the first defeat they would leave their Spanish and Portuguese allies to be killed, and run off to their ships bound for the Indies, Canada or Africa! And the Austrians? Name one battle won by the Austrians against us these last fifteen years! What about the Russians? Well, it was true that the Russians were . . . tougher. Invincible in Russia with their partisans and Cossacks behind them. But in battle formation faced with the Grande Armée – that was different! They had been beaten at Austerlitz, Eylau, Friedland and in Moscow. As for the Swedish, well they were just quasi-Russians.

These facile words did not reassure the floods of refugees pouring into Paris from the north-east.

The streets were often clogged with long columns of prisoners. Parisians crowded round to reassure themselves. And they found that the Cossacks on foot, the limping dragoons, the starving Austrians and the Prussians in their tattered uniforms were indeed less frightening than had been imagined. The people offering the prisoners hunks of bread had to withdraw their hands quickly for fear of losing a finger, such was the avidity with which the soldiers fell on the food.

Margont found it difficult to get through the streets. Because he was an officer he was hailed on all sides, or grabbed by the arm. 'Where is the Emperor?' 'Is it true that General Yorck's Prussians have devastated Château-Thierry?' 'What's the news? Tell us the news!' 'Where are your soldiers?' 'How many Austrians are left after all their losses in the last few weeks?' 'It's old Blücher we have to kill, he's the most dangerous, we can manage all the others! . . .' Margont did not reply. He would not even have stopped had the crowd not pressed suffocatingly around him. These people wanted him to appease their fears, but frankly he had his own to deal with. When he considered the situation, he imagined the Empire as a giant ship taking on water and listing increasingly to one side.

He finally reached his barracks in the Palais-Royal quarter. The sentry on duty tried to present arms, but his rifle escaped his grasp and landed in the mud. A soldier only since yesterday – he'll be dead tomorrow, thought Margont bitterly.

'It doesn't matter,' he called. 'The important thing is to learn to fire it properly.'

The National Guard had inherited the old principles of the militia – they had to admit as many civilians as possible to their ranks and they were to help the regular army to defend the country if it was invaded.

In the courtyard, it was bedlam. Piquebois – who had just been made captain – was surrounded by his men and was being harangued by an officer of the Polish *Krakus*. The officer had been fired on by a soldier of the National Guard, who had taken him for a Russian and panicked. Since the Russian campaign, all the powers had taken it into their heads to have their own Cossacks. The King of Prussia now had a squadron of guard Cossacks. And Napoleon wanted to 'cossackise' French farmers by transforming them into impromptu troops operating on the edges of the enemy forces. He also had his Polish *Kraku*s. They resembled their eponymous Russian counterparts, except for their headgear, which was a traditional, scarlet domed hat. Unfortunately, this detail was not sufficient to distinguish them from the Cossacks . . . Margont hastily saluted his friend, who was offering profuse apologies to the Polish officer.

Sergeants shouted commands at the disorderly line of soldiers of the National Guard, in their navy jackets and bicornes with the red, white and blue cockade. Men in civilian dress and clogs were also in the line, men who the day before had been labourers, millers, cobblers, carpenters, wig-makers, coppersmiths, shopkeepers, students, boatmen. The seasoned fighters were somewhere near Reims with the Emperor. All that were left in Paris were thousands of militia, the wounded, soldiers taken on the day before, conscripts who were too young, veterans who were too old but had been pressed back into service, and a few officers to try to whip that rabble into some semblance of an army. Plus the soldiers who were being punished by being transferred here . . . At that thought, Margont ground his teeth.

Since 1798, he had served in the regular army. And now, instead of being with the Grande Armée helping to stave off the abominations of an invasion, he was here! Thanks to his friend Saber and his damnable talent for strategy! Saber had been a lieutenant at the beginning of the Russian campaign and now he was a colonel! Such a promotion, obtained in a very short time, solely on the basis of merit, was not just rare but unheard of. He had been a captain at the start of the German campaign of 1813, during which he had distinguished himself several times. Then he had been a major at the Battle of Dresden and had participated in Marshal Victor's II Corps attack on the Austrian left flank, leading his battalion into a mad charge, holding back hordes of chasseurs deployed as skirmishers, overcoming and routing a series of Austrian units one by one and then pursuing the fleeing troops so that they crashed into the advancing enemy lines, throwing them into disarray. The enemy positions yielded one after another, collapsing like a line of dominoes. At one point Saber found himself at the head of the entire II Army Corps, which had earned him the nickname 'Spearhead'. In January 1814 the miracle he had been waiting for had finally materialised: he was promoted to colonel and had obtained permission from his previous colonel to transfer his friends, if they agreed, to the regiment he was to command. So he had taken Margont, Piquebois and Lefine with him.

Since then, however, he had become puffed up with monstrous pride. He had hardly arrived before he was bombarding his brigade general with advice. He wanted to reorganise everything, to promote some and demote others. The regimental regulations were unsatisfactory because of this, the cavalry were not up to standard because of that, they were not following the right routes, they were not aggressive enough, not warlike enough with the enemy, the food provisions were not worthy of the French army . . . Realising that the general paid no attention to his advice, he declared him 'an arrant incompetent and an imbecile' and addressed himself instead to the general of the division, Duhesme. The latter found himself with a choice: if he kept Saber, all the other colonels and generals would ask to be transferred! It was him or the others . . .

Duhesme got rid of Saber – or rather persuaded him to leave – by dispatching him to the National Guard of Paris, under the pretext that he was very good at training men. Marshal Moncey, who was second in command of the National Guard and was constantly begging for experienced officers to drill his multitude of militiamen, greeted him with open arms. So, in the end, Saber commanded his regiment for only thirty-five days. General Duhesme sent all Saber's friends with him.

Margont wanted to cut quickly through the disorganised crowd, but his appearance caused a stir and soon he was surrounded. News! Everyone wanted news; he just wanted some breathing space.

'I don't have any information!' he declared.

The guardsmen persisted. Yes, yes, of course he had information, he was a . . . Actually, what was he? He had two colonel's epaulettes, but bizarrely the silver braid was mixed with gold. His shako was also weird – there were two stripes at the top, one wide gold one and then one thin silver one. And his plume? In the infantry of the line, a colonel's plume was white, and a major's red. Margont's was half red, half white. He must be a 'half-colonel' or a 'major major'.

'Make way for the lieutenant-colonel!' boomed a captain.

Lieutenant-colonel? What was that then? Where did that fit in?

Margont beckoned over Lefine, who was explaining to the new recruits how to operate the 1777 model of rifle, modified in the year 9, and led him off to see Saber. The National Guard gloomily watched them go. Where was the Emperor? Were they winning the war or were they about to lose?

Colonel Saber was buried in his office. It looked like a library where a bomb had gone off. He was scribbling a letter whilst at the same time dictating two others to his adjutants. Although he was still friends with Margont, Lefine and Piquebois, his attitude towards them had altered since his dazzling promotion. He was so busy criticising those more highly ranked than he that he scarcely had time to look downwards. It was said that Marshal Moncey had almost choked on his coffee when he read the first missive Saber had penned to him. Fortunately for Saber, there was no one available to replace him. At that very moment Saber was writing a tenth letter to the marshal. Margont could not make out the subject but the handwriting spoke for itself: words running into each other through haste, paper tortured by the over-heavy pressure of the pen, a long list of indentations . . .

Saber thrust the paper at one of his officers.

'Add the usual greetings!'

He wouldn't do it himself because he was so furious with the marshal for not following any of his suggestions for the defence of Paris. Lieutenant Dejal conscientiously tried to imitate Saber's writing. He murmured, 'I remain your most trusted and humble servant . . .' Saber yanked the paper from Dejal's hand: his pen involuntarily traced a slanting line and, as if in rage, spat out a blob of black ink onto the light-coloured wood of the desk.

'Have you lost your mind? Are you also going to add that I will come and polish his boots? Make the formula less obsequious! Rewrite the whole letter! Something like "Yours faithfully" – since I am obliged to be loyal. But dress it up a bit; he's so sensitive!'

He pretended to go back to dictating to his other factotum, before finally glancing at Margont and Lefine, who were waiting patiently to attention.

'At ease. What's the bad news?'

Margont managed to get the two adjutant officers to leave. Then he explained, without going into detail, that he had been given a confidential mission and that he would like to use Lefine to help him. Saber was dismayed by Joseph's letter. He wondered why the commander of the army and of the National Guard of Paris had not included him in the secret. How did that august leader hope to succeed in anything important to do with Paris without the help of Colonel Saber? He concluded that Joseph was an incompetent, exactly like Moncey, General Duhesme and all the others, and he felt more alone than ever.

'Very well. I shall obey orders. Since Joseph is for once taking some decisive action, I shall not stand in his way!

Lieutenant-Colonel Margont, Captain Piquebois will replace you in your duties. I will notify him. You may take Sergeant Lefine with you. I hope your mission will be speedily completed. You may go now.'

He then called back his adjutant officers. Margont and Lefine were about to depart when Saber said, 'A secret mission . . . I don't like the sound of that. Look after yourselves.'

For a brief moment it was as if the old Saber had reappeared. Margont and Lefine went off as Saber's voice rang out, seeming to pursue them down the corridor.

'Lieutenant Dejal, have you not finished that letter to Marshal Moncey yet? Lieutenant Malsoux: letter to General Senator Comte Augustin de Lespinasse, commandant of the artillery and mastermind of the National Guard of Paris. "I still have not received the cannons which I am entitled to." That's the basic idea – make it a bit more formal and sign it with the absolute minimum of respect required by military hierarchy, which is much too generous to these charlatans. Lieutenant Dejal, still not finished with the marshal? My poor Dejal, don't let yourself be intimidated by the word "marshal". In fact you should get used to it, because you serve under me and . . .'

Margont and Lefine donned civilian clothes. Margont asked a soldier to take a letter to Medical Officer Jean-Quenin Brémond, who worked at the hospital Hôtel-Dieu, where he treated the French and Allied injured that were flooding into Paris. As he was putting the note in the envelope and sealing it with candle-wax to protect it from prying eyes, he was imagining Jean-Quenin's incredulous expression when he saw the request to join him at Colonel Berle's house, his uniform

by previous experiences of abandoned agreements, preferred not to involve themselves any longer in Napoleon's complicated and ever-changing diplomatic manoeuvres. All that remained of the French Oriental dream – which involved conquering Egypt, forming an alliance with the great Ottoman Empire and pushing back the English in order to seize India – were the archaeological treasures brought back from Egypt, the handsome hookahs that adorned the salons of imperial dignitaries and, for the soldiers who had fought at the foot of the pyramids, the taste of sand in their mouths.

A shutter had been forced open and a pane of glass shattered, so presumably that was how the murderer had entered.

'Is this room much used?' asked Margont.

'No, because it looks over that little lane, and besides, there are three other drawing rooms. It was used only when there were big receptions and so many guests we didn't know where to put them all.'

'And no one heard anything?'

He could immediately see why. To reach this room you had to cross the large drawing room, which had been deserted on the night of the crime, and then take a little corridor closed in by two doors.

Margont leant out of the window. He could not see the main road because of a dogleg in the lane.

'Do the sentries check here?'

'Yes. Every hour they walk round the building. The soldier on duty didn't notice anything. I discovered the colonel at about ten o'clock.'

'Take us to the study, by the route that the murderer must have taken.'

Mejun took them back to the main corridor, and painfully climbed a large stately staircase. On the second floor he led them down a corridor as far as the last door on the left. Margont, who was not used to such vast spaces, felt quite giddy. Lefine, on the other hand, found it exhilarating – it was the kind of house he dreamt of living in.

They had both prepared themselves for the sight of a murdered man. But nothing could have prepared them for what they actually saw. Berle had been mutilated with fire. His features had been burnt off, leaving a smooth, indefinable plane, red in places and black in others. The remains of a gag were still protruding from the mouth. The man's hands were bound behind his back, with rope.

'Are you certain this is Colonel Berle?' asked Margont.

Mejun's face lit up and Margont was annoyed with himself for having accidentally given the man false hope. He could see the servant's excitement at the thought that it was a plot: the colonel had been kidnapped and this unrecognisable body had been left here to cover up the kidnapping. Yet the old man did not really believe that. He freed a shirt-tail from the victim's trousers, his fingers moving slowly as if numbed by frost, and revealed a scar across the victim's left thigh. His answer stuck in his throat and he merely nodded.

'Have any documents been taken?' pursued Margont.

'Yes. The study was always cluttered with papers.'

Not a sheet of paper remained, although on the bookshelves piles of ill-assorted works were stacked on top of the lined-up books. Drawers had been pulled out, emptied and left open. Alas, the colonel had been a taciturn man and Mejun was not able to say what had disappeared.

The emblem of the Swords of the King had been pinned to the dead man's shirt. Caught in a ray of sunshine, the white material gleamed, like the glittering snowy summit of a mountain seen in the distance. Margont knelt down to remove the emblem and give it to Mejun, who accepted it, since those were his orders. But like Margont and Lefine, he did not think it right that an important clue was being hidden from the police. It appeared that the investigation was setting off in a devious manner. Margont tried not to mind about that. His two strongest qualities were also his worst faults. He was philanthropic and idealistic, as befitted a child of the Revolution – possibly, in its origins, one of the most utopian and naïve periods in the history of humanity. Margont tended to see everything as black or white, and here he was, plunged by Joseph and Talleyrand into a world of infinite shades of grey.

He sent the servant to watch for the arrival of the medical officer, then looked around the room. The bookshelves contained travel writing, military memoirs, works by Vauban, plays by Molière. Each of these books reflected part of the personality of their owner. Berle must have sat laughing at the adventures of poor Don Quixote, wondering if perhaps he didn't share some of his characteristics himself; he must have thought about those wild boars with human heads supposedly observed in this or that exotic country and depicted in Ambroise Paré's *Des monstres et prodiges*; perhaps he had dreamt of having an amorous encounter as he read Marivaux. Suddenly the body became the person, Berle, and that made it harder to bear the idea that he had been murdered.

'I wonder if he talked . . .' said Lefine.

'No,' replied Margont.

'How can you be sure?'

'Because he was already dead when he was burnt.' He indicated Berle's wrists. 'Look at where his wrists were tied. The skin is intact. If that man had still been alive while his face was being burnt, he would have tried to free himself, he would have struggled. His wrists would have been bruised and bloody.'

Lefine recoiled instinctively. Insanity frightened him more than barbarity.

'We must be dealing with a madman . . .'

'Possibly.'

Jean-Quenin Brémond arrived at that moment, in a hurry as usual. He removed his greatcoat, revealing his medical officer's uniform, which was of a lighter blue than the standard dark blue of the French army. His movements were hurried and nervous in everyday life but correspondingly slow and precise when he was practising medicine or teaching. So his life seemed to pass either too quickly or too slowly. Only a few days ago a colleague from the Army Medical Service had reprimanded him for spending too long tending to the Russian prisoners. Since then, as a protest, Jean-Quenin had worn a Russian medal given to him by a hussar from Elisabethgrad whose life he had saved. He was regularly at loggerheads with the military authorities, much like Margont and Lefine. And as his rages were famous, his aides, sentries and patients pretended not to notice the little blue ribbon with the strange silver medal.

Mejun appeared a little after Jean-Quenin. Margont asked him to leave them on their own, then explained to his friend what he wanted from him without telling him his first conclusions. The medical officer crouched down beside the victim. With his seventeen years' service in an army constantly at war, he was not shocked by what he saw. Recently, whatever he was confronted with, he had already seen worse. Always.

'This person was killed by a single knife blow straight to the heart. The attack was very precise and the murderer was certain that it was going to be fatal because he only struck once.'

He stood up to study the desk, then crouched down again and searched in his case for tweezers, which he plunged into the wound.

'The victim was sitting at the desk. His assailant came up behind him and must have put his hand over his mouth whilst stabbing him with his right hand. Yes, the direction of the wound means that the blow was delivered from behind by someone right-handed. I conclude therefore that the assassin is very familiar with the human body and its pressure points. Probably a doctor, a butcher or a battle-hardened soldier. I realise that doesn't narrow the field down much. The blood spattered the desk, then a little dripped onto the victim's clothes and the floor when the body was moved. But the heart stopped beating almost immediately, which explains why there is relatively little blood.'

He manipulated the corpse delicately with precise movements, undid the buttons, and struggled against rigor mortis to prise open the teeth.

'Astonishing. The man was killed first, then burnt! Look

carefully at his face – no blistering! Had the man been alive when he was burnt you would have seen blisters filled with serum, a liquid containing albumin, surrounded by red areas. You would also have seen damage to the oral cavity. He would have been obliged to breathe and so would have inhaled burning-hot air and flames. His tongue and pharynx would have been necrosed and would have suffered desquamation, that is, the superficial layers of mucous membrane would have come off in little strips, in squamas. And there would have been little ulcerations on the back of the throat. The mucous membrane on the epiglottis would have been red and engorged. You would have seen soot marks and a pinkish froth in the trachea and the gag would not have prevented that. A living victim would have breathed through his nose and that would have had the same effect as breathing through the mouth. As for the gag itself, of course it should have shown bite-marks. I've seen plenty of burns on the battlefield and in hospitals, and I can say with certainty: these burns were inflicted after death.'

'That's necromancy!' exclaimed Lefine.

'Hmm . . . Necromancy is consulting the dead to get them to give up their secrets. Yes, I suppose you could call it that! I'm a necromancing doctor. But that's thanks to my friend Quentin and his investigations.'

'I'm sorry, Jean-Quenin,' replied Margont.

'Not at all! Without you life would be monotonous . . .'

It was always hard to tell if he was being serious or sarcastic.

'Have you ever come across a crime where the murderer burns his victim after killing him?' Margont asked him.

'Never.'

'Neither have I. We'll have to find out whether the murderer was acting out of vengeance, or whether he was covering his tracks, or whether the fire had some special significance for him. Look around the room. There is a trail of blood from the fireplace to the desk, near where the body was found. At first sight it looks as if the murderer overcame the victim, bound and gagged him, dragged him over to the fire to burn him, and then, for some reason, took him back to the desk. The blood would have dripped in a trail as the body was dragged from the fireplace to the desk. But, in fact, according to what you've just told us, the blood flowed as the murderer dragged the colonel's body *to* the fireplace. Therefore, the murderer went to the trouble of taking the remains over to the desk to mask the fact that he had already killed the victim before burning him.'

Mejun erupted into the room, panic-stricken.

'The police are coming! You have to leave at once!'

'Investigators fleeing the police?' asked Jean-Quenin, astonished.

Margont was already dragging him by the arm towards the door.

'Oh, that's not the only paradox about this case, I can assure you . . .'

CHAPTER 5

THEY escaped by the back door and hurried away, plunging into the side streets to avoid the crowds, and talking in low voices. They did not want to be taken for royalist or republican plotters, or partisans of the Allies . . . Jean-Quenin left them, after insisting that they call on him again should the need arise.

Margont was having difficulty gathering his thoughts. Ideas were jumbled in his head, refusing to come together to form a coherent theory.

'We have to separate what the murderer wanted us to find from what he wanted to hide. He didn't want us to know the real reasons for his burning his victim. And what are we to make of the royalist emblem and those documents that were taken? Are they red herrings and the burns the real clue? Or the opposite? Or perhaps they're all linked? We're left with two leads: the royalist emblem, and the fire.'

'I find both of them rather worrying,' commented Lefine.

'Who is supposed to react to the symbol? And the burns?'

'We are! We're the ones trapped in this investigation!'

'Yes, but apart from us?'

Margont had been a bit slow in grasping what Lefine had meant. 'Fernand, I'm sorry to involve you once again in a complicated case, but I absolutely depend on you.'

'That's all right then. I knew that, but it's always good to hear it said. You can count on me! What use are friends if they don't help each other out? But if my services are effectively helping the defence of Paris – that's what all this seems to be about – I would very much like to be properly rewarded.'

'Meaning?'

'I want to be restored to the rank of sergeant-major!'

It was a long story. Throughout the last years, losses had been so heavy that veterans, as distinct from the masses of inexperienced conscripts, had benefited from numerous promotions. Since 1812, Margont had gone from captain to lieutenant-colonel, Piquebois from lieutenant to captain, Saber from lieutenant to colonel. Only Jean-Quenin Brémond and Lefine had kept their ranks. In the medical officer's case it was a reflection of the lack of respect accorded to the health services of the army. Priority and favours went to combatants. But as for Lefine, he had only himself to blame for his lack of promotion. In 1813 he had effectively been promoted to sergeant-major and the need for officers was so great that he was about to become no less than second lieutenant . . . when his major discovered that he was involved in a fraud.

He would present a requisition order for provisions for ten soldiers to a farmer or merchant. But afterwards he would falsify the document, and the requisitioner, who was in cahoots with him, would have him reimbursed by the army for an amount corresponding to food for twenty men. The practice was common. And besides, since the disaster in Russia, the soldiers were practically never paid! In fact, Lefine, like tens of thousands of other soldiers, was sliding gradually into poverty and he had used the money he had diverted in that way to feed and clothe himself. However, the major wanted to have him shot to make an example of him! The affair rapidly became confused. There was abundant proof of his guilt, but because he was facing a death sentence, Lefine maintained that he was innocent. As he had nothing more to lose he used all his devious talents, lying with such aplomb that the élite police, called in by the court martial, were completely taken in. The police were not in a hurry to convict Lefine since they did not understand why a man should be executed for so little, especially at a time when each soldier counted. Margont, Saber and Piquebois, of course, became involved and their respective ranks carried a lot of weight. But the major persisted, relaunching a trial that would have succeeded had it not been interrupted. Inadvertently, Saber had the last word by being transferred against his will to the National Guard and taking his friends with him. Lefine was the only one to dance with joy on hearing the news. However, the affair robbed him of the rank of sergeant-major and raised the prospect of him remaining sergeant *ad vitam aeternum*.

'I was the victim of a regrettable judicial error—' he began.

'All right! Don't bring up that business again. I promise you that if I succeed, I will not forget to ask Joseph personally for a promotion for you.'

'Thank you! So what do we do now?'

'We go and look together at the documents Joseph gave me. Then I will keep the ones I need and you will take the ones from the police and go and find an inn where you will live during this investigation. You're supposed to be poor, like me, so don't go and set yourself up in one of the best addresses in Paris at Joseph's expense. The lodgings they've found me are in

Faubourg Saint-Marcel at 9 Rue du Pique. I would like you to be nearby. This evening I'll go and meet Charles de Varencourt, whom I mentioned to you. I'm very suspicious of him. I'll tell you where and when I'm meeting him. You will also be there and you will spy on us from a distance without getting yourself noticed. You won't be able to overhear our conversation, but you should observe his expressions and gestures. Tell me later what you think of him. Also, try to spot if anyone is watching us. Maybe the Swords of the King suspect something and are having him followed, or maybe Varencourt will have had the same idea as I and will come with an accomplice . . . Afterwards you should follow him and then meet me at Pont d'Iéna, where you can report back to me.'

'Now that you're mingling with people who see plots everywhere, suddenly you've begun to think the same way!'

CHAPTER 6

MARGONT went to Palais-Royal, a district full of restaurants, cafés, sweet shops, gambling houses, money-lenders, theatres and perfumeries. Prostitutes propositioned passers-by under the arcades, trying to drag them up to the lofts above.

In Chez Camille, wine, beer, cider, tea, coffee and waffles were served. You could also ask an errand boy to fetch you a *bavaroise* from the famous Café Corraza; that way you could enjoy it at ease, since it was always packed over there. Margont, ensconced at a table, simultaneously skimmed *Le Moniteur* and *Le Journal de Paris*. He hoped to flush out fragments of truth by comparing the two papers. Alas, the first lied because it was the mouthpiece of the Empire, whilst the latter dared not say anything because it was not. Every time irritation gripped Margont, he gulped a mouthful of coffee. How did they dare to print such things? He imagined the progression of the words, which started out revealing the truth, then submitted to the censorship of the editor, the cuts and rewritings imposed by the owner of the newspaper, and those demanded by the censors and the Ministry of Civilian Police. He imagined lines being crossed out, hands tearing up entire pages, phrases being reworked to produce a text that was a shadow of its original self, with no subtlety, a Manichaean narrative. More passages crossed out. French losses melting away on the paper; Russians and Prussians perishing by the thousand under the pen blows of propaganda. Everything was fine! Better and better, in fact!

'Yet I'm not allowed to launch my newspaper!' muttered Margont.

But, of course, his determination to tell the truth would never get past the censors, and what sort of paper would that have made?

A man sat down at his table.

'Monsieur Langès!' he declared amiably. Since they were in public he had not used Langès's aristocratic title.

'Citizen Varencourt!'

Varencourt was enjoying the fake reunion with this friend who was not actually a friend and who was using an assumed name. Margont, on the other hand, was ill at ease. But the role he was playing, the dungeon in which he was trapped, was also his protection. So he immersed himself in his assumed character and smiled to encourage his new accomplice.

'It's a pleasure to see you, Charles!'

Varencourt served himself a glass of wine. He was dressed shabbily in ill-cut, drab clothes. But his self-assurance gave him presence; he seemed to have nothing to fear. He was a few years older than Margont, so about forty, with attentive blue eyes.

Margont took a look around the room. In spite of the fact that the café was crowded he had been able to sit a little apart. They would not be overheard so long as they spoke in low voices. He could not see Lefine but he was sure to be somewhere about. Margont never ceased to be amazed at his friend's talents.

Varencourt examined his glass by the light of the candle. The wine was improbably dark. He sniffed it curiously.

'I would say they've cut it with extract of logwood, bilberries and eau-de-vie. And perhaps even ink . . .'

He drank and grimaced as if an unseen hand was strangling him.

'Dreadful. So, you're the new investigator. I was worried they would send me another stooge. Monsieur Natai, the person I give my information to, who pays me, is obviously just a second-rate little official, an intermediary. He came to my lodgings this afternoon – which he promised he would never do! – and explained that I was to continue to pass on what I learnt to him, but that I would also have to meet someone else today, Chevalier Langès. To be honest, until now the authorities have not taken the Swords of the King seriously and have been concentrating their efforts on the Knights of the Faith and the mysterious Congregation. How wrong they were. Now that Colonel Berle has been assassinated, they send you. It's funny – you're not what I imagined at all. You don't look like one of those devious investigators from the imperial secret police.'

Margont said nothing.

'I've already given the police a huge amount of information,' Varencourt went on. 'So what else do you want to know?'

'Why didn't you warn them that Colonel Berle was about to be murdered?'

'I didn't know! It was Monsieur Natai who told me about his death.'

'Do you take me for an idiot?'

'If you were an idiot, they wouldn't have sent you. There are roughly thirty people in our organisation, perhaps more, and it is run by a committee with five members: Louis de Leaume, Honoré de Nolant, Jean-Baptiste de Châtel, Catherine de Saltonges and me. Although we have a leader, Vicomte de Leaume, all plans must be approved by a majority of the committee. Then they're explained to the other members, who have to carry them out. It was Baron de Nolant who proposed assassinating the people responsible for the defence of Paris. His plan was debated at length, then we voted and it was blackballed.'

'What does that mean, "blackballed"?'

Varencourt was astonished at that.

'You're not very up to date, are you? Did they not pass on all the information I gave Monsieur Natai? Louis de Leaume fled to London during the revolutionary years. Over there it's common practice for gentlemen to belong to several clubs. What kind of clubs? Well, they all have their own themes: philosophy, astronomy, insects, tobacco, the exploration of Africa, or the Indies . . . Actually, a nobleman has to be a member of a club to avoid ridicule. Because if you don't belong to a club, you become the laughing stock of the London nobility. So you put forward your application and the members vote on it. Each member puts a ball in a bag. If there is a majority of white balls: *welcome to the club*; if there are more black, you're blackballed, *bye-bye*. It's the last word in chic for a French aristocrat to blackball. It signifies that you are pure, an ultra, that you would rather flee to England than accept revolutionary France. So when our committee takes decisions we use the English voting system. It has the advantage of being secret. According to Vicomte de Leaume, that reduces tensions within the group. And the plan to launch a series of assassinations was blackballed – two white balls, three black.'

'And who voted in favour of the plan?'

'Honoré de Nolant, since he was the one who proposed it. I don't know who the other one was.'

'Apart from you five, did any of the other members know about the plan?'

'Not as far as I am aware, no. That's not how we work. The committee does not inform the ordinary members of the projects it's discussing, to limit the risk of leaks. Our leader is a cautious man. I've already explained all this to Monsieur Natai . . .'

'Tell me about your emblem, the lily and the sword.'

'It's the heraldic interpretation of the name of our organisation. Initially, our emblem was the traditional fleur-de-lis. Then Vicomte de Leaume decided to replace it with a fleur-de-lis in the shape of a spear. More warlike . . .'

'I've seen one. A cockade with a medallion and crossed arms.'

'You have? Where did you see it?'

Varencourt seemed surprised. But on the other hand, he was a gambler. He must be used to dissembling. As Margont did not reply, he explained, 'Vicomte de Leaume had some copies made and distributed them to the members of the committee.'

'I want you to give me one.'

'I don't have any. I didn't accept them. At the time, I was not acting as a police informer and I didn't want to have anything like that about me.'

Was Varencourt telling the truth? Margont hid his irritation.

He was finding it very hard to find any chink in Varencourt's armour. He would be able to begin to check what the man was telling him once he had been admitted to the group. Perhaps then he would find some hold over him.

Meanwhile Varencourt was saying suavely, 'At the moment, for reasons of security, the symbol is known only to the members of the committee. And to the people I have passed it on to, namely the personal police of Joseph Bonaparte, I mean, Joseph I of Spain. And I have also explained *that* to Monsieur Natai . . .'

'I haven't had time yet to study all the information you've passed on.'

Varencourt was worried.

'I see . . . Then why are we seeing each other now? What was the hurry for the meeting?'

'Well . . . because you have to get me admitted to the Swords of the King . . .'

Varencourt's eyes widened and he almost choked. The news was as hard to swallow as the doctored wine.

'You're joking!'

'No! Don't tell me you weren't informed?'

'Informed of what?'

They both mentally cursed Joseph and Talleyrand.

'You're not serious, are you?' demanded Varencourt. 'I refuse to lead you into the lion's mouth! You will be unmasked and we will both be killed.'

'My dear Charles, you refuse to take me and I refuse to go. The problem is that, in spite of that, it will happen. I have no choice and neither do you. These are the orders of our two friends, to whom we owe the pleasure of this enjoyable meeting.'

'We have to change their minds! They have no idea. Why do they need you to . . . when they already have me . . . ? Oh, I see, they don't trust me. It's just that, you see, it's virtually impossible to become a member . . .'

'You're going to have to get me in right at the top, on the committee.'

'Damn it, listen to yourself! It's impossible. You would have had to be a member for at least two months. They would have had to investigate you and you would have had to prove your loyalty.'

'I don't doubt it. I've already thought of a way round that. If I were indispensable, they would accept me immediately, and at the highest level, what's more.'

'I have to admit, I like your thinking. Do you play cards?'

'No! And now's not the time to talk about that sort of thing.'

'It's always time for gaming! Life's a game. At least that's the way I take it – it's easier to bear like that. But I am not interested in raising the stakes, and I must make clear to you that I refuse to play the game you propose.'

'Our two powerful friends will not accept that. If you refuse, they will put the police onto you. And they've already told me they'll feed me to the Cossacks . . .'

Varencourt was furious. But he continued to act like a chessboard king, proud and immobile as the opposing queen slipped forward to checkmate him.

'Right. I understand. But it will be very expensive,' he warned. 'I'm listening. What's your plan?'

'I've looked through some of the information you've provided, although only very quickly, and I see that another idea of the Swords of the King is to stir up the Parisians to support them, or at least to incite them not to take up arms if Paris is threatened. I suppose those cockades sporting your emblem are meant to act as a sign of recognition among your soldiers. But how do you plan to reach thousands of people? And how can you do that without the risk of being shot? You'll have to have bulletins and posters, but all the printing presses are under surveillance. That's how I can make myself indispensable. You can pass me off as a printer! I print theatre programmes, and posters for shows. Officially that's how I earn my living. But actually I'm only interested in printing because I've always had the idea of supporting the royalist cause using the most effective weapon in the world: words!'

'That's too perfect to be true . . .'

'That's why it will work! Because it's so perfect your friends will want to believe it!'

'You really should play cards.'

'I do have some notion of the printing profession. I've always dreamt of launching a newspaper . . . a real one,' he added, casting a rueful glance at the papers he had put on the table. 'How does admission to the heart of this group work?'

'Good question! That depends if they trust you or not. They will ask you questions: "Why do you want to join us?" "Who can vouch for you?" When I joined, they made me wait for two months while they investigated me. The investigation was satisfactory so my admission was only a formality. But the risk with trying to rush things is that they will be more suspicious.'

'Stop trying to make me change my mind; you won't succeed. You're the one who's going to recommend me. When someone wants to join, they must ask the person who is to nominate them questions about the group – who else is a member? What action has been taken?'

'We're not allowed to say anything, except that we're a royalist group who advocates action! We are the Swords of the King. Our leader is very strict about it: we're not to say anything else. Because if we had revealed more than that to those trying to join us, our group would have been crushed long ago. The imperial police are *very* efficient.'

'Are there any other ways you want to put me off?'

Varencourt shook his head. He wore a strange expression, halfway between anger and interest. He seemed to consider their situation like a roll of the dice from which he could either gain an enormous amount or lose everything.

'Our fates are linked but I know nothing about you, Monsieur Langès. Are you a policeman? No, you don't look like one. Policemen love order and discipline, which is not generally what journalists want. Are you a soldier?'

'These days, everyone is a soldier.'

'Are you an officer?'

'Ah . . . you'll have to find out.'

'At least tell me your real Christian name.'

'Quentin. Quentin de Langès.'

'You still don't trust me and yet your life depends now on my talents as a liar.'

Margont was nervous. 'And vice versa, Charles. Concentrate on convincing the Swords of the King to agree to meet me.'

He nodded towards the copy of *Le Journal de Paris*. 'Keep it. I've hidden the address where I can be contacted and a few details about me. You're supposed to know me, so learn the notes by heart and then destroy them. You'll see that we've met several times at various gaming tables in Palais-Royal. I've lost against you, owe you money and have signed an acknowledgement of debt. We have a meeting to discuss this and that's how we discover our common interest – the royalist cause. Happy reading! I'll wait for you to contact me so that you can introduce me to your friends. But don't leave it too long . . .'

CHAPTER 7

MARGONT left the café and wandered about the streets, hoping to throw off any spies that Varencourt, the Swords of the King or Joseph might have set on him. He couldn't be too careful. But the more he complicated his route, the more he had the feeling he was being followed. He started to see figures in every dark recess. At this rate suspicion would soon drive him mad.

He finally made it to Pont d'Iéna. The bridge had been built by order of Napoleon, who named it after one of his stunning victories against the Prussians in 1806. Old Marshal Blücher, who had commanded the Prussians troops, told anyone who would listen that as soon as he had taken Paris he would blow it up.

Margont pulled his collar up against the cold and moved away from the oil lamps like a wary insect fleeing the light. He went over to the greyish green waters of the Seine. A few weeks ago enemy shakos had suddenly appeared in the water, carried along by the current. Passers-by would stop, incredulous at the sight of the thousands of hats covering the surface and floating dreamily past. A few days after the appearance of the shakos, Parisians learnt that after Napoleon's defeat of the Austrians, Hungarians and Wurtembergers at Montereau, he had ordered his soldiers to fling the shakos of the dead and the prisoners into the Yonne. He thought that when the people of Paris saw them floating in the Seine, they would understand that a great victory had been won. But it would take much more than that to save France, and Margont imagined the Seine disappearing abruptly under a ground swell of three hundred and fifty thousand shakos.

He jumped when Lefine joined him. 'Were you there when I met him?' Margont immediately asked.

'Of course, as agreed.'

'Where were you hiding?'

'Here and there. I was mingling with the customers. I don't like the look of that Varencourt. He was too much at ease. Here we are with the world collapsing around us and he seemed not to have a care in the world. I almost envy him . . . In any case, he didn't spot me. And I didn't see anyone watching you furtively. At one point you made him very angry, and that was definitely genuine!'

'Joseph had "forgotten" to tell him that he would have to help me become a member of the Swords of the King. Where did he go after he left me?'

'Rue Saint-Denis, his personal address, according to the file we have on him. But he's very difficult to follow. He's always on his guard. What are you going to do now?'

'Go home. To my new home. And you're going to go and meet Monsieur Natai to tell him two things. That you're the man I've chosen to help me – you'll have to tell him where you can be contacted. Secondly, tell him that I need access to a printing works by tomorrow evening! He'll pass all that on to Joseph.'

Margont told Lefine how to find Monsieur Natai, explained

his idea and hurried on, not giving his friend any chance to comment. 'Next, get someone to spy on Charles de Varencourt. I'm sure you'll be able to find someone. Don't tell him anything, just pay him to watch our man. Joseph will reimburse you through Monsieur Natai. Do the same for all the members of the committee – their addresses are in the police reports. I will spend my time fine-tuning my act while I wait for Varencourt to give me the sign. If you need me, you know where I'll be. Have you had time to find lodgings?'

'Auberge Arcole, practically on your doorstep. The street doesn't even have a name, but it's on the banks of the Bièvre, between two tanneries. Monsieur Fernand Lami. What am I to Chevalier Quentin de Langès?'

'A soldier who served under me in the 84th. You support the King because you think that will earn you money and because you've had enough of the war.'

'A role *almost* tailor-made for me! I'll go and find Monsieur Natai tomorrow morning and see what reports he has for me. Then I'll be able to tell you all about them in the evening.'

'No. I don't think you should do that. I'm not supposed to know the members of the organisation. If you tell me a lot about them now, I'm worried I'll give myself away when I meet them.'

'I don't agree! The more you know about them, the better you'll be able to adapt your conversation and tell them what they want to hear, if they're going to accept you as one of theirs.'

'The first meeting with them will be fraught with difficulty. The strain of it might make me reveal something written in the police reports . . .'

'You'll just have to be careful! And if you do ever make a mistake, you can always say that Charles de Varencourt told you about them.'

'No. That's against their rules and you can't assume they're stupid. The Revolution tried to paint the aristocracy as imbeciles and degenerates. But it never does to underestimate your enemies. No, I've made my decision. My strategy is going to be to get into the skin of my character as much as possible, and Chevalier Quentin de Langès doesn't know much about them. So it must be the same for Lieutenant-Colonel Margont. You mustn't talk to me about them until after I've met them for the first time. That leaves you enough time to study as many police reports as possible. Afterwards, in my other meetings with them, if I mention something I'm not supposed to know, then I'll be able to say that I researched them after I had been admitted to the group. That's exactly what Chevalier de Langès would do.'

'Well . . . all right, perhaps you're right. You decide – it's you who has to be Quentin de Langès . . .'

Rue du Pique looked unprepossessing. It was dirty, and the smell! The emanations from the tanneries, hide-makers and dye works mingled with the stink of mounds of rubbish . . . Number 9, which had been converted into an inn, was so dilapidated it looked as if it might crumble to the ground at any minute. Margont presented himself to the owner as Monsieur Langès and was given the key to a room under the eaves.

He studied the documents Joseph had given him. To help

him memorise the events of his life, he imagined them unfolding before his eyes. When he was capable of reciting the life of Quentin de Langès, he burnt anything compromising and got rid of the ashes.

The room had been suitably furnished before his arrival to suit his new persona. But he spent a little time rearranging things so that they better suited his own preferences. He chased away the cockroaches that scuttled under the floorboards at the approach of his candle, leafed through the books and scribbled notes in some of them, went to the window and hailed a water-carrier, who brought him up a bucket filled with water from the Seine.He ground his teeth when he opened the trunk. All the clothes were brand spanking new! He decided to throw them away and go to a second-hand clothes shop the next day. He would also buy a Bible. He thought about his situation, he was worried . . . He felt like a ferret about to be released into an earth filled with foxes and expected to pass himself off as one of them.

CHAPTER 8

A FTER three days spent trying to perfect his royalist persona
and avoid being observed, Margont was no longer quite
himself. He was so successful in his new role that little by little
he was starting to lose his bearings.

He went to 'his' printing works, Imperial Press (previously
called Crown Press, but hastily renamed during the Revolution),
just beside the Botanical Gardens. Joseph and Talleyrand had
arranged everything very cleverly. Above the modest doorway,
a metal sign with a representation of a newspaper indicated what
the premises were. You went down a few steps to reach a large
room furnished with a classic printing press with twin wooden
frames, a 'one movement' Didot and Anisson press, a Nicholson
cylinder press – the last word in printing, a dream! – and
various broken presses, which were there merely to furnish
parts for those that functioned.

The manager, Mathurin Jelent, was the only one to know the
truth about Margont. He had been secretly passing on
information about the printing press to the imperial authorities
for years, denouncing customers who wanted to print illicit
documents: anti-government pamphlets, unauthorised newspapers, unofficial proclamations . . . He had also undertaken to
act as a link between Joseph and Margont, who wouldn't then
have to rely solely on Lefine and Natai. Conveniently, the
owner of the print works lived in Lyons and never visited,

contenting himself with drinking the profits away. This allowed Jelent to introduce Margont as a new associate. Margont told the employees – two typesetters and two printers – that he had come in person because he hoped to make money out of the current situation.

Margont helped lay out the pages, handling the characters and getting his fingers covered in ink. He familiarised himself with printing and learnt about all the parts of the process: choosing the paper and the typography, setting the type by pushing the characters into the slots of the coffin, inking the formes, placing the virgin sheets between the frisket and the tympan, folding and feeding the whole thing under the plate of the press, turning the handle to activate the screw . . .

He felt like a matryoshka, one of those Russian dolls he had seen in Moscow. On the outside was Monsieur de Langès, a man interested only in turning a profit. Inside there was the royalist secretly preparing posters calling Parisians to sedition. And inside that was Quentin Margont, his true self, who had to be kept well hidden.

Nevertheless he derived real pleasure from printing. He turned out invitations, the new menu for the Beauvilliers restaurant in the Palais-Royal arcades, and proclamations from the Imperial Government. He imagined he was working on the newspaper he had wanted to start for so many years. Instead of printing 'eel pie', 'turbot stuffed with rose' (new recipes and unusual flavours were all the rage) or 'English green beans', he imagined the letters spelling out headlines such as 'What has become of Liberty?' 'Will the war ever be over?' . . . The words danced in front of his eyes and the lead characters relaid themselves in his mind, printing his dreams.

When he was out and about he took care to throw possible spies off the scent. He forced himself to look with contempt at soldiers, at the Colonne de la Grande Armée in Place Vendôme and at the Arc de Triomphe, which was already very impressive, even though it was still only half its projected height of fifty metres. He ground his teeth when he had to go down Rue Saint-Honoré, turning away to avoid looking at the Église Saint-Roch, where on the orders of a certain General Bonaparte, royalist rioters had been felled on the steps by a hail of cannon fire. He trained himself to banish the name 'Napoleon' from his thoughts and to replace it with 'Bonaparte', 'the tyrant', 'the ogre', 'the upstart', 'the usurper' . . .

Once a person starts to act contrary to their own instincts they end up losing sight of their true selves. Margont was astonished to notice how far the attitudes he adopted for appearances' sake started to influence his thoughts. As a result of continually acting like a royalist, he started to wonder whether the restoration of the monarchy might not in fact have some merit. It would mean an end to war, which in turn would mean that many people who longed to do something else could finally leave the army. But to think like that was heresy for a republican like him! How could he even consider abandoning the ideals of the Revolution? He was like an actor who plays a role each evening with such success that he eventually becomes consumed by it.

His daily meetings with Lefine were all the more precious; they were his one link with reality.

Eventually, one evening, someone knocked at his door. It was Charles de Varencourt. He was very pale and drawn, and had lost his swagger.

'They've sent me to fetch you. You haven't changed your mind?'

'Not at all.'

'What bothers me is that by gambling on your life, you're gambling on mine as well!'

Margont did not reply. His decision was irrevocable. Joseph and Talleyrand were right: he had to meet the royalists himself. While Margont was struggling to conquer his fear, Varencourt shrugged, apparently accepting the situation with fatalistic resignation.

'They're waiting for us,' he concluded.

As they were walking through the darkened streets, Margont again had the impression that he was just a pawn on an enormous chessboard. A pawn about to embark upon an audacious bluff . . .

CHAPTER 9

THEY reached the heart of the Saint-Marcel district. Varencourt was walking briskly, obliging Margont to fall in behind him, and grabbing his arm at regular intervals to make sure he followed him down a little side street, before setting off in a different direction again. Margont was lost but did not dare ask any questions. A door opened on their right and they dived into a house. There was no light inside and Margont felt as if he had been swallowed by the dark maw of a Leviathan. His silhouette, however, seemed to have been left framed in the doorway, backlit by an oil lamp. Someone bounded up behind him and held a knife to his throat. With his left hand, his attacker seized Margont's right wrist to stop him trying to free himself or reaching for a weapon. The door shut again.

'You are a spy, Monsieur,' said someone in front of him.

Margont was terrified and waited in vain for a candle to be lit.

'Our friend Monsieur de Varencourt has told us about you, but as he admits himself, he barely knows you,' the stranger went on. 'So we're going to ask you some questions. Depending how you answer, we might be able to spare your life . . .'

The voice belonged to a man accustomed to being in charge. The intonation, rhythm and phrases were designed to command, to destabilise and to let Margont know his lies would be flushed out. The words uttered by the voice pierced straight through him.

'I can't see anything . . .' stammered Margont.

'You'll be able to see even less when I've cut your throat,' murmured the man holding him.

'You say that you own a printing press . . .'

'It's the truth!'

'That's just the problem. The Tyrant is cunning, and he controls everything that's published. You claim to be one of us but you have a printing press? These places are watched by the Director of Printing and Bookselling, but also by the police. There are some policemen whose sole task is to control printing, books and newspapers! And yet you want us to believe you've deceived them all? Absurd! We've had you followed. Admittedly it wasn't easy. It's true that you do have access to a printing press, Imperial Press, but all that proves is that you have the protection of the police.'

Margont wondered if Charles de Varencourt had sold him out. But it was too late to ask him. He could not retreat; he would just have to press on with his role. And with bravado! 'If Napoleon takes so much care to—'

'Bonaparte! The coronation of 1804 is not legitimate! Napoleon does not exist!'

'All right . . . If Bonaparte takes so much care to control the printed word, it's because it's his weak point. And that's just where we should strike him! A friend of mine who's a duellist taught me that way of fighting.'

'What do you mean?'

'I don't doubt Bonaparte's military talent. It would be difficult to defeat him on the battlefield. Unless he had no more army left! So we have to convince the French to abandon him.'

'Interesting. But you didn't answer my question.'

It was so dark that Margont could not even make out the outlines of anyone there, and he could not accommodate what he was saying to the expressions on people's faces or to their demeanour. He had to rely on that over-confident, arrogant, domineering voice, with its ironic intonations. He was on the edge of a cliff and about to be thrown into the void. But his survival instinct had always been strong. Even with a knife at his throat, he refused to give up.

'I served for several years in the Grande Armée. Like many other gentlemen. After I was wounded, I had to return to civilian life. I devoted all my efforts to obtaining authorisation to acquire a printing works. As I had distinguished myself during the Russian campaign, several officers were willing to vouch for me. I had to grease some palms as well but eventually my tenacity paid off. Oh, there are certainly one or two employees who spy on me for the police. But gradually the police have ceased to suspect me, so for a long time now I have felt quite safe. In the end they put my years of emigration in Edinburgh down to a youthful error. Do you know how the praying mantis captures its victims? It moves so slowly that its movements are imperceptible to the insects it preys on. It's only when it is very close that it suddenly strikes the fatal blow. I have overlooked nothing. I returned to France in 1802 and, for all those years since, I have inexorably, step by step, put my plan into action. I have found out all about printing and I have acquired a print shop. It took twelve years of effort! The imperial police don't pursue things for that long, I can tell you.'

'How long have you had the print shop?'

'For a year. I must emphasise that I am only an associate, but my partner knows nothing about my real intentions. Until recently, I practically never went there. Had I showed up there too often, the police would have become suspicious. All I did was spend the meagre profits when we were lucky enough to have any. But I go there much more often now. The situation is more favourable to us. It's time for us to take action!'

'What is it that you want?'

'Two things. The return of the King!'

He stopped talking. The man with the knife pressed harder with his blade. But paradoxically Margont drew strength from the gesture.

'Well? What's the second thing?' insisted the leader.

'The gratitude of the King . . .'

'What insolence!'

' "Audacity, more audacity, always audacity!" ' replied Margont, quoting Danton, one of the most hated revolutionaries. That might have seemed a suicidal tactic, but he was trying to lead the discussion in an unexpected direction and catch the men off guard. He would probably die if he were to try to beat them at their own game, so he was making up his own rules.

No one answered him so he went on: 'Before the Revolution, my family lived peacefully on its lands. But I knew that life for only a few years. Then I had everything thrown at me. My family was massacred and our château burnt; I was forced to wander from place to place . . . I was very young when I emigrated to Scotland. I planned to return to my homeland as an officer, with other royalist émigrés and an English army. The

English held out the prospect of that dream, but they never fulfilled it. It was too risky, too expensive . . . And although they did want to see their old enemy brought to its knees, they never really trusted us. They were still annoyed with us for having resisted them so fiercely in Quebec and partly blamed us for the loss of their American colonies . . . In Edinburgh, I lived in terrible conditions. So because I was sick of never having enough to eat, and of being treated like an undesirable, I took advantage of the great amnesty of 1802. Like many others I returned to my country, swore an oath in front of a prefect and here I am. I was *pardoned* for having been an émigré, as if I had committed a crime! I enlisted in the Grande Armée because I had no other means of supporting myself. I even envisaged serving the Empire, I admit. I wanted to become a general. But that dream also went up in smoke. I have found my roots again and I want the King to be restored to the throne. However, I'll be frank, I would like to be rewarded for my services.'

'You're a mercenary!'

'Yes, but a mercenary for the King! What is wrong with wanting to rebuild the ruins of my family château? I want to have the life I lived before; I want the life I had before the Revolution!'

Even in the inky darkness Margont could tell that his argument had struck home. His adversary had taken a blow, and Margont would have to follow up his counterattack before his opponent had time to regroup. 'It would be wrong to think that Bonaparte can't win again!' he exclaimed. 'The fellow has more lives than a cat! He was said to be finished in 1805 but then there was Austerlitz, done for in 1806, but then there was Jena.

He was crushed at Essling in 1809 and then went on to win at Wagram. The King needs help! Against Bonaparte, but also against the Allies! Bernadotte is not content just with Sweden, he wants to become King of France! And what if the Tsar or the Emperor of Austria accepts a compromise and proposes to leave Napoleon his throne? Or if they decide to organise a regency until the King of Rome is of an age to govern and become Napoleon II? No! If the Allies feel that the French are abandoning Bonaparte they will fight to the bitter end. And, if we, the noblemen of France, are indisputably linked with the victory, we can ensure that Louis XVIII will prevail!'

'I don't like you, Monsieur, but you're not lacking in courage.'

'And we need courage! We need to stir up the French! But for that, they have to be able to hear us. Let's blanket Paris with posters!'

'Why do you need us?'

'I can't act on my own. When I print my proclamations, it will be at night, in secret. I'll need accomplices to keep watch, then to put the posters up. Besides, we will need to do more than that to make an impression. I think you yourselves have some ideas for action. So in conclusion, I . . . I . . . um . . .'

'In conclusion?'

'Well, I'm not sure how to put this without annoying you. I would like to do all I can for the King . . . but I have never met him and I don't want my services to go unnoticed.'

'You want us to put in a good word for you with His Majesty?' the stranger asked, stupefied.

'Exactly. And where's the harm in that? I'm not making any

comment on human nature, but if Louis XVIII accedes to the throne, which is his by divine right, people all over France will rush to court him. Those who betrayed the King or who did nothing will shamelessly take the credit along with the real heroes of the Restoration. Who will bear witness to what I have done? Why is it shocking to want to be rewarded? Can you swear on the Bible that neither you nor anyone else present doesn't hope for compensation for your good and loyal service?'

'That's not what we are about. We aren't acting just for our personal gain!'

'Nor am I, but . . .'

'Why don't we light a candle?'

The blade moved away, liberating Margont. When the halo of flame appeared in a yellow ball of light, his eyes filled with tears.

CHAPTER 10

THE man who had interrogated Margont must have been about forty-five. He looked as commanding as he sounded. He held himself proudly, he was clearly impassioned and he seemed poised to fling himself into battle. There was an impressive energy about him. Had he chosen to serve the Empire he would certainly have been high up in the hierarchy, either civil or military. But he had decided to support the King, and his 'Grande Armée' was merely a group of perhaps thirty, and instead of gliding through the enemy palaces he had seized, he was hiding from cellar to cellar. He was a sort of fallen angel precipitated into limbo alongside royalty. Although he was an idealist, he must have suffered from not occupying a rank commensurate with his talents. Margont's argument about the need to be recognised had shocked him because it had hit the nail on the head . . . The emblem of the Swords of the King was pinned to his jacket over his heart. Margont looked at it briefly, as if he were seeing it for the first time, and noted that it corresponded in every particular with the one he had seen on Colonel Berle's body.

'I'm Vicomte Louis de Leaume.'

'Delighted to meet you!' said Margont, massaging his throat.

'Baron Honoré de Nolant.'

Nolant was overcome with embarrassment. It is not every day you are introduced to the person you almost murdered a few minutes earlier. He was a little younger than Louis de Leaume, and thin, but Margont was not taken in by his fragile appearance, knowing how easily he had been overpowered by him. Nolant did not look directly at Margont and appeared distracted, lost in his own thoughts.

Varencourt looked pale. He did not dare move, as if he had not yet realised that the ordeal was over.

He turned to Margont and said, 'Incredible! You're even more of a gambler than I am!'

He laughed, bringing colour to his cheeks, but the rest of his face was still as pale as porcelain.

A third man, who had been silent up until then, introduced himself: 'Jean-Baptiste de Châtel.' He was posted just inside the door, as if to intercept Margont should he try to flee. He was a little older, but not yet fifty, with a bony face and searching, narrowed eyes. He was so emaciated he looked ill, or as if he had endured many years of deprivation.

Margont realised he had been put in front of a sort of tribunal. Everyone had been listening to him and when Louis de Leaume had proposed lighting a candle, any one of them could have sentenced him to death by replying 'no'. In the meantime Jean-Baptiste de Châtel did not look happy. He had contemplated refusing the light!

'Monsieur de Langès, perhaps you would like to suggest a suitable quotation from the Holy Bible. What do you know of the word of God?'

'Thou shalt not kill,' replied Margont, looking at Honoré de Nolant.

'That's a bit short.'

Margont now felt trapped in the persona he had just projected. It would not do to appear merely as a pushy trouble-maker. He would have to temper the showy opportunism he had displayed with a demonstration of faith to win over the idealists present. Jean-Baptiste de Châtel looked as if he might be susceptible to this. So Margont pressed on.

' "Seeing he despised the oath by breaking the covenant, when, lo, he had given his hand, and hath done all these things, he shall not escape. Therefore thus saith the Lord God; As I live, surely mine oath that he hath despised, and my covenant that he hath broken, even it will I recompense upon his own head." Ezekiel, Chapter 17, verses 18 and 19. He who breaks a covenant offends God and breaks away from him.'

Jean-Baptiste de Châtel's expression was transformed, like a block of ice turned suddenly to vapour. He seemed about to take Margont in his arms. 'Good, very good!'

Margont had spent four years in the Abbey of Saint-Guilhem-le-Désert studying the Bible under the iron yoke of the monks. He had almost become a monk himself, against his will. So it would be hard to trip him up in his knowledge of theology. To lie effectively was it not best to lead your adversary onto territory that you were sure of?

'What do you know about the Antichrist?' Châtel demanded.

Margont thought he was trying to trip him up by asking him about an unfamiliar subject. ' "And he shall subdue three kings. And he shall speak great words against the most High, and shall wear out the saints of the most High, and think to change times and laws." Daniel . . . I can't remember which chapter . . .'

Jean-Baptiste de Châtel was jubilant. 'Magnificent! A real believer! So, Quentin – I may call you that? – as you know the Holy Scriptures so well, do you not agree that Napoleon is the Antichrist?'

Margont was dumbfounded and wondered if Jean-Baptiste was making fun of him. His reaction caused Jean-Baptiste's joyous demeanour to falter somewhat.

'But it goes without saying, Monsieur de Langès!'

Margont was taken aback by such an extreme theory. Jean-Baptiste de Châtel took immediate offence and did not address another word to him. Their alliance had lasted all of the time it took to recite a couple of verses of the Bible, and Margont's clever tactic had been turned against him: far from making a friend of Jean-Baptiste, he had turned him into an enemy.

'Has our zealot finished his sermon?' demanded Louis de Leaume with such irony that his words were like a slap.

Clearly it was not permitted for a mere member of the group to monopolise the conversation at the expense of the leader. The Vicomte's words had been designed to reassert his authority. But far from being called to order, Jean-Baptiste de Châtel gave Leaume a sardonic smile, provoking him even further. He was openly delighted at having roused Leaume's temper, and his attitude made everyone else ill at ease. Leaume chose to ignore him. Margont wondered if the cause of the animosity between the two men was just rivalry, or if there was not more to it. Jean-Baptiste had a strange way of staring at the Vicomte in an insistent manner. Leaume turned to Margont.

'What do you want in exchange for your help?'

'I want everything. I want to be on the committee of the Swords of the King.'

'To be on the committee, you have to have been a member for more than two months, and have done something to prove your loyalty.'

'Nearly getting my throat cut in order to meet you – doesn't that prove my loyalty! As for your two months, I don't have the patience to wait, and in any case, we don't have two months. The outcome of the war will be decided in the next few weeks. If my offer doesn't interest you, no matter. There are many other royalist organisations: the Congregation, the Knights of the Faith, the Friends of Order . . . The King will reward the men who help him the most and I'm going to become one of those men, with you or without you.'

'We have our regulations, Monsieur.'

'I'm sure you do. But you're not the kind of man to let regulations stand in your way.'

Louis de Leaume looked at him with a new eye. 'How perceptive you are . . . Perceptive people are dangerous, because they won't be appeased by the lies that would satisfy others. Why do you wish to become part of our group? The Knights of the Faith, for example, are better known; why not go to them first?'

'There are too many of them. I would be lost in the mass. I would scarcely be heard and I would be nothing but a second-rate pawn, and I absolutely won't have that! If you admit me to the top of your organisation, to your committee, my printing press can be heavily influential in your success. It's up to you.

Now it's time to see if you really are the man of action you claim to be.'

'I accept you as one of us, in effect as a member of our committee. I take full responsibility for the decision.'

Leaume had not asked the opinion of any of the others before deciding, thus demonstrating that he was in charge. Varencourt and Honoré de Nolant were delighted and shook Margont's hand in a show of brotherhood. Jean-Baptiste de Châtel merely nodded coldly at him, keeping his distance.

'Now that you are one of us, there is one more person you should meet,' said Louis de Leaume. 'All the members of the committee should know one another. We'll have to go upstairs.'

Margont almost stumbled on the stairs. He was pale as he regained his balance. He had just guessed why the other conspirator had waited upstairs while they interrogated him. It was because that person had not wanted to be present at his execution.

CHAPTER 11

THERE was no furniture in the room upstairs and it was freezing and soulless. This nocturnal meeting was its only moment of life. It would be abandoned immediately afterwards; it was just a stage in the exhausting game of hide-and-seek around Paris.

A woman welcomed Margont in, relieved at the way things had turned out. She was about forty, possibly older. She was beautiful but her long hair was pulled back in an old-fashioned chignon, her face was unadorned by make-up and she wore no jewels; her dress was drab. It appeared to Margont that she was hiding her beauty – had it brought her misfortune in the past?

She looked at him with a strange intensity; her blue eyes seemed to pierce his soul. It was as if she were probing his character, trying to see the real Margont. He felt scorched by her gaze, as if his lies were burning up in his soul.

'Chevalier Quentin de Langès,' he said, bowing to escape her inquisitorial gaze.

'Mademoiselle Catherine de Saltonges. So here you are, one of us. We thought you were a spy.'

The irony in her voice let him know that she did not trust him.

'Monsieur de Langès used to be a soldier and he owns a printing press!' said Vicomte de Leaume.

'So I heard.'

'If opinion had been divided, would you have voted for my life or my death?' Margont asked her.

She lowered her eyes, as if she found him desirable.

'How can you say that? I wouldn't have . . . I . . . Not I! But I don't like you, Monsieur. What you say is a mixture of truth and falsehood. That sickens me.'

Her face expressed disgust, as if Margont's lies had released a rotten odour.

'Have we finished discussing my admission?' he asked. 'Let's move to action! And with God's help we will win the battle! I propose we—'

'We'll decide nothing now!' Catherine de Saltonges cut him off. 'You're going rather quickly, Chevalier.'

'Not as quickly as the situation is going!'

Leaume intervened. 'We'll contact you. Members of our group are strictly forbidden to see each other outside official meetings for any reason at all. Everyone adheres to that rule on pain of death. Do you understand?'

'Yes, but what if I need to get hold of you? I must be able—'

'That won't be possible,' put in Jean-Baptiste de Châtel. 'We'll leave first.'

Catherine de Saltonges and Honoré de Nolant left, followed by Jean-Baptiste. The Vicomte hung back. He unknotted his scarf, looking at Margont.

'Monsieur de Langès, don't underestimate our determination.'

He then revealed a mark. In the Pacific Islands the great explorers like Cook had discovered a method of indelibly marking the skin, and had brought it back to Europe. The prestige of these adventurers and the French taste for exoticism had made tattoos popular. In the past, Count Tolstoy, on his return from Oceania, had shown off his tattoos in the salons of St Petersburg, after which the Russian nobility had also embraced the practice. Legend had it that Catherine the Great had had herself tattooed in a very special place . . . Old Marshal Bernadotte had 'Death to kings' tattooed on his chest during his revolutionary years. Yet now he had become the hereditary prince of Sweden and dreamt of beating Napoleon and becoming king of France . . .

Louis de Leaume had chosen a strange motif. It was – Margont drew closer, frowning – yes, it definitely was a dotted line like the ones tailors and dressmakers draw on their material before they cut it. But this line stretched round Leaume's throat, indicating where it should be cut . . .

'I will fight to the end, Chevalier. I have learnt to live permanently with the blade of the guillotine round my neck!'

With that he went out and disappeared into the night.

Margont waited with Varencourt.

'Did you know the welcome that was waiting for me?'

'No, I didn't, I swear to you! If they had . . . Anyway, if you hadn't convinced them you were genuine, I wonder what they would have decided to do to me.'

He was finally beginning to show his full colours. Margont stared at him openly.

'Who followed me to the printing press?'

'I don't know.'

They left and Varencourt closed the door behind them, whispering, 'Don't bother having this house watched. They'll never come back here. Vicomte de Leaume never lets us return to our meeting places. And he imposes even stricter rules on himself – he never sleeps twice in the same bed.'

'Who does this house belong to?'

'To one of the many French noblemen living in exile, waiting for Napoleon's fall. They left all their property and possessions in France. Part of it was pillaged or seized during the Revolution and the period after. But there are still places like this. Vicomte de Leaume lived for two years in London. He made several rich contacts there and he's kept in touch with them. As a result, he has dozens of keys to hovels like this one. The noblemen sit sipping brandy in their London clubs, perfectly happy to fund the Vicomte's activities, as long as he's the one who takes all the risks. If Louis XVIII does become king one day, these generous benefactors will be able to impress His Majesty with the important role they played in the restoration. In fact all they're sacrificing is some gold and some broken-down shacks they inherited or rented or bought in the early years of the Revolution with the idea of hiding in them or salting away their possessions. If we win, they will receive honorary service charges, rents . . . But as for the Vicomte, he can only play with what's in his hand. His only cards are his ideas, but what's at stake is his life. He's well aware of it too, don't you think? That's why it was so clever of you to have mentioned your desire to be rewarded! He really drank that in! One Vicomte de Leaume is worth fifty Langèses!'

'And a hundred Varencourts.'

But Varencourt did not rise to the taunt.

'Now you know why the Vicomte is head of our organisation

– because he created it and, more especially, because he has access to money, which is after all the sinews of war!'

As they moved further away from the building, they were both relaxing a little.

'In any case, bravo, you made a good impression on them,' said Charles de Varencourt.

'Is that meant to be a joke?'

'Not at all. They all distrust each other. You have to put yourself in their shoes. Jean-Baptiste de Châtel lost ten members of his family in the Vendée, royalists killed in battle or civilians gunned down in reprisals or massacred by the infernal columns of that criminal of a general, Turreau. Vicomte de Leaume also lost everything: parents, lands, fortune . . . In addition, in 1793 he was the leader of a little group of royalists called the Loyalists – they were all arrested. Every day, through the tiny window of his cell, he saw the heads of his companions falling under the blade of the guillotine. He made himself watch, convinced that it would help him vanquish his fear and behave with bravado as he mounted the scaffold. He tried to imagine what he might do to make a lasting impression, something that would get him noticed and that would be a public slap in the face of his enemies. You must have worried him when you cited Danton. No doubt he thought about Danton as he sat in his prison cell. He hated him. But he certainly wanted to emulate him on the day of his death. Danton went up to the executioner and said: "Don't forget to show my head to the people, it's well worth seeing." And the executioner did! Everyone had already forgotten the names of the people who had ordered Danton's death, but his last words would be remembered for ever.

Vicomte de Leaume managed to escape a few hours after he appeared in front of the Revolutionary Tribunal – the tribunal that had, it goes without saying, condemned him to the guillotine. Believe me, when he talks about it, it's as if it happened yesterday. All that is just to explain that when you know what they have lived through, you cease to wonder at how fanatical they have become. Violence breeds repression, repression breeds violence. To put an end to the vicious circle, perhaps we have to try to forgive, or at least to accept the past. But it's so difficult . . .'

'And what about you, Charles? What have you lived through?'

Varencourt reared back and clenched his teeth as if he had just been hit and was preparing to retaliate. 'I won't answer questions like that!'

'All right . . . Well, here's another type of question. What proof of loyalty did you give that allowed you to be accepted onto the committee?'

Varencourt pretended to calm down and laughed like a child.

'You must know that I can't answer that either. You would have to put it in your report to Joseph and he would fall off his chair.'

Paris was ill lit, although it was worse in other European capitals. They walked by the light of the moon, passing under lamps that had been blown out by the wind or had run out of oil. Margont was trying to control himself, but he was very angry.

'You said nothing during that trumped-up half-trial!'

Varencourt replied jovially, 'You were wriggling like a snake, hissing and trying to bite!'

'That amuses you?'

' "I am quick to laugh at everything so as not to have to cry," said Monsieur de Beaumarchais. If only because he said that, I would have liked to meet him.'

'They didn't tell me about any of their plans!'

'That's because they're cunning. They each know part of the picture. Just because they've allowed you in at the top doesn't mean that they're going to tell you everything about every-thing. That would be much too dangerous! Logic dictates that all the members of the committee should know each other – and so they do – otherwise it would have been impossible to take coherent decisions and then to apply them. But they don't call on you until they think you're going to increase the chances of a particular plan succeeding. So even I probably don't know some of the projects that have been submitted to Vicomte de Leaume and I know only about ten of the thirty members of our organisation. Maybe there are even more than that, in fact. Or perhaps fewer . . . Only Louis de Leaume knows everyone. But he will never let your Joseph take him alive.'

'How many times have you met the other members of the committee?'

'There is barely a meeting a month, except when we are planning a project. Now stop asking questions. I've already told everything I know to the police; look at my reports. From now on we'll see each other only at group meetings. Leaume told you that we are expressly forbidden to see other members of the group outside the meetings that he himself organises. So you and I will not meet on our own any more.'

'I'll be the one to decide that!'

'No! Listen to me: clearly you have been plunged into a world you don't understand at all. I don't know if that's a good or a bad thing. The main thing is that here you are, still alive. Do you know why Louis de Leaume was almost guillotined? It was because the police spotted one of the Loyalist group. And since the Loyalists were in the habit of meeting up just to have a drink because they were friends, when the police saw one of them, they had them all and they were all arrested. Every one of them! So I repeat: we won't meet alone again!'

'You're hiding something from me!'

'Don't worry, everything I find out, I'll sell.'

'How can you—'

'Stop! I won't debate ethics with you. We would be wasting time. Besides, I would greatly appreciate it if you would stop showing your contempt for me.'

As they were less and less able to bear each other's company, they separated.

The cramped, miserably furnished room plunged Margont further into despair. He flopped onto the bed and extinguished the candle. The darkness was like straw on the fire of his fear, which immediately flared up. He could not stop thinking about the blade he had been threatened with. He could see it, a luminous line coming through the darkness, making straight for his neck. The more he told himself it was over, the more he pictured the blade. He could actually feel it against his neck, more vividly than when it had really been there. He decided to fight his reaction. To give himself courage, he ran through his real motivations. To defend republican ideals! Liberty! The Constitution! Equality between men! And so the dirty, dark little room with its imaginary dancing knife was filled with the great, inspiring ideas of the Revolution.

CHAPTER 12

THE man sat opposite the drunkard, not looking at anyone. Everyone at the Boutefeu was engaged in shady business – there was no other reason to come to such a dive. The place was so disreputable that the police did not venture here, unless Savary, Napoleon's Minister of Civilian Police, gave repeated orders and voiced his anger if they were not carried out. So when they came, they came in number, backed up by soldiers of the municipal guard, on foot and mounted. But no one worried very much about this eventuality: the police always took care to warn their informers, who let everyone know in advance. That way, there were no riots and no wounded. The police would arrest a few prostitutes, who let themselves be taken with good grace, and Monsieur Savary could reassure the Emperor that order reigned in Paris.

The drinker sat up, not as drunk as all that. 'I'm waiting for a friend.' He spoke with a Portuguese accent.

'I am that friend.'

'In that case, you're welcome at my table.' He smiled and drank some beer, happy that the exchange had passed off exactly as his intermediary had told him. He was missing three fingers on his left hand, which lay exposed on the table. He had lost his fingers to a cannonball during a naval battle off the coast of Portugal. His sloop, *A Corajosa*, had been wiped out by the frenetic cannon fire of *L'Amélie*, a French frigate.

'I have what you need, *senhor*. But it was much harder to come by than I expected. It was bad enough that I had to go to the Amazonian jungle, but what was worse was that even though I had already bartered with the Indian tribes there, they still didn't trust me. I risked my life dealing with them! And the ocean! There was a storm in the Atlantic, the like of which I've never seen . . . It felt as if the sky was sucking up the sea to drink it, the waves were so high. And I've been a sailor for sixteen years! Then getting across France . . . The English, the Spanish and the Portuguese will all tell you that Napoleon's on his knees, only they've all forgotten to tell him that! I was almost arrested, I had to grease the palms of soldiers . . .'

'How much more?'

'Ah, *por Deus*, at least you know what you want!'

'More than you can know. How much?'

'I should ask for four times as much, but I'll settle for triple the amount.'

'You can have double.'

'No, no, *senhor*, with all due respect: triple. If we can't agree on a price, you can always dispense with my services and go yourself to our viceroyalty, Brazil, to get what you want.'

The thought of that made him laugh. But he added: 'Believe it or not I'm not just motivated by money. I also want a return to the monarchy for the French. As long as Napoleon is over-thrown, any king will do – Louis XVIII, Bernadotte, even a fish: "King Fish" . . . Napoleon has invaded so many countries, perhaps he's forgotten Portugal, but Portugal hasn't forgotten Napoleon.'

The man gave in and handed over almost all the money,

under the table. In exchange he received a bag full of little receptacles.

'That isn't triple, but it's more than double. I had foreseen that you would be greedy, but not that you would demand quite that much.'

'Do you really think you're going to succeed, *senhor*?'

The man smiled in reply. It was a strange smile, a mixture of joy and ferocity. The sailor was leaning back in his chair now. He displayed his left hand again. It looked like a pale starfish a shark had taken a bite out of. 'In your case,' he said, 'Napoleon has taken much more than just three fingers . . .'

The man walked through the disordered crowd without taking in what he was seeing. There was a profusion of National Guardsmen, farmers from Picardy, Champagne or the Ardennes, perched with their families on carts filled with their furniture, and people standing about hoping for news. He had waited months for that meeting! Finally! Finally! But had he really obtained what he needed? If not, he would have to think of another plan.

He reached an area of the city where there was a concentration of butchers. In 1810, Napoleon had ordered that five abattoirs should be built outside Paris. But they were not finished yet, and the killing areas – the parts of the city where slaughter was authorised – were not sufficient to feed Paris with its fondness for red meat. So the capital's butchers continued their old practices. They slit their beasts' throats by the dozen in the courtyards of their shops and the blood ran into the streets.

The man wondered if it was a prophetic vision of the Paris of tomorrow, when the city would be bathing in the blood of Parisians, Russians and Prussians, like Venice, but with blood instead of canals.

The butcher's shop he went into was just like all the others. The animals were bleating and mooing in a nauseating odour of blood. Blood, blood, blood everywhere – it was as if he had walked into the mouth of a Leviathan that was devouring the world. An apprentice butcher recognised him and came to meet him. The man merely nodded and followed the young man towards the pen, where they would be away from prying eyes. As agreed in advance, he handed the apprentice a twenty-franc piece, but when he asked the boy to leave, the apprentice refused.

'I want to see what you're going to do to the animals.'

'Go on now, you won't get any more. The person before you took everything.'

The employee still hung around, curious. The man protested, but eventually gave in because he was short of time. He opened the bag that contained eleven little terracotta pots. Eleven possibilities of success. He took a needle from his pocket, picked up the first pot and pulled out the stopper, releasing a strong vegetable odour. The butcher was amused by these strange manoeuvres. The man plunged the point of the needle into the black, syrupy liquid, which gave off such a pungent smell that it seemed as if the little pot magically contained a whole miniature virgin forest. He was so emotional that his hand trembled as he injected the thigh of an ox. The animal did not react. The man threw the needle into the straw, far away so that he would not poison himself, closed up the pot and put it in his pocket. He moved with cold precision. He took a new needle and went through the same procedure with a second pot. Still no reaction. He did it again. Failure. He tried again. Still no result. His gestures were exactly the same each time, like an automaton. Only the odours of the substances varied – strong and smooth, sharp and lingering, like soil in a forest after a storm . . . A few seconds after the seventh injection, a *frisson* ran through the ox, and its back legs began to tremble, as if the temperature had suddenly dropped. The trembling spread through the rest of its body and the enormous 120-stone ox, opening its mouth but unable even to moo, collapsed on its side. Stiff. Dead. The man swivelled round and pricked the butcher in the arm. The effect was even more immediate and the boy fell before he understood what was happening to him. His mouth was wide open, but he was no longer breathing.

The man packed away his equipment and left. There were so many people of all types about that no one paid him any attention. He was filled with joy. He had what he wanted and the poison was even more effective than he had heard. His confidence knew no bounds. Now he could kill at a touch, like a god.

CHAPTER 13

ON 20 March Margont paid an errand boy to take a note to 'Monsieur Lami'. The message was coded, using a method he had perfected with Lefine in the past to while away the hours of boredom in the bivouac. The note, when decoded, simply said, 'Meet me at midday chez Marat.'

They met at the appointed hour on the outskirts of Paris, at the foot of the hill of Montmartre, 'Mount Marat', as it had sometimes been called during the Revolution. Lefine still mockingly used the old-fashioned appellation. Margont was delighted to see his old friend. He felt himself again.

'Are you sure you weren't followed here?'

'Certain, and you?'

'I'm certain as well. I'm expert now at complicating my route – needs must. Well, it's happened! I've met them!'

He recounted the events that had led to his admission to the organisation, and what Charles de Varencourt had told him. 'And what about you? What have you learnt about our suspects?'

Lefine sat down and leant against a tree, in the shade. Margont followed suit. The birds were singing at the tops of their voices, as though to hurry the arrival of spring.

'Everything I'm about to tell you comes from the police files that have been "enriched" by Charles de Varencourt's reports. Sometimes I was able to add to the information with my own research.'

'Which police? There are so many . . .'

'Joseph's personal police. They're the ones controlling the investigation. But they've also used information gathered by Fouché's police when he was Minister of Civilian Police but had also developed his own networks, and by the civilian police—'

'What do they think of Charles de Varencourt?'

'They think he's trustworthy and worth listening to. He's furnished information that the police have been able to double-check against information they already had. So they know he doesn't feed them nonsense.'

'Right. I'm listening.'

'Let's start at the top with the leader, Vicomte de Leaume. Varencourt has already told you a good deal about him. But do you know how he escaped?'

'No, tell me!'

'He pretended to be dead. It sounds simple when you say it like that, but when the gaolers see a prisoner is apparently dead they stab the body with a lance or bayonet. All the fakers yell immediately or writhe in pain. But Louis de Leaume didn't move a muscle. As it was during the Terror, when there was killing and maiming left, right and centre, the guards thought he had succumbed to his injuries. He was thrown into a communal grave with the guillotined bodies of the day and the bodies of the poor wretches who had died of starvation in the streets. When night fell he pulled himself out from under the dead bodies.'

Margont could not help imagining the scene. He saw the man extricating himself from the decomposing dead bodies – his silhouette, illuminated by the pale light of the moon, looking more like a ghost than an escapee. The thought was chilling. 'Where did the gaoler wound him?' he asked.

'What a question! I haven't the faintest idea.'

'The scar would be a way of identifying him. Because where's the proof that the real Louis de Leaume climbed out of that mass grave? Someone could have usurped his identity . . .'

'I asked myself the same thing, but the police dossier backs up that version of events. And what's more, the description you've just given me corresponds to the one the Revolutionary Tribunal gave at the time of his trial.'

'I see. Go on.'

'He was believed to be dead. But instead of adopting a new identity and changing his life, Leaume once more joined a royalist group, the Alliance, and under his real name! He eventually came to the notice of the Commune police three years after his death. There was an investigation into the exact circumstances of his demise, which concluded that he had in fact escaped alive.'

'That was all he had left: his real name. He had no family, no house, no money, and not even any country . . . I don't know if he's an impostor or if the real Louis de Leaume did escape and keep his real identity, through pride, to defy his enemies and humiliate them by letting them know that he had fooled them. But I can tell you this. If someone pretends to be dead, is wounded, thrown in a communal grave and spends hours entombed under corpses, when he finally gets out of the charnel house, he's no longer the same man. Perhaps that's the reason Louis de Leaume kept his real name. He wanted to keep a link with the man he had been before his ordeal.'

Margont had spent his childhood steeped in religion, and now he thought of Christ, who had also been 'dead'. To confirm it, a legionary had wounded his right flank with his lance. Could one consider Louis de Leaume like a sort of perverted Christ, resurrected not to love, but to avenge himself?

Lefine disliked speaking of death. He therefore moved swiftly on to the next phase of Louis de Leaume's life. 'In 1796, he left the Alliance because he found its members too moderate. He emigrated to London where he spent at least two years. The police lost track of him until he reappeared in Paris in January 1813, where he formed a new group, the Swords of the King. That's all I can tell you about his past. As you know, I have many "friends", some reputable and others less so. But I have not managed to hear any mention of him. So this Leaume knows the capital extremely well!'

'If he's the murderer, you can understand why he left the symbol of his group on the corpse. If you had seen them dithering about me . . . He would be the type to cut to the chase to force them all into action. But why the fire?'

'They wanted to cut his head off, he burns their faces . . . And I do agree with you: after you've escaped from a grave, your ideas must become somewhat warped.'

'That's not what I said. I was only emphasising that an ordeal like that would change you.'

'Well, anyway, I wouldn't trust him if I were you. Because if he finds out who you really are . . . He's sure to have left his mercy behind in the communal grave. That's all I've found out about him.'

'You don't know anything about his stay in London?'

'No. All our suspects live very secretly, so the facts are incomplete.'

'The facts are like the people: you just have time to glimpse them in silhouette before they disappear again into the shadows. Tell me about Charles de Varencourt.'

'Again, almost nothing is known about his past. He was born in 1773, near Rouen. His family belonged to the Norman nobility. Nothing else is known about them. In 1792, he emigrated to England. And after that we have very little. He claims to have lived in London. In January 1814, he contacted the police and offered to sell them information. As he distrusted the civilian police, he approached Joseph's personal police force. He knew the names of some of them because the royalists kept tabs on the people hunting them. Joseph's agents accepted his offer. He had to provide them with a variety of his own documents. He showed them his passport, which stated that he had returned to France in 1802.'

'Ah, the great amnesty of 6 Floréal, year 10. Just like me.'

'Exactly. And, as you know, it is widely acknowledged, given the level of corruption at the time, that many of those passports were handed out to royalists who did not actually return to France until much later. As Varencourt did not tell them anything concrete about what he did in France between 1802 and 1814 – he said he travelled around the country earning his living by playing cards – it's quite possible that the documents are fake. That's what the police suspect. In any case, thanks to that "valid" passport, which "proves" that he was pardoned for his crime of emigration, he lives comfortably at home, whilst Louis de Leaume, Honoré de Nolant and Jean-

Baptiste de Châtel are on the run and spend their time moving from house to house.'

'Right. And what have you found out about the Charles de Varencourt of today?'

'I arranged for two men to take turns keeping an eye on him day and night, as agreed. I went back to see Natai – I wish you'd seen his face when I asked him for a hundred francs to pay the men.'

'A hundred francs? That's going it a bit. You're taking a cut, I assume?'

'You misunderstood when I said "I wish you'd seen his face". He recognised that this was an extraordinary situation and found my bill quite normal – I just had to sign a receipt in the name of Gage, the pseudonym I use when I go and see him. For months now soldiers have not been paid, yet any old spy employed for less than ten days can walk away with a hundred francs! That's nearly five months' sergeant's pay!'

'Fernand, for heaven's sake! The Swords of the King might come across you. If you have all that money on you, they'll know immediately who you're working for!'

'Don't worry, I've already spent it all. I may be greedy, but I'm not stupid. I paid the men – four in all, because there were also two men watching Catherine de Saltonges – and I bought a present for a lady friend.'

He smiled disarmingly. Margont, who was always in a ferment of projects and ideals, sometimes envied his friend his nonchalant approach to life.

'Let's go back to Charles de Varencourt,' continued Lefine. 'No one ever visits him. But he often goes out, so he's almost never at home. Unfortunately, he is practically impossible to follow. For example, he will suddenly begin running and, obviously, the person who's following him can't do the same . . . He sometimes manages to lose my men. Sometimes I go myself to keep watch outside his house. I've tried to follow him three times but lost him. But yesterday I got Natai to tell me that Varencourt was coming to see him that day, to collect his traitor's salary. Natai refused to say exactly how much it was, from which I gathered that Varencourt is even greedier than I am. I hid opposite Natai's office. Varencourt came to get his money and immediately went off to gamble. He was so impatient that he wasn't as cunning and careful. He was trying quite hard, like the other times, but he must already have been thinking about the hands he was going to play, and this time he didn't manage to lose me.'

'Are you sure he didn't spot you?'

'When I follow someone, they only see me if I want them to! First he went to Quai des Miramiones, opposite Île Saint-Louis, to a cabaret, La Gueuse du quai. He seems to be very well known there. Everyone greeted him by the name Monsieur Pigrin. And his nickname seems to be King Midas because he's so lucky at cards that everything he touches turns to gold! I wish I was like that. He joined a table of whist players and began betting, betting, betting . . . I was having a drink with a bunch of drunkards who were all telling me their misfortunes, either real or imagined, and I was able to watch him discreetly. You should have seen his face as he looked at his cards. Such nervous excitement, such impatience, such rage . . . Oh, yes, the card-demon has him in its grip. And it's a hell of a demon, I can tell you! He won more often than he lost, and left with his winnings. He didn't seem worried about being set upon for the money – he must be armed. He didn't go far, only to a second bar, very small, Le Louveteau. I didn't go in there; it would have been too risky. So instead I asked a passer-by where I could find a game of cards. He gave me a few addresses of the best-known ones, La Commère, Le Sultan du feu . . . I went to the closest, which was Le Sultan du feu. What a strange name!'

'That's what the Mamelukes called Bonaparte during the Egyptian campaign, because our infantry fired on all the devils opposing them.'

'Who do you think came in half an hour later? He joined the other players like a starving man feeding his hunger. The more he plays, the more the card-demon reinforces his hold over him.'

'Like eau-de-vie only makes a drunkard thirstier and thirstier . . .'

'But this time he didn't play whist. He played vingt-et-un and he took huge risks. At first he accumulated winnings. But as he was pushing his luck, he began to lose. I did notice one thing. There was something that gave him more pleasure than winning. It was when he began to win after having lost a lot. It was very striking. When that happened, he was exultant.'

'Interesting. As if he prefers climbing back up a slope to climbing it in the first place.'

'That's a complicated way of saying what I've just explained clearly. That's you all over, that . . .'

Margont could easily imagine Charles de Varencourt busily studying his cards. When he spoke, he always seemed to be bargaining, to be engaged in a game.

'What did he do next?'

'At about six o'clock, he went to Faubourg Saint-Germain, Rue de Lille. Having played with the poor, he then went to play with the rich. He knocked on the door of a baroque-looking abode with moulded columns and statues of naked beauties supporting a large balcony – exactly the kind of house I dream of! A valet opened the door to him and greeted him with a bow, but not a deep bow. I had the impression that the owner of the house considered himself superior to Varencourt but that he nevertheless enjoyed his company. The servant said: "Monsieur le Comte would be delighted to play cards with you today but he would like to make clear that this time he will shuffle the cards himself." Varencourt agreed and went inside.'

'Perhaps he cheats sometimes and that's why his host wanted to deal the cards himself . . .'

'Other players arrived. There was an old aristocrat in a powdered wig, his face whitened with make-up, with one of those horrible tufts of hair on his chin. You could have sworn that he had inadvertently fallen asleep at Versailles and woken up twenty years later thinking, where the devil is Louis XVI? What's happened to the court and the Swiss Guard? Next to arrive was a captain of the National Guard, jingling his money in his hand. Finally a couple of bourgeois arrived at the same time, boasting of their success in the games they had just played.'

'They must have thought that swaggering would bring them luck. As if they were saying to Luck, "You remember us, don't you? We spent such good times together the last time . . ." What superstition!'

'I think they were all addicted to gambling. I did some research on the owner. He's the Comte de Barrelle. Imperial nobility. Sixty-three years old and never leaves the house. Varencourt came out three hours later looking depressed. Not bitter or angry, more despairing. I'm sure he had lost everything. He went home and sat up late. When every other house in the street was in darkness, there was still a candle burning in his bedroom window.'

'What's his house like?'

'He rents an attic. As small as a pigeon house.'

'I'm living like a pigeon too. How can he bear to live like that when he doesn't have to? The police are giving him vast sums of money!'

'He prefers gaming. And all this time soldiers aren't receiving any pay!'

'Everything froze during the retreat from Moscow . . . Going back to Charles de Varencourt. Why is he addicted to gambling?'

'Is there always a reason?'

'Not always. But sometimes. If he's the murderer, why the fire? There are too many blanks, too many gaps in what we know about the suspects. Time is not on our side, and yet we mustn't fail! The situation is already bad enough.'

Margont looked up the hill of Montmartre. From up there, the whole of the capital could be seen. It was the key to Paris. If the enemy captured it, they would mount large-calibre cannons on the top of it and they would be able to bombard the city. There should have been swarms of crack soldiers on the hill, building redoubts. When an ant hill is threatened, it covers itself in ants. The same should have gone for the heights at Saint-Germain, at la Villette, at Buttes-Chaumont and at Nogent-sur-Marne. From 1809 to 1810, when Wellington, the commander-in-chief of the British troops, had been operating in the Iberian Peninsula, he had erected fortifications at Torres Vedras to protect Lisbon. Margont had seen them with his own eyes. Ditches, pre-ditches, traps, bastions overlapping each other, entrenchments flanking the assailants, little fortresses . . . More than a hundred redoubts and four hundred and fifty cannons, all in three stacked lines! A triple line of defence, three raised fists, warning the French to stop! When Marshal Masséna came face to face with them, leading his sixty thousand men, he had indeed stopped short. He and his general staff had spent entire days trying to find ways through the blockade, had reached the conclusion that . . . it was impossible, and had ordered his troops to retreat. Wellington had triumphed without even having to fight. He had prepared for battle so comprehensively that he had won before it had even started! That's what should have been happening here! Paris should have been encircled by a triple line of defence like at Torres Vedras, and Montmartre should have been made into a great redoubt, more fearsome than the famous redoubt at the Battle of Borodino! But instead, the only activity came from the first butterflies fluttering around the five windmills on the hill.

'I've discovered some surprising things about Mademoiselle de Saltonges,' said Lefine, continuing with his report. 'I can't really believe that a woman would have the guts to burn off the face of a corpse, but—'

Margont burst out laughing. But it was a disturbing,

desperate laugh; he was laughing instead of crying. His friend looked at him uncomprehendingly as he tried to shake off a childhood memory. He was thirteen, walking in the streets of Nîmes, gradually rediscovering the world after four years being shut away in the Abbey of Saint-Guilhem-le-Désert. But the 'real' world was nothing like the paradise of his imagination. Without explaining why, his mother was taking a series of back routes. She was trying to hide the guillotine from him. The Terror was raging at that time and people were being executed in their thousands – for not being revolutionaries, or for not being revolutionary enough, or for being revolutionary but not in the correct way. Alas, she did not know that the residents of the Esplanade, where the 'National Razor' was normally set up, had complained about the smell of blood, so it had been moved. And that was how his mother came to lead him to the very spectacle she had tried to spare him. The sight he had briefly glimpsed would haunt him for ever. He saw women going up to the heads. Heads without bodies, bathing in bright-red blood. And these women, who calmly knitted as the executions were carried out, were aiming the points of their needles at the eyes of the freshly decapitated heads. A black screen suddenly cut off his vision. His mother covered his eyes with her hand to prevent him seeing any more. She fled, pulling her son by the hand, running as if the guillotine itself were chasing them. It was the only time in Margont's life when he had briefly wondered whether he should not return to the Abbey Saint-Guilhem-le-Désert of his own accord . . . He thought again about Louis de Leaume extricating himself from his shroud of corpses. Had he also seen those decapitated and mutilated heads? Yes, certainly!

But no hand had descended to protect him. He had looked at them, his gaze searing into their unseeing eyes.

'My dear Fernand, it's usually me who's the naïve one. But this time, it's the other way round. Your misogyny is misleading you. Catherine de Saltonges is as much a suspect as the others, believe me. When I met her, she seemed to want to avoid being present at my . . . at any violence towards me.'

He still could not articulate exactly what he had been through, as if the ordeal of his admission to the Swords of the King had become an absess that was going to go on getting worse.

'But it was obvious that she was just pretending. Had any violence occurred, she would happily have produced her knitting needles.'

Lefine grasped the reference. He had heard about 'the tricoteuses'. Although the nickname was used generally to mean the women who had come, during the Revolution, to listen to the debates at the National Convention, to keep an eye on the elected representatives and to participate in the debates with cheers or booing, it also evoked a much more sinister group, tiny but bloody . . .

'She married Baron de Joucy in 1788 at the age of seventeen. Her family were keen on the marriage because the Baron was a good catch. And she was keen on the marriage because she was in love. A good marriage and a love match! But the dream was short-lived and the awakening brutal. The Baron was an inveterate seducer, a regular Casanova, and he cheated on her endlessly – with her friends, her servants, with mothers, with their daughters, with prostitutes . . .'

'Surely that's a slight exaggeration?'

'Well, it's probably true that the rumours were exaggerated. But I managed to find a former servant of the household, one Guerloton, who had thrashed the Baron when he found him in bed with his wife! The Baron didn't press charges, for fear of publicity. He merely terminated the employment of the valet and his wife. Happily for the Baron, he now lives in London, because were he to return he would find someone waiting for him who would not stop at thrashing him this time . . . The saddest thing was that Catherine de Saltonges was oblivious. She didn't think that her pregnant servant was anything to do with her husband. He came home at all hours because of his "business affairs". Her husband flirted constantly with beautiful women. But she saw nothing, suspected nothing.'

'Her education can't have prepared her for such things. It must have been all crochet and the Bible . . .'

'All Parisian nobility was laughing at her behind her back, which delighted her husband, making him all the more desirable in the eyes of certain women. But one day in September 1792, Catherine de Saltonges cancelled a shopping trip unexpectedly because of a storm.'

'A storm that was the prelude to an even more violent tempest. I suppose she went home and discovered her husband in the arms of another woman.'

'That's exactly what happened. In her own bed, what's more. She ran away to her parents, who tried in vain to send her back to her legitimate husband. In their eyes, as in his, the couple had been married before God for better and for worse.'

'She being the better and he being the worst . . .'

'She changed completely after that. She had previously been shy and self-effacing; now she was transformed into a formidable woman. She decided to divorce! She was one of the first to make use of the famous law of October 1792 permitting divorce. Her grounds were her husband's "notorious disorderliness of morals". Can you imagine the reaction of the two families? Not to mention her husband's reaction. Up until that point the Revolution had not troubled the Baron much. Of course, he feared the revolutionaries, but he would never have thought that the Revolution might harm him because of his wife! She was brave enough to appear before the district tribunal; since it was not a case of divorce by mutual consent and since the Baron denied the accusations she brought against him, there had to be a trial. A baroness who wanted to divorce! It caused hilarity amongst the revolutionaries and there was a hue and cry amongst the aristocracy. To his horror the Baron became the laughing stock of his peers! Catherine de Saltonges had succeeded in reversing the roles. She pressed on with the trial despite pressure from her friends and family. The revolutionaries make an example of the case, the newspapers wrote about it endlessly . . . I was able to track down a witness at the trial, an old soldier who had been allocated guard duty at the district tribunal. He told me that the trial became a spectacle. When the baroness was expected, reinforcements of soldiers were called in. The crowds grew ever thicker and had to be pushed back to let her through. On the one hand there were some daring priests and hordes of anxious husbands come to boo and hiss. On the other there were revolutionaries and hundreds of women of all ages! Catherine de Saltonges arrived, outwardly serene. She advanced through a barrage of insults, spitting, cheering and applauding. Then she answered the questions put to her. She repeated to the tribunal everything her so-called friends had hastened to tell her after she had discovered her husband's true nature. Each of her husband's infidelities became a weapon for his spouse to use against him! She repaid blow for blow. Several times the sessions degenerated and the tribunal had to be evacuated. But each time, she returned, composed, as if she had forgotten the threats and brawls of the previous session.'

Margont was perplexed. Lefine's description did not fit at all with his memory of her. He had the feeling that the more he learned about the woman the less he knew her. 'I don't know if I would have had her daring, in the same situation.'

'Well, I know that I wouldn't. I would have left with the silver. The district tribunal found in her favour. Her husband emigrated to London, officially because of revolutionary fury, which was set to increase, but also to escape public derision.'

'Well done, Fernand, good work!'

Lefine looked pleased. When he was complimented, he thrust his chest out like the fabled crow, though he would never have opened his beak and let the cheese fall out . . .

Margont grew thoughtful.

'What you've told me explains some of her behaviour. When I met her, I had the impression that I disgusted her. I had never encountered such a reaction before. Having been deceived for such a long time made the betrayal she suffered much worse. She must have developed a hatred of lies. I think she's on the lookout for lies everywhere and in everyone she meets. And she's discerning – she picked up that I was not being honest with them. I'm going to have to be very careful when she's there!'

'If she poses the most danger to you, why don't you seduce her?'

'What a despicable idea!'

'If she's in love she will be blind to—'

'I don't like the way you treat people like pawns.'

'And how do they treat us?'

'You can't see her burning off the face of a corpse . . . but I'm not so sure . . . In any case, she's certainly a strong character. She introduced herself under her maiden name and none of the members dared call her "Madame de Joucy", even though they probably all disapprove of the divorce.'

'She's the only other member whose address we know. She doesn't seem to be aware that the police are investigating her. She lives in Faubourg Saint-Germain – I'm having her house watched.'

'Are you using trustworthy men, as I asked?'

'Yes, I can vouch for them. They haven't discovered anything very interesting about her daily life.'

Margont rose. 'Let's go and stretch our legs.'

They went towards the hill of Montmartre and started to climb it slowly. It was so easy at the moment . . . but should the Allies arrive at the gates of Paris, they would inevitably attack Montmartre. And so with every step, Margont imagined he was already stepping over the enemy corpses that would litter the slopes.

'What did you find out about Honoré de Nolant? I know nothing about him, other than that he was the one the group had allocated to slit my throat, if necessary. So obviously he is capable of killing. Perhaps he has already done so . . . He's the one I know the least, but at the same time he's the most dangerous.'

'You're right to fear him, because he has done some unpleasant things. The police reports contain some interesting facts about him. His family belongs to the nobility of Champagne. As an adolescent he was part of Louis XVI's entourage. He used to read to the King and perform other similarly useless services. Nolant really was a good friend. But he was quick to spot the change in the prevailing wind, and after 1790 he began to pass information secretly to the members of the National Assembly who were drawing up the new constitution. He passed on the details of the lives of the King, Marie-Antoinette, the dauphin . . . According to what I read, he was the first to reveal the disappearance of the King and his family on the night of 20 June 1791 . . .'

'The flight of the King, that ended at Varennes, when a postmaster, Jean-Baptiste Drouet, recognised Louis XVI.'

'Honoré de Nolant was cunning. By the time he had raised the alert, the royal family was already on the road. He claimed that he reacted as soon as he had noticed that the King was no longer there. But I think he was hedging his bets. Had Louis XVI been able to escape abroad, Nolant, who was certainly aware of the plan and had perhaps even helped with arrangements, would have been rewarded. But once the King was arrested, the revolutionaries stopped treating Honoré de Nolant as merely a spy and welcomed him as a real revolutionary. He changed his name to "Denolant" and had a dazzling career. In 1793 he spied on behalf of the Committee of Public Safety, the bloodthirsty alliance – Robespierre, Couthon, Saint-Just – that wanted to guillotine every Frenchman!'

'Another spy? Varencourt, me, now Nolant . . .'

'If you stick your hand in the hornets' nest, you shouldn't be surprised if you keep coming across hornets.'

'The Swords of the King must be unaware of all that. They would never have accepted such a man into their ranks! They must know only part of his history.'

'Afterwards he worked for the Revolutionary Tribunal. So he might well have had reason one day to write out the name Louis de Leaume, adding after it, "Condemned to death by guillotine." When Bonaparte was proclaimed emperor, Honoré de Nolant became an imperialist and denounced the partisans of the Republic. He had gathered many contacts during his time as part of Louis XVI's entourage, and then amongst the higher revolutionary echelons. Which was why Fouché, when he was head of the civilian police, decided to take him into his ministry where apparently he was very useful. He helped put together dossiers on the royalists, on revolutionaries and on republicans who were opposed to the Emperor. But in January 1810 people started to suspect that he was embezzling money. Honoré de Nolant immediately disappeared – from one day to the next! The police realised he had been making fools of them. He had claimed to have numerous informants who would only deal with him. But most of them did not actually exist and Nolant simply kept the sums he was supposed to pay over to them for himself. In exchange for the money, he invented republican plots, assassination plans . . . it was all hot air. Expensive with it. The civilian police hate him.'

'He can't have walked away empty-handed, and I'm not only referring to money. He must have joined the Swords of the King complete with dossiers of information. That's why he was accepted onto the committee! He's the reason they are so well informed. Thanks to him they continually avoid detection by the police! He must have given them the names of the investigators in charge of tracking royalist organisations, and the names of their informers . . . Perhaps he still has friends in the Ministry of Civilian Police, who continue to keep him informed. Now I understand why Joseph and Talleyrand chose me. It's because I have nothing at all to do with any of the imperial police forces.'

'That's all I have on Honoré de Nolant.'

'The group must be suspicious of him. They make him pay for his treachery by giving him the dirty jobs. He's obliged to prove his loyalty by spilling blood. He's a professional traitor: a royalist, a revolutionary, a republican, an imperialist and then a royalist again . . . It must have been he who realised that the best way to disrupt the defence of Paris would be to murder those in charge. He understood the situation from the inside. He must have been the one to suggest Colonel Berle! So at the very least, he was an accomplice to the crime!'

'Calm down . . . you're in a state!'

'At least the others are following an ideology. Even Charles de Varencourt is loyal to his passion for gambling. But Honoré de Nolant . . .'

'If he's arrested, the police will hang him. Unless the army has him shot before that.'

'I can't see any connection between him and fire.'

They reached the summit of Montmartre and Paris stretched out before them. Louis XIV had stamped his mark on the city with his grandiose architectural schemes: the golden dome of the Invalides shimmered like a second sun – sparking off dreams that were immediately quenched by fear – Place Vendôme . . . Napoleon had done the same, to tell the world that he was as great as the Sun King: with the column in Place Vendôme, the Arc de Triomphe still under construction, the Église de la Madeleine imitating a Greco-Roman temple, the opening up of Rue de Rivoli, the bridges of Austerlitz, Iéna and des Arts . . . Paris was starting to look like a vast chessboard on which the rich accumulated palaces and other playthings like so many sumptuous pawns.

'And finally, there's Jean-Baptiste de Châtel. He was born in 1766, to a noble family from Orléans. He entered the Cistercian Abbey of Pagemont in the Loiret at an early age. He wasn't like you: he really wanted to become a monk. But he soon got himself expelled by the Abbey, discreetly, on the pretext of ill health, because the Church wanted to avoid a scandal. Why do you think he did that?'

'I spent four years in an abbey and you're asking me why? I could talk all day on that subject! Because he wanted to see the world, because he had fallen in love, because he wanted to have children, because he was attracted to women, or men, or he'd lost his faith . . .'

'No, it wasn't any of those things. It was because he wanted to reform everything: the running order of Mass, the ordination of priests, the functioning of the Vatican . . .'

'A reformer?'

'Yes, but a conservative reformer. He found the other monks didn't pray devoutly enough to God and that Pope Pius VI and Louis XVI were too moderate.'

Margont shook his head, incredulous.

'Pius VI, too moderate? You mean that Jean-Baptiste de Châtel was more royalist than the King and more Catholic than the Pope? How is that possible?'

'Well, here's an example. He wanted to ban all religions other than Catholicism.'

'Wonderful! He wanted to ignite religious wars! What else?'

'He was adamant that atheism should also be banned, and that education could only be provided by priests; he campaigned for renewed crusades to liberate Jerusalem.'

'Oh, so that's why the other members refer to him as "the crusader". He's a bigot!'

'In 1791 he was keen to escape revolutionary France and considered the French clergy were too soft, so he went to Spain. He made an impressive start there: he was admitted to the Abbey of Aljanfe, near Madrid, where he became the heir apparent to the abbot. In fact, many of the Spanish clergy shared his views that the French religious community was too moderate. His intransigent sermons were very appealing.'

'But I wager he rapidly overtook even the most fanatical Spanish.'

'He did indeed. In Spain, you don't take liberties with Catholicism, and in 1797 he was imprisoned by the Inquisition, accused of heresy because some of his interpretations of the Bible diverged from dogma. For example, he stirred up controversy about Christ's poverty. According to the Bible, Christ had no personal or shared possessions. And it follows from this that the Catholic Church should also take a vow of poverty.'

'That's a long-standing debate that worries the Catholic Church a great deal. In the Middle Ages, Franciscans were frequently burnt at the stake merely for raising the question.'

'His trial lasted three years.'

'That's incredible!'

'It's because he defended himself so vigorously. He used his theological knowledge to confound the Inquisitors, he contested every point and argued ceaselessly. He kept going back to what he called the original Bible – that's to say the most ancient texts in old Hebrew, in Aramaic and Ancient Greek – and referring to what he considered translation errors.'

Margont was astounded. He himself was quite capable of insolence – it was a typically revolutionary characteristic – and so he was always impressed when he heard about someone even more daring than he.

He said, as much to himself as to Lefine, 'So in fact, he was saying to the Inquisitors – the most fanatical of fanatics – that they had the wrong Bible and he had the correct one, so he was the only man on earth to have access to the word of God.'

'I would have loved to see that! And because inquisitorial trials are scrupulously recorded, the Inquisitors were obliged to answer him. Besides, Châtel drew attention to the irregularities in his trial. He knew all about inquisitorial proceedings because he believed that the Inquisition should be re-established in all countries. During his time at the Abbey of Pagemont, he had worked on updating the proceedings – although no one had asked him to. Apparently he was already assuming that he would be the new inquisitor general of France.'

'But where did he find the time? Monks are busy all day long: praying, listening to sermons in the chapterhouse, working, praying again, reading the Holy Scriptures, listening to the word of God . . . They rarely have even short periods of free time.'

'It doesn't say in police reports how he found time.'

'He must have done it at night . . .'

'At the end of the trial the Spanish Inquisition condemned him to death. But the sentence was commuted to life imprisonment after an appeal was made to the newly elected pope, Pius VII. Châtel rotted in a Madrid gaol, dying a slow death while reading the Bible the Inquisitors were happy to let him have. It was Napoleon who eventually saved his life in 1808 when he suppressed the Inquisition after he besieged Spain.'

'Châtel wasn't very grateful. He thinks the Emperor is the Antichrist. I thought he was joking when he said that, but now I'm sure that everything he said he meant literally.'

'The police lost track of him after he was freed, and I haven't been able to do much better. He only reappeared in 1813, in Paris, as a member of the Swords of the King. I can't see any link between him and fire either.'

'He doesn't get on with Louis de Leaume. He can't accept anyone's authority, so he's uncontrollable. I think even waging a campaign of murders would be too mild for him. What are his real aims, I wonder.' Margont was lost in thought for a moment. 'They all have lives that reflect the period we're living through: turbulent, full of confusion, contradictions and periods of wandering . . . And we all believed that after the Revolution, everything would get better . . . What do you know about the other members who aren't on the committee?'

'Not very much. They are a mixed bunch: monarchists, rabid believers whom Jean-Baptiste de Châtel convinced to join the Swords of the King with his sermons, refugees from other dismantled royalist groups . . . The biggest group are opportunists who've become royalists because they can see the tide is turning.'

'What did Charles de Varencourt really tell Joseph's agents?'

'There's a whole police report on the subject. Very little on the committee members, because he claims they all keep their life stories to themselves. He only supplied new information on Vicomte de Leaume, whom he said had spent at least two years in England, living with friends in the Strand, the heart of the French royalist community. Paradoxically, what Varencourt really gave away was himself. The police had managed to identify all the members of the group – except him! Varencourt had believed that they already knew about him before he betrayed himself, but it wasn't true.'

'That was clever of him!'

'He confirmed what the police already suspected – that the Swords of the King were planning to foment a popular uprising in favour of Louis XVIII.'

'It's a fashionable idea. Especially amongst monarchists. A

bloodless revolution that would sweep away the republican-inspired empire and restore the King. A sort of inverted Revolution, which would overturn all that the revolutionaries had put in place. Although that seems to me pie in the sky, just a way of refusing to face reality.'

'And the group's emblem. There again the police had their suspicions. The white cockade is deemed too popular by aristocrats, so the secret royalist societies like to develop their own devices of recognition. But Charles de Varencourt gave a detailed description of their emblem. And finally he revealed their proposed campaign of assassinations. But you'll be furious when I tell you that although Varencourt supplied a list of eleven victims, Natai didn't give it to me. He told me that his superiors were adamant that you shouldn't discuss it with Varencourt.'

Margont managed not to lose his temper. 'What?'

'Look, it's not surprising if you think about it. Joseph must judge that it's not necessary for your investigation and he wants to limit the risk of the list of names circulating . . . especially if his is on it! Right, that completes my report.'

'Thanks, Fernand! Your help is invaluable! Try to continue finding out more about our suspects. The first one of us who has something new should get in contact with the other.'

Lefine left. Margont stayed for a while, lying on the grass at the foot of one of the windmills, enjoying the gentle breeze and looking out across Paris.

When he went into his room Margont noticed that it had been searched. He was always careful before he went out to put some of his possessions in designated places. Some of these had been moved. His books were no longer piled up in the same order as he had left them; his mattress was touching the wall, although he had left a small gap. The intruder had been very careful and nothing had been stolen, so without these little indicators Margont would not have noticed anything. And the more he thought about it, the less sure he became . . . Had his books and mattress really been moved? He could not ask his landlord, who, even had he noticed anything, would have denied seeing anyone enter. He ran his hand over the pile of books, trying to prove to himself that their arrangement felt different since his meeting with Lefine. He often believed he was being followed when he was outside. By one of the Swords of the King? By a policeman who took him for a royalist? Or maybe someone with personal motives? He could not tell if he was imagining it all.

He hurried over to his chest. He had hammered a little nail inside it, right at the bottom, on the left, and had attached a thread to it. Before leaving, he always took the thread out of the chest and attached it to a notch on the lid. Once he was back he would untie it. This time the thread had been broken. So someone really had rummaged through his room. He felt strangely comforted by the knowledge – he was not losing his mind. Not yet anyway . . . His grip on reality seemed to be hanging by that thread.

CHAPTER 14

I T was 21 March and Napoleon was surveying the Bohemian army under the command of Generalissimo Schwarzenberg, from the heights of the plateau south of Arcis-sur-Aube. The Emperor blinked, incredulous. He had defeated the Allies over and over again, and this was the result! Those massed ranks blanketing the horizon. A hundred thousand men at the very least. Divisions, methodically formed into giant rectangles, made up a spider's web awaiting the attack of the French army. But the latter comprised only thirty thousand soldiers, since some of the troops had been scattered during manoeuvres and battles . . . Napoleon had thought the Austro-Russian force was retreating! They *had* to be retreating. He continued to scour the hordes for signs of disorder, or for movements backwards . . .

Finally he reached the inescapable conclusion. It was the French who would have to retreat. But in which direction?

The most obvious solution was to withdraw to Paris, to protect the capital. But what would the Allied armies do then? They would unite into one, having learnt the dangers of operating separately. Schwarzenberg's Bohemian army would join forces with Marshal Blücher's Silesian army, and they, reinforced by other diverse troops, would both be joined by the nearest units of Bernadotte's Army of the North. The French would be ignominiously forced back to Paris . . . Several members of the imperial general staff advised retiring to Paris, but only because they could not envisage any other course of action.

Napoleon then took one of the most important decisions of his career. He had been plotting the manoeuvre for several days and had discussed it with his marshals, who, in the main, opposed it. They considered it too complicated and, above all, too risky. But it offered the only possibility of victory, and so that day Napoleon decided to press ahead with it. The French army would not turn back towards Paris; it would go round the Allied army to threaten its rear. The enemy needed vast amounts of supplies to feed and equip such a quantity of troops. And the Emperor was counting on his own prestige. The enemy feared him when he was in front of them, so what general would dare turn his back on him? His tactic would sow panic in the Allied ranks. He wanted to force his enemies to pursue him. He would also be leading them away from Paris, towards the east, where he would rally fresh troops who were stationed in strongholds. But the danger of the tactic was obvious: no one would be defending the road to Paris. It was a gamble, a throw of the dice.

CHAPTER 15

MARGONT was radiant, his fingers ink-stained and his hands full of paper. Around him typesetters and printers bustled about, brushing purposefully past him. The print shop was a hive of productivity pouring out ink like honey. They had received several orders that they had to fulfil as quickly as possible. Restaurants were changing their menus. In 1800 on the eve of the Battle of Marengo, Napoleon – then merely Bonaparte – had eaten a delicious dish: chicken with a tomato sauce flavoured with little onions, garlic and crayfish. After the battle, the recipe had been renamed 'chicken Marengo' and was to this day very popular. It was as if the flavour of the sauce was enhanced by the glory of the victory. Inevitably today innkeepers were offering 'beef Olssufiev', reflecting Napoleon's resounding defeat of General Olssufiev's small élite army at the Battle of Champaubert, which had set off an astonishing series of victories. But Margont knew that there were dozens of other Olssufievs waiting in the wings.

Margont had suggested an unusual typeface for a ball invitation and was reading the proofs. He was yet again imagining he was printing his newspaper. His fingers manipulated the lead letters with the ease of a master. As he was checking the phrases, his imagination was creating others, all with the word 'liberty' in them. This double personality was mixed with a third, that of a royalist. Margont was trying to find the most convincing posters supporting a restoration. The more he succeeded in that the more he would gain the confidence of the Swords of the King. But it would be a double-edged victory. What if the Swords of the King, in their enthusiasm, teamed up with other royalist groups? What if Paris found itself blanketed with posters? How ironic if Margont's success in his mission should bring about the thing he most dreaded.

Mathurin Jelent knew that Margont was playing a role, but although he passed Margont orders and went through the accounts with him, his face never betrayed what he knew. He was completely at ease.

A street urchin burst into the print shop. He was scrawny, but arrogant and aggressive, like a cockerel ruling the roost. One of the employees picked up an iron bar, which had been part of a now useless press, and put it over his shoulder. Bands of marauding children were plaguing the capital, terrorising passers-by . . .

'M'sieur de Langès, your friend Fernand wants to see you; he needs money urgently. Otherwise, he's in danger of being chucked in the Seine . . .'

Margont followed him out, seizing his hat and coat on the way. The lad led him to a small street in Faubourg Saint-Germain where they found Lefine, who rewarded the boy with a coin.

'What's happened?' demanded Margont.

The debt story was their code for an emergency. Lefine told him that they were very near Catherine de Saltonges's house. Actually the house belonged to her parents, who had withdrawn to the country to flee the scandal surrounding their daughter's divorce.

Saint-Germain had once been a favoured address of the nobility, but that had all changed after 1789. Many of the landlords had emigrated to escape the Revolution, abandoning their houses, which had been seized, declared national property and resold. Now diverse social groups co-existed: aristocrats, republicans grown rich from the whirlwind of events of the last few years, dignitaries of the Empire – Marshal Davout, Prince Eugène de Beauharnais, Cambacérès – and armies of functionaries who worked for the Ministries of War, the Interior, Culture, Foreign Relations . . . It all made an astonishing mosaic of royalist white, republican blue and imperial gold.

Lefine gestured towards the child and said, 'Let me introduce Michel. He and his brother have been keeping a watch on Catherine de Saltonges for me.'

Margont could not believe his ears. 'He's one of the trusted men you're relying on?'

'Yes, he is! When you're worried about being followed, you turn round all the time trying to see if anyone looks suspicious. But who would notice a brat, and a beggar at that? Michel, tell Quentin what you saw.'

'That woman, she's acting very strangely . . . She hasn't stopped crying since yesterday. This morning she went out twice, alone. She took a few steps along the street and then started crying, changed her mind and went back inside again.'

In the print works, the child had spoken the language of the street urchin, now he expressed himself more clearly. He delighted in deceiving everyone. Just like Lefine!

'The third time, she went to Rue de la Garance. That's in Faubourg Saint-Antoine. She tried to make sure no one followed her but I was always right there. It was easy! A woman let her in. I'd say your woman stayed about an hour. Then she came out again, crying and very pale! You would have thought she was about to mount the scaffold. She went home four or five hours ago. I wasn't sure if I should, but I alerted Fernand . . .'

'You were right. What did she go to do in Saint-Antoine? Right, Fernand, you stay here in case she comes out again. And, Michel, you take me to the person she went to see.'

'That's dangerous,' Lefine declared.

He dared not say any more in front of Michel, who seemed to be looking off distractedly into the distance, a sure sign that he was listening for all he was worth. Margont had already weighed up the pros and cons. It was true that the woman he was going to meet might inform Catherine de Saltonges of his visit. But he could always claim he was trying to find out about the other members of the committee, as surely they were trying to find out about him. His investigation was not progressing as quickly as the military situation. He was running out of time and he was obliged to act and ready to lower his guard a little.

'Let's go, Michel,' he ordered.

CHAPTER 16

As Margont knocked on the door, he had still not worked out a plausible reason for his visit. Unusually for him, normally so methodical and careful, he was improvising. A woman of about fifty answered the door. She smiled in a friendly manner. There was no doubt that here was the woman Michel had described. She invited him in, without asking any questions as if it were the most natural thing in the world.

The living space was cramped but very clean and tidy. Margont was intrigued by the way it was laid out. The room they were in seemed to serve as kitchen and bedroom, with an impeccably made and tucked in bed. But a closed door indicated that there was another room. The premises were like the woman who lived in them: pleasant and welcoming. She offered Margont a seat. Why is she at such pains to make me feel at home? he wondered. The chair she had proposed for him was arranged in such a way that he was not looking directly at the door of the other room. But nor was the woman hiding it, it was simply discreetly out of sight. Margont guessed that this was no coincidence. Everything here was carefully worked out. The clue to the mystery lay behind that door.

'May I know who recommended me?' asked the woman. She was smiling at him, but her question was pointed.

'A woman friend of mine . . .'

'It's always "a friend" who recommends me. But I need to know who exactly. Otherwise I won't be able to help you.'

Firm but kind. A rather extraordinary person. Had she been a man, Margont would have assumed she had been a soldier. She was used to dealing with awkward situations. And the way she had invited him in – he could have been a burglar. She must know how to defend herself. Or else what she did forced her to act in this open way. If she had tried to seduce him he would have concluded that she was a prostitute. Perhaps she was a go-between? Had Catherine de Saltonges come here to prostitute herself in a room behind that mysterious door? But that hypothesis ran counter to everything he felt he knew about her! Had her husband corrupted her into behaving as he behaved? Margont blushed at the thought and his discomfort reassured the woman.

'Don't be embarrassed, Monsieur. It's quite normal, but rest assured I won't say a thing.'

That was just the problem . . . She was waiting for a response. I'd better just bluff, like Charles de Varencourt, Margont said to himself. 'It was Mademoiselle Catherine de Saltonges who recommended you.'

That reply put the woman completely at ease. 'Is she all right? I was worried about her.'

'She's still crying a great deal . . .'

'That's understandable. When you discover you're having a child, you worry and panic and wish that it didn't exist, but once it's gone, you wonder if you've made the right decision . . .'

An abortionist! Catherine de Saltonges had come to have an

abortion. Who was the father? Why had she not kept the child? Margont was bursting with questions.

'She was very unsure . . .' the woman said.

Her sentence ended in an uncertain silence. She wondered if she were not giving too much away. Margont reflected that she might know who the father was.

He ventured: 'Um . . . the father . . . I don't know if she told you a bit about him . . .'

'Yes, she did confide in me, she had to tell someone. I do feel she should have told him about the child – he had a right to know. If he had supported her, I'm certain she would have kept the child. At the beginning she told me he couldn't be there because he had business to attend to, but later she admitted that he was not aware of the child's existence. She felt that he had suffered enough and that he would neither be able to welcome the child, nor to take responsibility for the decision not to keep it. She was distraught that she had fallen pregnant so quickly, when she had previously been married for four and a half years without it ever happening. She said that despite her age, she hoped one day to have another child with her lover, but that next time they would be able to keep it and bring it up. Together. What a tragedy! The father must have been through terrible times.'

She was eaten up with curiosity and hoped to get him to tell her more. Margont looked worried.

'We are very concerned about him. Did she explain why?'

'No, she told me almost nothing about him. Not even his name. When she came the second time, when I performed the procedure, I said to her, "Another married man who makes fine promises and then decides he doesn't want to leave his wife." She laughed bitterly and replied, "Exactly right! Except that his wife is dead! And how do you leave a dead person?"'

'It's a very sad story . . .' He was trying to be as evasive as possible.

Burning to know more, she said: 'All she would say is, "He's already lost so many of his family and now he's about to lose someone else without even knowing they exist. Fate is conspiring to kill his children before they are born." Isn't it awful?'

She leant forward so as not to lose a single word of the confidences she thought he was about to whisper to her.

'Yes. But just now it's Mademoiselle de Saltonges I'm worried about. She's so pale and weak . . . Did she bleed much?'

'Inevitably, since the pregnancy was more than two months advanced . . .'

Finally, regretfully realising that he was not going to reveal anything further, she decided to change the subject. 'But what about your case, Monsieur?'

Margont floundered for a moment, then pulled himself together. 'No, in the case of my lady friend, she's only in her first month.'

'In that case it's possible that a concoction of plant extracts and a massage of the stomach will be all that's necessary. If that doesn't work, or if you leave it too late, I'll use a needle. But I'm experienced. If your friend decides to use my services she will have to give me her name. Her real name, because I will check . . . I need to know. It's my way of ensuring that there's no trickery, that you're not a policeman . . . Also, sometimes when

I discover the identity of the person I choose to withhold my services. You would be astonished to know the celebrated and powerful people who contact me. Even the wife of a marshal . . . In those cases, I always refuse, whatever price they offer me. But you can count on my complete discretion.'

The room behind the door made its presence felt more than ever. Catherine de Saltonges had been there, eaten up by doubt; the odour of her blood still impregnated the air; women had died in there . . .

'I'll think about it,' he announced. He rose, adopting the air of a man who had been reassured and who was going to confer the life of his loved one to a woman he barely knew. They said goodbye to each other cordially and Margont took his leave. He had not even revealed his name. As he crossed the threshold he shivered under the glacial caress of those who had died in the house.

CHAPTER 17

ONCE he had sent Michel away, Margont relayed every-thing to Lefine. As he was talking, a bitter taste filled his mouth as if he had bitten into a plum without checking whether it was ripe. He was upset that he had been drawn into the private life of Catherine de Saltonges. He had barely finished his account before he launched into his hypotheses.

'In leaving her lover in ignorance of her pregnancy, she lied to him – by omission. And she did that even though she has a horror of lying!'

'Well, you're playing at espionage and you're cheating and manipulating even though, ordinarily, you vaunt the merits of sincerity, honesty and loyalty . . .'

'The world has become a giant fools' playground where everything is topsy-turvy. Do you think the father is a member of the Swords of the King?'

'I think it's very likely, since they're the only people she keeps company with. According to the police, since her divorce she doesn't see her old friends any more. Michel and his brother have been watching her since the beginning of our investi-gation: she often walks in the public gardens or in Faubourg Saint-Germain, but she never goes to visit anyone, nor does anyone visit her.'

'She's been pregnant for more than two months. The child

must have been conceived around the beginning of January. She hesitated a while before deciding to get rid of it. If the father really is one of our suspects, it's possible that he was the murderer. If that's the case, does she know? Was she his accomplice? She told the abortionist that the father had business to attend to. She also mentioned that he had already lost many close relations. That could be Louis de Leaume or Jean-Baptiste de Châtel . . . But the others must also have seen family members disappear during the Revolution. We don't know enough about the pasts of our suspects, I've already told you that.'

'I'm doing my best to find out! They don't know anything about your past either, otherwise—' Lefine stopped short, looking embarrassed.

Margont was reminded once again of the risks he was having to run for this affair. He had fought all over Europe, against the Austrians, Hungarians, Russians, Prussians, English and Spanish . . . and yet he could easily be killed right here in Paris by a Frenchman. Apparently Fate had a sense of humour; how it must laugh seated with Death in that tavern at the end of the street, drinking to his demise as it watched him through the window. These sombre reflections were chased away by a flash of inspiration.

'The father will go and visit her! Even if he hasn't guessed what's wrong he must have noticed that something is. She can't be her normal self! If he loves her, he must be worried about her. Or else she will go and visit him. She almost died and she's lost a child she wanted to keep! She needs the man's support. I'm going to stay here. Call Michel back so that he can help me.'

'And I suppose I'm going to have to try again to find out more about our suspects . . .'

Margont was not very good at surveillance. Waiting exasperated him. He tried to make use of the lost hours by thinking about his investigation, especially about the evening he had met the committee of the Swords of the King. Perhaps an important detail had escaped him. In light of what he now knew, the memory of that meeting took on a different hue. Who could be the tormented lover of Catherine de Saltonges? It was Louis de Leaume who had addressed her to introduce Margont as the new recruit. Was that a sign of connivance between them? Or had he merely been the one to speak because he was the head of the committee? It was probably not Honoré de Nolant . . . Catherine de Saltonges seemed to have a horror of murder; she would not have allowed her lover to be the hangman of the group. Although . . .

Michel was amused to see how Margont, who was obviously a soldier – he had a scar on his left cheek and his assured manner spoke of success in dealing with dangerous situations – could not bear the enforced inactivity. Michel, on the other hand, was enjoying it. He was being paid to do nothing – what could be better?

'You're going to give us away, Boss,' he told Margont with his most ironic smile.

'Don't call me "Boss".'

'The boss is the person who pays, Boss. If you don't stop walking about and turning in circles, someone is going to notice us. You need to melt into the crowd – but you hate crowds.'

'Because they don't move fast enough. You're right, though, I'll try to calm down.'

Half an hour later he was less calm than ever. He was on the point of returning to the printer's when the door opened. He hurriedly hid out of sight. Michel was aghast. 'It's a good thing your woman is still crying and can't see anything much, otherwise she would be wondering who that man was, pressing himself against the wall and dirtying his overcoat just as she was coming out.'

'You stay here, Michel.'

'Happy to.'

Margont followed Catherine de Saltonges. He had not taken offence at the brat's comments. He knew the child was right, and tried to behave like someone out for a stroll like everyone else. He raised his collar and crammed his hat down on his head to make himself unrecognisable at first glance, hoping it would be assumed that he was feeling the cold. The crowd also helped to make him less noticeable.

Catherine de Saltonges was making her way along Boulevard Saint-Germain in a strange fashion. Sometimes she would walk quickly, at other times she was almost stationary. She was riven with indecision. She branched off towards the Seine, reached the embankment and went over to the river, moved closer to the river, then closer still . . .

She's going to throw herself in, thought Margont. What should he do? Save her and ruin all his efforts to be accepted by the Swords of the King? Call for help? Catherine de Saltonges leant over the green, glacial water. An invisible thread seemed to pull her backwards. Nevertheless she continued to walk along the embankment. It was as if she was walking along beside Death and finding it surprisingly soothing. Finally she turned back and went across the old Saint-Michel bridge, which now resembled a plucked peacock. In 1809, the sixty houses that had been built on the bridge two centuries before were all destroyed.

When she reached Île de la Cité, she crossed the cathedral square and went into Notre-Dame. Margont went in as well and kept to one side so that he could slide discreetly from pillar to pillar. Although thousands of churches and abbeys had been devastated, pillaged, transformed into stables or stone quarries with ready-made stones, or even into the Stock Exchange (the Paris Stock Exchange had been installed in the church of Petits-Pères from 1796 to 1807), Notre-Dame had been left relatively unscathed. It was in fact where Napoleon had been crowned emperor of the French on 2 December 1804.

Catherine de Saltonges's steps resounded with surprising force, as if the burden she was carrying was weighing her down. She looked tiny amidst the vertiginously tall columns. In the gloom, the multicoloured windows gleamed, transmitting the light of God to man through their images.

She went into a chapel and knelt down – or rather fell to her knees – and joined her hands. She was motionless, so wrapped up in prayer that it seemed as if she had been changed into a pillar of salt. Christ looked down at her from his Cross with such compassion that he might have been about to rip his hands free from the nails to hold her in his arms.

Moments passed. When she eventually moved again it was

to bow, as if she were about to prostrate herself. Then she rose and returned shakily through the cathedral. She stopped at the intersection of the nave and transept and looked up at the dome where there was a painted medallion representing the Virgin holding the baby Jesus in her arms, against a starry night background. Catherine de Saltonges repressed a sob.

But when she reached the light of the entrance, she began to walk firmly. She must not reveal her wounds and hurt to the world. Ever.

Margont hesitated. Instead of following her, he went back to the chapel. At the foot of the cross, in the middle of the lighted tapers, were three little objects, nestling next to each other. A folded woman's handkerchief, a button, and a golden bracelet just big enough to fit the wrist of a baby . . .

Margont stretched out his hand, feeling as if it were being devoured by imaginary insects born of his guilt. The button was gold-coloured metal, like the button from a uniform. But it had been beaten with a flat object. Not with a hammer, in which case it would have been cracked and crushed. The heel of a shoe? Unfortunately the motif was unrecognisable: perhaps a number or a letter, an emblem, or two symbols intertwined.

Margont decided to leave the two other items since they did not tell him anything he did not already know. The bracelet would soon be stolen. Catherine de Saltonges had not wanted to keep the jewel she had intended for the newborn. But she had not been able to bring herself to give it to someone else, or to have it melted down or to throw it away. Instead she had offered it up to Christ in the hope that he would authorise a mother come to pray to him to take it for the wrist of her child.

Margont knelt on one knee and scraped the edge of the button on the ground leaving a light tracing of gold dust. Then he slipped it into his pocket.

He went out and caught up with Catherine de Saltonges, who was walking slowly home. He reflected on the strangeness of the little family: a woman who had almost thrown herself into the Seine, a child dead before it was born and a man of whom nothing was known but this damaged button.

CHAPTER 18

THE needles were lined up on the table along with the terra-cotta pots. Their geometrical neatness reassured him. The first needle had been soaked in curare forty-eight hours earlier, the next one thirty-six hours, then thirty, twenty-four, eighteen, twelve, nine, six, five, four, three, two and finally one hour previously. He picked up the oldest one and went over to the rabbit he had bought at Les Halles. The animal was trembling in its cage, trying to squeeze out through the bars . . . The man injected it. The beast squealed and began to leap about its prison. The movement should have accelerated the circulation of blood and hastened the action of the poison. But the rabbit continued to thrash about and bang into the sides of the cage. Failure. After forty-eight hours the curare must have evaporated or mutated on contact with the air and was no longer effective. He had expected problems like that . . . Little was known about curare, partly because it was so hard to come by and partly because there were so many variants.

He took the next needle and injected his victim again. Another failure. The animal's movements, more erratic than ever, contrasted with the irreproachable order of the lined-up needles. A third attempt led to a third failure. Had the product deteriorated in the pots? A fourth injection, still no result. He started to lose his temper. He would have liked to wring the stupid rabbit's neck, making its vertebrae crack so that it would be rendered as motionless as the other objects in the room. But he controlled his mounting rage. He was used to doing that.

The four-hour needle was effective: instantaneous death. So once the needle had been soaked in curare he would have to try to take action within four hours. That was not very much . . . As a result he would have to have the pot with him, in case too much time elapsed and he had to impregnate the needle again. What did it matter? He had the poison, everything else was just a question of organisation and method.

CHAPTER 19

MARGONT was pacing about his room. After the wide open spaces of the desert during the Egyptian campaign and the endless plains of Russia, he was suffocating in his chicken coop. Sometimes the interplay of his vivid imagination and the shadows contrived to change the colours in the small space. The walls took on a slight ochre hue and seemed to close in on him, crushing him, and transporting him back to his monastic cell at Saint-Guilhem-le-Désert. Lefine, stretched out on his straw mattress, seemed to belong to another world. Margont had insisted that he come back with him.

'Can I go now, Chevalier?' Lefine now asked sarcastically.

'No, I need you.'

'It's not very nice of you to keep me here.'

'There's no more time for being nice. Or rather, we have to be nice in a different way.'

Lefine got up smartly, like a cat bounding to its feet as it scented danger, and went over to his friend. Margont looked him in the eye.

'You're not obliged to agree to the plan I'm about to propose.'

'I want to refuse already . . .'

'We're in a race against time because of the military situation, and I fear we are being overtaken.'

'Of course, Joseph's limping devil . . .'

'If people realised that the war was at our doors, they would be out buying everything edible and the cost of food would soar! But prices haven't gone up, not by a sou! All Paris is blind! Almost no one is preparing defences. Our ill-preparedness offers a wide margin of manoeuvre to determined monarchist groups . . .'

Lefine reflected that here was a fantastic business opportunity. Perhaps he could buy chickens today and sell them for five times the price in two weeks?

'What is your new plan that apparently involves me?'

'As a result of all that they've been through, our royalists are adept at protecting themselves. I'm under no illusion – their acceptance of me is only partial. They're prepared to listen to me, but they won't reveal anything to me. Everything is partitioned; each member knows something that his neighbour doesn't and vice versa. The group functions a little like a chest of drawers full of secrets where each person has access only to his own two drawers. Only Louis de Leaume has an overview of all the plans of the group – and I'm not convinced even he knows everything! I've been accepted onto the committee, but I haven't been told a word about the plan to carry out a series of murders to destabilise the defence of Paris. I must admit I had hoped that they would be so keen to enlist my help that they would have told me more. Of course, they're suspicious of me. But they're also anxious to act. So, to sum up, the group are working on two plans. The first is to distribute propaganda to rouse part of Parisian society to support the King. The second is their campaign of murders – but fortunately some of their members are not yet in favour of that. But what if they have a third plan?'

'What makes you think they might?'

'Louis de Leaume and Jean-Baptiste de Châtel are both men of action and prone to violence, albeit for different reasons. They're ultras, and the two plans I've just mentioned are probably not extreme enough for them.'

'Isn't killing people enough proof of the group's intransigence?'

'No. Not for fanatics like them.' Margont added, 'I feel I understand those two, you know, because I share one of their defining characteristics – idealism! Of course, our ideals are not the same. Which means I feel both close to them and repelled by them. Nothing is more beautiful than idealism. But there is nothing worse either. If you consider history, idealism has resulted in great progress, in leaps forward and improvements . . . but it has also brought untold carnage and other abominations. For these two men the two plans are not enough to quench their thirst for action.'

Lefine tried to gather his thoughts. Half an hour ago he had had a clear picture of the situation. Now he was confused. His mind was like a calm pond into which Margont had just thrown his hypotheses, stirring up mud and silt.

'But Charles de Varencourt keeps us informed, and he likes his money, that fellow.'

'Maybe he doesn't know about it. Or maybe he's frightened to speak, or else he's waiting for the best moment to exact the highest price . . . Or perhaps he's playing both sides to make sure he doesn't lose out, whoever wins.'

'I don't always understand what it is that you want me to do . . .'

'When things aren't moving fast enough, sometimes you have to administer a kick to the ant hill. '

'And I suppose I'm the kick.'

'The group is like a liquid bubbling on the fire of events. If we wait until the flame is big enough to show itself, it will be too late. So I propose to add an ingredient – that's you! – to create an instability that will force them to lower their guard.'

'Oh, I see, you want to play the alchemist! But do you know how many of those, by playing with sulphur in the hope of turning lead to gold, blew themselves up with their concoctions?'

'You're not obliged to accept. If you agree, all you have to do is stay with me. I know that I'm regularly watched, so eventually they will spot you. If you don't agree, you are free to leave now.'

Lefine was more torn than ever. His instinct for survival was shouting at him to make for the door. But there was another part of him . . . He always worried that if confronted with a difficult situation, Margont would not escape without his help. And he did not want to lose his best friend. Because once the Napoleonic dream had been comprehensively shattered, once everything had collapsed and the Revolution was nothing but a distant memory that no one dare evoke, what would be left for him apart from Margont, Saber, Brémond and Piquebois? Whilst Margont thought in the abstract terms of universal ideals, Lefine thought in concrete terms of his own wellbeing. Margont was trying to look as if he were thinking through his hypotheses, but Lefine could see that all he was thinking about was whether or not his friend was going to accept. Although Margont had tried to produce elaborate justification, sometimes he was easy to read, even though he was unaware of it.

'All right, I agree. But it's going to cost Joseph dear! They're going to have to pay my wages for the end of 1812, for 1813 and for the beginning of 1814, with interest on top!'

'Thank you, Fernand! But then who will have access to the police reports?'

'That will still be me. I'll just make sure that it is impossible to follow me when I go to see Natai.'

'Very good. All you have to do is to be seen with me from time to time and the Swords of the King will soon notice you. Let's take stock. How far, in fact, have the police got?'

'I read a copy of the report from the inspectors of the civilian police in charge of investigating Berle's death. Their inquiry – interrogations of the servants, friends and relatives, verification of his fortune, and reading his correspondence – has revealed nothing. No liaison, debts, no enemies so annoyed with him that they would mutilate him and assassinate him . . .'

'Why do you put it in that order when we know he was burnt after death? Haven't the inspectors of the general police discovered that?'

'No.'

'Have they finally heard that there was a royalist emblem pinned to the victim?'

'Not that either.'

'Joseph has divided the investigation in two, and only we know both parts.'

'It's us he's counting on,' said Lefine. 'As we thought, nothing of value was taken. The only things that disappeared were the colonel's notes on the defence of Paris. The civilian police have ruled out the possibility of a privately motivated crime and have reached the conclusion that the murderer or murderers were royalist partisans. The inspectors have reached the point where we started.'

Margont told him what he had discovered that day. Then he tossed the button to Lefine with a challenging look. Lefine caught it, clapping his hands. He examined it carefully, turning it over slowly close to his eyes.

'It's a military button . . . There's a number or a letter, or several . . . It's too worn to see . . .'

He looked disappointed. The button hid the solution to an enigma, but was like a nut they were unable to crack.

'So you also think it's the button from a uniform,' said Margont. 'But hundreds of soldiers wear uniforms with decorated gold buttons. The foot artillery of the Imperial Guard have buttons that are decorated with two crossed cannon barrels surmounted by the imperial eagle. The grenadiers of the Old Guard also have the imperial eagle on theirs. Our friend Jean-Quenin still has his button from 1798, even though it's no longer regulation, and it has the words "Military hospitals" and then "Humanity" with a Phrygian cap above it. His other buttons have a staff entwined with a serpent surmounted by the mirror of prudence and surrounded by an oak branch and a laurel branch. Customs-house officers are similarly decorated, but I don't know the exact details. The light infantry have the number of their regiment inscribed inside a hunting horn. Normally they're silver, but I can't be certain that there aren't any light regiments who have gold buttons. Just as the infantry of the line is supposed to have gold buttons but several regiments have silver ones. And I have no idea about other buttons – the navy, for example, or the engineers . . .'

'We don't get paid but we all have these expensive uniforms. Why can't all soldiers have the same buttons? And anyway, the regulations for uniforms are not always respected. Each regiment has its own foibles and traditions and variations according to what comes to hand. If Saber suddenly says, "I want all my soldiers to have uniform buttons with the number of our legion in roman numerals preceded by an 'S' for Saber," we'd all have to pay for them from the little money we have left . . .'

'Perhaps we're barking up the wrong tree. Perhaps it's the button from an expensive civilian suit. I don't know what a count or a baron would have worn under the *ancien régime* . . . You've got so many contacts, do you know anyone who could help us?'

'I know the perfect person. I have a friend who works in the commissariat. If anyone knows about military buttons, he does.'

'I'm relying on you. Then there's the fire – what clues can we draw from that?'

Margont brandished a Bible. Lefine remembered being dragged, in tears – of rage! – to church by his father who hoped that God would put the little miscreant back on the straight and narrow. Ever since, he had given the Holy Scriptures as wide a berth as possible. Margont, on the other hand, was turning the pages with the practised ease of a preacher. 'Job, chapter 1, verse 16: "While he was yet speaking, there came also another, and said, 'The fire of God is fallen from heaven, and hath burned up the sheep and the servants, and consumed them; and I only am escaped alone to tell thee.' " '

His fingers flicked back a bit further. 'Leviticus, chapter 10, verses 1 and 2: "And Nadab and Abihu, the sons of Aaron, took either of them his censer, and put fire therein, and put incense thereon, and offered strange fire before the Lord, which he commanded them not. And there went out fire from the Lord, and devoured them, and they died before the Lord."'

Lefine felt uncomfortable. He did not believe in God. But if He did in fact exist and if the Bible was His word, He did not seem exactly 'the God of bounty and love' which He was usually taken to be . . . Margont, undeterred, went on and his apparently random quotes started to form a coherent and unsettling whole.

'Deuteronomy, chapter 5, verses 23 and 24: "And it came to pass, when ye heard the voice out of the midst of the darkness, (for the mountain did burn with fire,) that ye came near unto me, even all the heads of your tribes, and your elders; And ye said, 'Behold, the Lord our God hath shewed us his glory and his greatness, and we have heard his voice out of the midst of the fire: we have seen this day that God doth talk with man, and he liveth.'"'

'Isaiah, chapter 66, verses 15 and 16: "For, behold, the Lord will come with fire, and with his chariots like a whirlwind, to render his anger with fury, and his rebuke with flames of fire. For by fire and by his sword will the Lord plead with all flesh: and the slain of the Lord shall be many."'

More pages turned. The more the passages mounted up the more impact they made as if each were a fire, which, added to all the others, formed a blazing inferno.

'Jeremiah, chapter 5, verse 14: "Wherefore thus saith the

Lord God of hosts, because ye speak this word, behold, I will make my words in thy mouth fire, and this people wood, and it shall devour them."

'And finally, of course, Revelation, chapter 8, verse 5: "And the angel took the censer, and filled it with fire of the altar, and cast it into the earth: and there were voices, and thunderings, and lightnings, and an earthquake." What do you conclude from all that?'

'That I prefer to think about the button . . .'

Margont slammed the Bible closed. 'Fire has a double symbolism in the Holy Scriptures. It is either a positive force, the incarnation of the Word of God, the Holy Spirit, the Spirit of God . . . Or, it's the opposite, the illustration of his all-powerfulness, the instrument of his anger, the Anger of God . . . And supposing Jean-Baptiste de Châtel believes he's been charged with a divine mission? To overcome the Antichrist, Napoleon, with fire.'

'But what exactly is the Antichrist?'

'A man in the pay of the devil. He starts off quietly, then launches into a frenetic series of conquests. "He shall subdue three kings" – according to Daniel – and will himself become a king. His power will grow still greater and will spread "over all kindreds, and tongues, and nations," as Revelation says.'

'There are strange similarities, actually . . . coincidences . . . but that's all that would be needed to stir up a religious fanatic.'

'He will wage war on God and the Church – Napoleon annexed the pontifical states to the Empire and, by his order, Pius VII spent almost five years in a supervised residence, at Savone, then at Fontainebleau. He will try to pass himself off as a god. But his reign will not last. God will easily and rapidly overturn it. Most of that comes from Revelation, also known as the Apocalypse of St John, because it's the coming of the Antichrist that sets off the Apocalypse.'

He paused for a moment before going calmly on: 'Jean-Baptiste Châtel seems to want to follow the Bible to the letter. Because of that, when I immerse myself in the Bible it's as if I can read his thoughts . . . If you think about it, it's hardly surprising that he has nothing in his head except for the Holy Scriptures. He spent several years imprisoned by the Inquisition with only the Bible for company.'

'So you think that's the "third plan" – to assassinate the Emperor with flames?'

'Aren't the damned supposed to burn in hell? It's a suggestion. Châtel would have mystical motives but the other members might support it for political reasons. However, there is someone else who might well be influenced by the Bible . . .'

'Who's that?'

'Louis de Leaume. Like all aristocrats, his childhood would have been steeped in religion. His family must have taken him to church, spoken of God, quoted the Bible . . . I don't know how much importance he attached to his faith at the time. But later he was in a way dead, and then brought to life again. He pulled himself out from amongst the dead . . . It's unimaginable that he would not have made a connection between his resurrection and that of Christ. So the question is: what sort of connection exactly? Did he just see it as a coincidence? Or a sign from God? Did it tip him into religious fanaticism as well?'

'One should never mix religion and politics . . .'

148

'How right you are.'

'Alas, not right enough, obviously. How did you find all those passages in the Bible? You couldn't have read it all.'

'I spent part of my nights reading it. But I was able to find the parts I wanted quite easily because I know it well. My years of apprenticeship in the monastery have proved very useful.'

As far as Lefine was concerned, Margont's religious training constituted a useless episode from his past, a splinter he had given up trying to remove from Margont's soul. Margont, on the other hand, drew great strength from it, more than he would have liked to admit.

'I'm sure we haven't explored the fire connection sufficiently,' concluded Margont. 'We're going to have to find another way of approaching this investigation . . .'

They agreed to meet the next day and Lefine left.

He had not been gone many minutes when there was a knock at the door. Margont grabbed a pistol and pointed it straight in front of him.

'It's me again,' Lefine called.

Margont opened the door and Lefine crashed into him, pushed from behind by several people. The little room was suddenly overcrowded. There was Louis de Leaume, Jean-Baptiste de Châtel and Honoré de Nolant, as well as two other men whom Margont did not know. They were all armed and Margont's pistol was immediately seized, much to Vicomte de Leaume's delight.

Lefine declared: 'I brought a few friends . . .'

CHAPTER 20

Louis de Leaume was exultant, as if he and Margont were playing a game of chess and he had just checked his adversary. 'Who is this man?' he asked Margont, pointing at Lefine.

'My name is Fernand Lami, Monsieur le Vicomte,' the latter replied. 'I know everything and I'm one of you.'

Jean-Baptiste de Châtel smiled ironically. 'Oh, but you don't know everything . . .'

Margont noticed that this comment annoyed Louis de Leaume, and took it as another sign that the group was preparing a third plan, which he had not been told about. Lefine kept his cool.

'I've known Monsieur le Chevalier de Langès for many years. We served in the same regiments, the 18th and then the 84th. Facing death together inevitably forges bonds . . . You want a return to the monarchy? So do I! Not for the same reasons, but so what?'

'And what are your reasons?'

'I want an end to war so that I can leave the army and work for Monsieur de Langès, as he's promised me. I'm going to look after the forests on his future lands! A well-paid but not too taxing job. Perhaps my ambitions are small, but that is my dream.'

'You hid him from us,' Louis de Leaume told Margont.

He seemed unwilling to address someone of the lower classes. That irritated Margont but he knew he had to take it in his stride and pretend to find it normal.

'But Monsieur le Vicomte, you hid those men from me.' He indicated the two unknown men who had started to search the room. They lifted up the mattress, turned the pages of the books, moved things around, emptied the trunk . . .

'They're other members of our group—' began Louis de Leaume.

'We haven't time for that!' interrupted Jean-Baptiste de Châtel.

Margont felt that Châtel was playing a tactical game. He continually provoked Vicomte de Leaume. If the latter should lose his temper he would discredit himself – who would want a leader incapable of controlling himself? But if he did not react, he would gradually lose his authority because it would look as if he were unable to oppose Châtel. The Swords of the King were not a homogenous group, but a fragile coalition, perpetually on the verge of splitting apart.

Honoré de Nolant searched Lefine. He found a knife and a pistol, which he placed on the floor. As he patted Lefine down, he felt something in a pocket. He pulled out the gold button and looked at it, but put it back without comment. Margont was searched by Châtel, who then said to him, 'Chevalier, you won't mind if we go straight away to your print works?'

They set off, leaving behind the two members Margont did not know, to continue their search. Margont was not worried, though: apart from fleas and cockroaches, there was nothing to find . . . But Joseph had been right to forbid him to have the police reports himself. As for Joseph's letter, they would have to be very clever to flush that out . . .

When they got outside, five more people surged out of the shadows of the adjacent streets – determined-looking men in the prime of life. Two of them returned to the shadows to keep watch to protect their accomplices inside the inn. The three others fell in behind the group, but at some distance, forming a rearguard, ready to close in, in case of danger.

Margont watched and memorised everything. He was witnessing a display of force on the part of his adversaries. They were better organised than he had previously thought. They were apparently capable of leading a little troop into combat. Were they aiming for some spectacular show of force? In October 1812, during the retreat from Russia, while the Grande Armée was in complete disarray, General Malet, a republican officer imprisoned for his hostility to the Emperor, had launched a mad attempt to overthrow him. Wanting to restore the republic, he had escaped from the madhouse where he was being held, and embarked on an audacious series of escapades. He pretended to be General Lamotte and had gone to a barracks and announced that the Emperor had been killed in Russia. His aplomb and assurance had convinced the 10th cohort of the National Guard. Then he had liberated two other republican generals and arrested Pasquier, the Prefect of Police, and Savary, the Minister of Civilian Police. But the Governor of Paris, General Hulin, had refused to support Malet, who responded by shooting him in the jaw. Eventually Malet had been arrested, then shot after a brief trial, but he had well and truly shaken the imperial throne. If Louis de Leaume were as daring as Malet, he would have a much greater chance of success, since he had more resources and the Emperor's situation was much worse than in October 1812. It all depended what plans he was pursuing.

On the other hand, the fact that the Swords of the King had sought to intimidate Margont was also a good sign. They would not have bothered had they not needed him and perhaps feared him.

The streets, cold enough to make their teeth chatter, were lit by the moon, which resembled a block of ice floating in black water. But Margont was burning inside, heated by the passion of his thoughts. Varencourt was notable by his absence. Was that proof that the group did not trust him? Or was he off leading another operation?

The little printing press came into sight. How Margont loved it! But he was seized by a sudden fear. What if Joseph had asked his police to keep watch on the place? If a guard spotted them and told his superiors that several of the people they were searching for had just appeared, the place would soon be alive with the sound of gunfire . . . Margont was annoyed with himself for dragging Lefine into danger with him.

In a little lane nearby a man stepped out from under a porch. He nodded to Vicomte de Leaume, who had stopped, but now went on again.

CHAPTER 21

THEY swarmed into the room. The cold air intensified the smell of ink. Honoré de Nolant lit as few candles as necessary. The unaccustomed nocturnal activity might attract the attention of the police, especially since printing presses were kept under close watch.

The faces, lit by the pale trembling light of the candles, looked eerie. To Margont's amusement, Jean-Baptiste de Châtel resembled a ghost.

'So Monsieur de Langès: where have you hidden the posters you promised us?'

'Where no one can find them.'

Honoré de Nolant had already begun moving piles of paper about and searching behind the presses.

'Show us where,' commanded Louis de Leaume.

'Here,' replied Margont, tapping his forehead.

'Are you pulling my leg?'

'In here, neither the police nor the printer's employees can stumble across them . . . Let me demonstrate.'

Margont launched into a sort of dance. He had to give the impression that he was working quickly, whilst actually moving as slowly as possible. He prepared the press, installed the paper, started the ink flowing, aligned the lead characters . . . The Swords of the King tried to follow what he was doing, but printing was more complicated than it looked. Besides, Margont was making it more complex than necessary. He was like a bee flitting from flower to flower. Honoré de Nolant tried to help him by picking up a line of characters. Inevitably, he was instantly stained with ink. He looked at his hands in consternation. In the gloom, the ink looked like blood. It was as if he had just stabbed someone. Was he thinking of a crime he had committed? His appalled expression said a great deal . . . He began to wipe his hands on his coat, his fingers pressing the material so tightly that his knuckles were white.

Margont seized the crank with both hands and pushed it vigorously. He loved that moment. The words did not yet exist, at least not visibly. It was the press that made them appear. He waited longer than was necessary. Finally he freed the sheet and presented it triumphantly to the others. He had printed in enormous characters:

THE KING, PEACE!

'That's it?' queried Jean-Baptiste de Châtel in astonishment.

'Yes. Short and sweet – it's perfect!'

'What about God? And the legitimacy of the King? And the loyalty of the people to their sovereign?'

'Too long, too heavy, too complicated . . . The French want peace.'

Vicomte de Leaume took the little poster. He beamed. One of his plans was coming to life in front of his eyes! 'It's magnificent! Anyway, we're going to have several different types of poster . . .'

Then suddenly he took Margont in his arms. It was an

unusual gesture for an aristocrat. It was more like the embrace of brothers in arms. 'Chevalier, excuse us for doubting you! You are an extraordinary man!'

His face was transformed. His vigour, which had struck Margont the first time he had met him, was more obvious than ever. He seemed capable of overcoming any obstacle. Yes, he had definitely kept the passion that had saved his life. He must have worn the same expression as he clawed his way through the putrefying corpses to drag himself out of the communal grave. How could such a man serve Louis XVIII? He should have been a general for the likes of Alexander the Great, but instead he was under the orders of little Louis . . .

'More!' he exclaimed.

Margont set to work. Lefine, Honoré de Nolant and Louis de Leaume came to lend a hand. Châtel, meanwhile, strolled slowly around, looking about him scornfully. The idea of covering Paris with posters did not interest him. Margont spent far too long brushing the characters with ink on the pretext of distributing it properly, using several different types of typography to make the same poster, taking care to centre a sheet badly so that he had to redo it . . . In spite of his efforts, the pile of posters grew little by little. Louis de Leaume picked up a pen and frenetically scribbled a draft. 'What do you think of this?'

Parisians!
Take up arms
and overthrow the tyrant!
Down with Napoleon! Long live Louis XVIII!

'It's good,' Margont complimented him.

Louis de Leaume's choice of words said plenty about what he was planning. Honoré de Nolant also suggested some wording.

> Throw off the imperial yoke!
> Spray the Eagle with bullets!
> Long live the King!

Even Jean-Baptiste de Châtel eventually took a pen and wrote his own poster. He did not need to think about what he wanted to say, it was obvious to him.

> People of France
> Support the return of your King!
> It is the will of God!

How hateful, thought Margont. That expression, 'It is the will of God!' had been used by Pope Urban II in 1095, during his famous speech calling for a campaign to free the Holy Land. His harangue had played a major part in sparking the First Crusade. And that familiar way of addressing himself directly to the French people – what breathtaking arrogance! As for the words 'your King': as if it was obligatory to have a king at all . . .

A piercing whistle sounded from the street. Baron de Nolant and Jean-Baptiste de Châtel blew out the candles, plunging the room into darkness.

'What's happening?' whispered Lefine.

'Silence!'

They heard footsteps coming towards them. Margont waited anxiously for his eyes to become accustomed to the dark. But still he could not see anything. He began to worry. What if someone attacked him here, taking him by surprise? Perhaps one of these men was the murderer they were looking for. Had Margont been unmasked? Was the murderer going to come over and stab him to death? Margont stretched his arms out in front of him, hoping to detect an assailant who might be creeping towards him. He started to move silently forward, but at the same time he was annoyed with himself – he had become prey to his own fears.

A long moment later, there was another whistle, shorter and sharper. Honoré de Nolant lit a candle again. 'We're off now,' he announced. 'Chevalier, we'll need more posters. You can print them when the printing press is open again.'

'No, that would be too risky. Every printer has a police informer on the staff and I don't know who ours is. Besides, the censors and the police often drop in to check up on us. It's better if I print them on my own. I'll be able to do a few at a time. I should be able to do hundreds eventually . . .'

'Very good,' Louis de Leaume agreed. 'In any case, it's best if we don't come here again.'

They left, abandoning Margont and Lefine, who had to put everything back in place so as not to arouse the suspicions of the employees. They would, of course, take the posters with them.

Once they were on their own, Lefine said to Margont: 'I would love to see Joseph's face when you tell him how you used the print works he put at your disposal . . .'

CHAPTER 22

O N 24 March 1814, the Allies held a military council not far
from Vitry. Confusion reigned once more. What should
they do? No one could agree, but they had to stick together
because Napoleon would certainly exploit any disunity. The
day before, some Cossacks had captured a cavalryman on his
way to deliver a letter to the Emperor. The note was from
Savary, the Minister of Civilian Police, and was full of anguish.

> We are at the very end of our resources, the population is
> restive and wants peace at any price. The enemies of the
> Imperial Government are everywhere, fomenting unrest,
> which is still only latent, but which will be impossible to
> repress if the Emperor does not succeed in keeping the
> Allies well away from Paris by drawing them after him
> away from the gates of the capital . . .

That was all very well, but what if it was a trap? What if the
Allies turned their back on Napoleon to march on Paris, and
then found their communications threatened or cut off. They
would have to be sure they could seize the capital quickly.

The Tsar was hesitating. He had been foolhardy at
Austerlitz, and that had precipitated the Austro-Russian army
into a Napoleonic trap, with catastrophic results. But on the
other hand, during the Russian campaign, most of his soldiers

felt he had been too cautious. Even now, many people considered that the French could have been beaten at the Battle of Borodino had Alexander and the chiefs of staff had more faith in their soldiers. That was an absurd point of view, of course, but everything always seemed simpler when you looked back. So, as much as he told himself that he would be prudent and not repeat the errors of Austerlitz, when he thought of how his beloved Moscow had been destroyed, he longed to set his army charging against Paris. Or against Napoleon. There again, thinking about Austerlitz . . . Astonishingly, that day, his advisers were unanimous. It would be Paris!

The Tsar had long dreamt of taking Paris in revenge for Moscow. So, Paris!

Schwarzenberg, the generalissimo, showed himself to be modest that day, which was unusual for someone of his rank. He had just been beaten by Napoleon's little army; many other generals would have been in a hurry to try to take their revenge. But Schwarzenberg judged that the Emperor was a better tactician than he, and that he would be better off avoiding fighting him. So it was Paris.

Frederick William III, King of Prussia, was of the same opinion.

The decision was almost taken. It was heads Napoleon, tails Paris, but the coin was still spinning, although leaning heavily towards Paris. General Winzingerode, a German in the service of the Tsar, who had the reputation for being the best Allied sabre-fighter, had an idea that made the Paris plan even more appealing. He suggested marching on the capital, but making Napoleon think that they had decided to go after him. He proposed that he himself would head towards Napoleon with ten thousand cavalry, mounted artillery and infantry, and behave exactly as if he were commanding the advance guard of the Allied army. His idea was greeted with enthusiasm.

So it was definitely Paris.

CHAPTER 23

O<small>N</small> 25 March, Napoleon found himself near Wassy and wondered what his adversaries were planning to do. He had sent detachments of cavalry on reconnaissance trips in all directions – to Bar-sur-Aube, Brienne-le-Château, Joinville, Montier-en-Der, Saint-Dizier.

Finally he spotted the enemy. Near Saint-Dizier. The Emperor was triumphant, believing that the Allies were starting to turn back to protect their communications. Keen to keep up the pressure on them, he immediately launched his army in their direction, believing he had the advance Allied guard in his sights, when in fact all he had was the very back of the rearguard.

At the same time, several leagues away, Marshals Marmont and Mortier, who had been separated from Napoleon by the encounters and manoeuvres of the previous days and who were trying to rejoin him, noticed that the Bohemian and the Silesian armies – two hundred thousand soldiers altogether – had come to station themselves between them and the Emperor. They withdrew immediately, pursued by the Allies. In less than forty-eight hours, they were attacked from all sides, and lost eight thousand men. But, unexpectedly, the National Guard, whom the enemy did not take seriously, fought with determination and to good effect, allowing Marmont and Mortier to continue their heroic retreat. They were left with only one option – to retire to

Paris. This they did, bringing with them an unexpected escort.

Napoleon fell with such speed on Winzingerode that he was rapidly able to overwhelm him. From 26 March, the French cavalry vigorously fought off the Cossacks. The cannon fire of the mounted artillery, already in place, began to overpower the Russians. Winzingerode was delighted to see that his plan was working, but he was a victim of his own success. There were too many French, too quickly! He wanted to establish a solid position in Saint-Dizier to contain them. It was of the utmost importance that he should hold firm and continue to deceive the Emperor. But the French were already in battle formation – Macdonald, the Imperial Guard – when Marshal Oudinot's infantry burst in a torrent from the forest of Val and headed for Saint-Dizier. Winzingerode was rapidly ousted from the town, losing men and artillery, then pushed back again, and battered some more. The dragoons of the Imperial Guard and some Mamelukes galloped after him, charging everything in their way. The French army followed the cavalcade and set upon Winzingerode just as he was gathering his troops back into order; Napoleon thought he had caught the Bohemian army by the scruff of the neck, and so he went at them with all the force he could muster. But he found himself holding nothing but a handful of straw, a scarecrow, a decoy . . .

CHAPTER 24

On 26 March, Margont was again summoned to see Joseph Bonaparte and Talleyrand. As they could no longer meet in the Tuileries, Mathurin Jelent had given him the address of a private house on Île Saint-Louis.

It was barely ten days since their first meeting, yet the two dignitaries frowned when they saw Margont, wondering if this was really the same man they had sent off on their mission . . . Their spy was in old, outdated and not very clean clothes. But he had an affected, haughty air about him. He was holding a riding crop and seemed ready to lash anyone who did not obey his orders speedily enough. He looked like a baron holding a salon in the ruins of his château, devastated by the Revolution.

He was so supercilious that Joseph could not help exclaiming, 'All right, that's enough of that now!'

Talleyrand, on the other hand, applauded quietly. 'What a transformation! I would have you work for me any day.'

'But the question is, would I want to work for you?' replied Margont.

'How far have you got, Lieutenant-Colonel?' demanded Joseph.

The commander of the army and of the National Guard of Paris had spoken in a honeyed tone, but Margont had detected irony. There was poison in the honey. Margont guessed that he would be severely reproached, but he calmly presented a succinct report. When he stated that he was sure the Swords of the King were plotting an armed insurrection, as Charles de Varencourt also claimed, Joseph became agitated. Paradoxically, he seemed much more worried by the few thousand enemies hidden in Paris than the hundreds of thousands of enemies threatening the French army. He was convinced his brother would be able to handle the coalition, whereas the enemy within was his responsibility.

'But there's something more worrying,' added Margont.

Joseph and Talleyrand looked surprised. Margont told them of his suspicion that the Swords of the King were planning something else as well. Talleyrand immediately accepted the hypothesis. Did he know something he was not revealing? Joseph, however, reacted violently, like someone who has had his fill of bad news and only wants to be told reassuring things.

'What could be worse than a campaign of murders aimed at disrupting the defence of Paris, Lieutenant-Colonel?'

He had pronounced the last word as he might say the word 'cockroach'.

'I don't know, Your Excellency. But believe me, at least two members of the committee, Louis de Leaume and Jean-Baptiste de Châtel, will not stop there. They are after something more grandiose, more spectacular.'

Talleyrand seemed lost in thought and was no longer looking at Margont. 'So we are dealing with a hydra, each of whose heads poses a different threat, with the most prominent heads concealing the most dangerous . . . What a diabolical strategy . . .'

It was amazing to hear Talleyrand use the word 'diabolical', since he himself was nicknamed 'the limping devil'. Just a coincidence? Or had he said it on purpose, implying that he too was capable of spawning hydras? Margont was reflecting on this possibility when Talleyrand turned to him and smiled, as though he could read his thoughts.

Joseph was in a state. Catastrophes were piling up around him at alarming speed: when would the damned avalanche finally stop?

'When one is confronted by a hydra, one must cut off all its heads at once,' he murmured. 'You have to get them all! Not one must remain! Let's decapitate the lot and hope that the body, deprived of its heads and paralysed by fear, becomes incapable of action. Lieutenant-Colonel, we're changing the aim of your mission. For the moment, forget about the murder of Colonel Berle, you—'

'Forget about the murder?' exclaimed Margont.

Joseph replied sharply, 'Be quiet! Just obey orders.'

'I can't—'

'Imbecile! You tell us the worst is to come? It's already happened! Count Kevlokine has been assassinated. In Paris, by a member of the Swords of the King. We don't know exactly when or why. And you, who're supposed to have infiltrated them, noticed nothing! We needed that man, do you hear? We could have tried to negotiate with the Tsar! Now that hope is gone!'

Margont's confusion made Joseph even angrier and he was almost shouting. 'The Tsar's agent, you half-wit! He was murdered by the group you were supposed to be keeping an eye on. We found the symbol of the Swords of the King on his body. And he was burnt, just like Colonel Berle! So it's the same murderer, the one you were meant to unmask. The one who has succeeded in wiping out the only moderate amongst our enemies, the man we hoped to negotiate with! How is it possible that you didn't know that Count Kevlokine was in touch with the Swords of the King?'

'They don't trust me . . .'

'You'll have to find a way round that! So, let's sum up: the only two things you have succeeded in doing are, one, to have some theories about a mysterious and hypothetical third plan, and two, to allow them to print a hundred posters calling on Parisians to revolt against the Emperor.'

Margont wondered if he was about to be carted off to the Temple prison, or to the one at Vincennes . . .

'I couldn't do any more! I—'

Joseph silenced him with a gesture. 'Redeem yourself by allowing us to arrest all the leaders of the group. We waited, thinking you would identify other members and that you would soon discover who the murderer or murderers are. We had also hoped you would have had the opportunity to help us lay our hands on Count Kevlokine. You've failed us in all three ways, whilst the war has continued to go against us. We're going to have to adapt to the new situation—'

He broke off before continuing more calmly, 'We're not going to arrest Mademoiselle Catherine de Saltonges at the moment, because her accomplices would soon know about it. So I've had your printing press put under surveillance. We haven't done that so far to minimise the risk of your identity being discovered. But from now on we can't afford to be so careful.

We'll still take precautions but if the royalists notice our presence, you're going to have to act as if you didn't know about it, make something up . . .'

That was easy for Joseph to say. He made it sound like child's play!

'You will inform us of the time and place of your next meeting,' he went on.

'But I never know when they'll be! One or several members simply turn up at my lodgings—'

Joseph brushed that aside with a sweeping gesture.

'Don't bother me with details. Improvise! When the Emperor is in battle, he says to one of his generals, "Take that hill and hold it firmly to protect our right flank." And the general does it; he doesn't spend the day saying, "All right, Your Majesty, but with how many soldiers? Who should be in command? What battle formation should I use? Must I just use my infantry or can I use cavalry? When exactly should I take the hill? How long will I need? And why me?" Show some initiative! With all those posters you've allowed them to print, they must be starting to take you for a royalist, because, frankly, I'm beginning to wonder myself!'

Margont was furious. Don't reply, don't reply, the man's an idiot, no point in replying to an idiot, he repeated to himself.

'Either they'll come and fetch you at the printer's, in which case you'll have to warn Jelent. At any rate, I've told you that my agents will be keeping watch on the place and will follow you while others will go and alert my soldiers. Or they'll come to your lodgings, which I will also put a watch on. Rest assured, my police know what to do!'

Margont was becoming more and more uneasy. And he was forced to admit that he had not spotted that he was under surveillance. Joseph concluded, with a forced assurance that made him sound more confident than he was, 'And Catherine de Saltonges and Monsieur de Varencourt are now both being spied on day and night. Ah, Varencourt! The most sensible thing you've said so far is that you don't trust him – we don't either! He's never told us about a third plan; he demands money all the time . . . He does not know that we've decided to arrest everyone. Nor does he know that we're watching his house. Only his house, because he's impossible to follow! So that he doesn't suspect anything, we've led him to believe that we want more information about the group and we've promised him an extra sum of money – twenty thousand francs. Monsieur Natai reported that when Charles de Varencourt heard about that, he was overjoyed. How grasping! The operation will be supervised by Natai's superior, Monsieur Palenier, who has been kept fully informed.'

Talleyrand leant towards Margont and whispered: 'At our first meeting, we promised you five thousand francs. Of course, it's not the money that motivates you . . . And the imperial finances are unfortunately not what they were. But on the other hand, it would be quite unfair to offer twenty thousand francs to a traitor and only five to a loyal man. So we would like to ask you: do you also want twenty thousand francs if you succeed in your mission? You only have to ask.'

The tortuous experiment was typical of Talleyrand. It was designed to show that an idealist was as corruptible as the next man, it's just that his price was higher.

'Your Excellency,' replied Margont, 'I will be quite happy with Imperial Press and the authorisation to launch a newspaper. I propose to use the money to buy—'

'You're still harping on that? That's not just an obsession, it's an illness!' raged Joseph. 'But it's agreed, help us throw them all in prison and you can have them both – your newspaper and your machine to make it with!'

Margont hid his pleasure, which was immediately replaced by a new worry. 'What will happen to the prisoners?'

Talleyrand narrowed his eyes. 'Ah . . . scruples. Well, they won't be executed and they won't be tortured. Our enemies have captured as many of our men as we have of theirs, so everyone treats their prisoners well.'

That was a highly partisan view, and might be true for the upper echelons, but simple soldiers, NCOs and subaltern officers had endured appalling conditions in Spain, on English pontoons, in damp Edinburgh gaols, in Russia . . . Yet neither Joseph nor Talleyrand would take the risk of condemning these royalists to death. Not while there was a chance that the Allies might win. Because to hang those men would be to hang themselves with the same noose . . .

'There's already been enough bloodshed,' Joseph assented. 'Only the man or men responsible for the murders of Colonel Berle and Count Kevlokine will be punished with the death penalty, and then only after a fair trial.'

'How will you make sure that everyone is arrested?' asked Margont. 'Even when the committee meets, you never know how many are present and how many are keeping watch outside. And there's a lot of them – thirty, perhaps more . . .'

'Well, we'll send more than a hundred! There will be a company of the National Guard standing by day and night, ready to intervene, as well as my agents. Wherever your meeting takes place, it will be well surrounded – very well! We will be able to arrest everyone quickly.'

Margont could already picture himself caught right in the middle of generalised shooting.

'But, Your Excellency, you're going to set off exactly the kind of insurrection you're trying to avoid!'

'That will never happen! Faced with superior manpower, they will give themselves up without resisting.'

'That's exactly what they won't do!'

'Our decision is taken! At the critical moment, if one of the fanatics wants to open fire, it's up to you to make them see reason. You should let yourself be arrested along with the others. You'll all be taken to different prisons. Each prisoner will be alone in his cell. We'll lock you up too, so as not to arouse their suspicions about you. But of course, you will be freed immediately afterwards.'

'And Charles de Varencourt?'

'He will also be freed. But a little later, after we've established that he really is on our side. If we discover that he failed to pass on any information, he'll find the key to his cell at the bottom of the Seine.'

'I'm going to have to examine Count Kevlokine's body.'

'We knew you were going to ask that. This time the civilian police got there first. Unfortunately they discovered the symbol of the Swords of the King. I've personally made sure that they won't broadcast the fact. There's a policeman waiting for you in the next room. He will take you to where the count's remains were found. Everything has been left as it was found. You will find Inspector Sausson there – he's also from the civilian police so he does not know that my secret police are on the trail of the royalists. He only deals with criminal investigations. He will receive you alone and tell you everything he knows. I have expressly forbidden him to question you and he does not know who you are or why you are involved . . . He has understood that, as far as he is concerned, you don't exist.'

'But that might not be true! The civilian police also sell information about royalists. I run the risk that someone sees me at the scene of the crime, and describes me physically—'

'You have nothing to fear, because with your help we'll be able to annihilate the Swords of the King very soon. You may leave now.'

Margont reached the door, but then turned back.

'Your Excellency, may I know whether Paris is threatened?'

Joseph was stupefied by his insolence; Talleyrand was amused. The lieutenant-general wanted to reprimand Margont and tell him that there was no risk to Paris, but he was so tangled up in his anger and his lies that it was the truth that emerged from his mouth.

'They're coming . . .'

He then added firmly: 'So make sure that we're not stabbed in the back while confronting the Allies.'

CHAPTER 25

THE policeman said nothing as he took Margont to the Marais, not far from Place des Vosges. He marched sullenly ahead without looking back once; perhaps he was hoping to lose him 'accidentally'. He was so put out by having to look after this officious parallel investigator that when they arrived and Margont asked him to go to find Medical Officer Jean-Quenin Brémond at the hospital Hôtel-Dieu, he replied with disarming indolence, 'I'm afraid I won't be able to find him.'

The words were like flints rubbing together in Margont's mind, causing sparks of fury to light his eyes. The man quickly changed his mind and hurriedly set off to find the doctor.

Behind its sober façade, the house harboured a stunning luxurious interior. There was a Mazarin desk covered in brass marquetry, a gold table with a white marble top, silver candlesticks, Dutch paintings, Gobelins tapestries of mythological scenes . . . Margont felt as if he had opened an oyster apparently like all the others, only to find pearls rolling in every direction at his feet. Count Kevlokine did not seem to have led the difficult wandering life of the leaders of the Swords of the King. What's more, he ran far fewer risks. Had he been picked up by the police half an hour earlier Monsieur de Talleyrand and Joseph would have received him in the Tuileries Palace. Rat-ridden cellars for the ultras, palaces for the moderates.

A man came over to Margont. He was twenty-five or twenty-six, well turned out and fresh-faced with an impatient, slightly aggressive manner. 'I'm Inspector Martial Sausson.'

'Delighted to meet you,' replied Margont without introducing himself.

'I've been told not to ask who you are, why you are investigating or whether you have any information that I don't—'

'Exactly.'

Margont thought he could almost see black clouds of anger emanating from Sausson.

'Here's my report, Monsieur Unknown. This morning a servant by the name of Keberk comes to work for his employers Monsieur and Madame Gunans, a rich bourgeois couple, well, not so rich now that the Emperor has imposed a blockade on England. The Gunans made a fortune in maritime trading. Keberk tries to open the servants' door with his key. It doesn't open, which is very unusual. At night his employers bar the entrance, but early in the morning they remove the bar so that Monsieur Keberk can enter using his key when he arrives. It is the first time he has encountered such a problem in all his fifteen years of service. Keberk is alarmed and knocks at the door, shouts through the windows then runs off to tell the police that his masters have been murdered. As the house is in my area of jurisdiction, I come in person, accompanied by two of my men. I look about and discover that a shutter at the back has been forced open. I take the decision to enter the house with Monsieur Keberk. I find no sign of the Gunans. But I do discover the body of a man whom Monsieur Keberk says was called Monsieur Melansi, a friend of his masters. I use that word "masters" because that's the word Keberk used. But I recognise immediately that the victim is Count Kevlokine, who everyone has been searching for and whose description had been circulated to all the police stations in Paris. Monsieur Keberk seems not to understand when I tell him this. I think he was fooled by his employers about the man's real identity. I follow the procedure required when Count Kevlokine is spotted – I immediately inform the King of Spain, His Majesty Joseph I.'

He finally drew breath. Lord knows he had spoken quickly!

'Up until that point everything had passed off normally. But then an investigator named Palenier suddenly bursts into my police station. He hands me a letter signed by His Majesty Joseph I himself, giving me the most peculiar orders . . .'

He tried to find a more diplomatic way of putting it. 'The most astonishing orders I have ever received. In summary: I must touch nothing, I must await a mysterious unknown man – you! – whom I must tell everything I know without asking any questions! And – the bitter cherry on the cake – Palenier then takes the letter back out of my hand. When you have gone I am to – by order! – forget everything, as if you never existed!'

Margont could well understand Sausson's fury; he had felt the same way at his first meeting with Joseph and Talleyrand. It was like looking in a mirror and seeing his image of ten days ago.

The policeman went on even more hurriedly: 'I interrogated Monsieur Keberk while I was waiting for you. His employers received many visitors: society contacts, friends, clients, relatives, debtors, creditors . . . He claims not to know whether the Gunans were in contact with royalists or not. But I'm sure they were; why else would Count Kevlokine be at their house? He had been staying here for a week, never went out, but had streams of visitors. It was a good hiding place. He would have been expected to find refuge with monarchists, or aristocrats . . . not with an apparently unobtrusive bourgeois couple. I'm going to do my best to find out who all those visitors were, but it's not going to be easy. There were several people every day and Monsieur Keberk is giving nothing away. I'm waiting for reinforcements from the Minister of Civilian Police, to help me find out more. My two theories are as follows. The first is that the Gunans woke up this morning and found that Monsieur Kevlokine had been murdered by someone who had broken into their house during the night. They then took fright, and feared they would be accused of the crime or arrested by the police for consorting with an enemy agent. They fled in disarray, taking their housekeeper and a servant who both lived with them. My second theory is that for some reason I don't know they were the ones who killed Count Kevlokine. Whatever the case, they are no longer here and nor are their two servants. Some personal belongings are missing: clothes, combs, jewellery, little things the couple were fond of . . . If you would like to follow me . . .'

He led Margont into a large bedroom of unbelievable luxury with paintings in massive golden frames, marquetry furniture, Sèvres or Dresden porcelain, and Persian carpets. The count's body lay near the fireplace, not far from a four-poster bed. He looked about forty-five and had been gagged. He was very fat with reddened cheeks that contrasted with the pallor of his skin. His hair was so grey it was almost luminous. The man's appearance corresponded closely to Talleyrand's description of Count Kevlokine. In the heavenly setting, with its gold and other bright colours, his burnt arms formed two horrifying lines of red and black. His hands had been bound with one of the curtain ties, which had in its turn been burnt. He was wearing a nightshirt, a long, white quilted goose-down housecoat and breeches – normally the outfit of a man first thing in the morning, but also used to sleep in by men who worked all the time. It was comfortable enough for sleep, but allowed one to leap out of bed if awoken suddenly in the night, all ready for work without having to get dressed. His feet were bare.

Margont went over to get a closer look at Kevlokine's face. Unlike Colonel Berle's, it was unscathed. Margont turned round and saw that Sausson was watching him attentively, trying to work out what he was thinking from his gestures.

'They forgot to give me the order to close his eyes,' said the policeman sardonically.

Without asking him to leave, Margont went on with his investigation. The badge of the Swords of the King was pinned to the count's nightshirt, on his chest, like a decoration. It was exactly the same as the symbol that Margont had noticed on Colonel Berle. The count's serene face contrasted with the state of his arms, devoured by fire. Margont could not, however, see any mortal wound.

A brouhaha broke out in the street – there were cries and exclamations. Margont recognised one of the voices and hurried over to the window, completely forgetting he was supposed to keep himself hidden. Jean-Quenin Brémond and the policeman who had gone to find him were surrounded by four men. Jean-

Quenin was showering them with invective. Although extremely kind to his patients, colleagues and friends, he was often impatient with everyone else. His guide had been obliged to raise his voice to explain to him that he was from the civilian police. At that point several people who had been lying in wait surged out of the adjacent little streets to come and surround them.

'Imbeciles! What're those political oafs getting involved for?' Sausson cursed. 'And that other idiot, who came in the front instead of using the back door as usual!'

He opened the window with such force that a pane smashed on the hook for the curtain tie – but it looked as if the glass had been shattered solely by the force of the policeman's fury.

'Let them through!' he yelled.

The assailants scattered like cockroaches surprised by a light. The next instant there was not a sign of them. But Jean-Quenin continued to shout insults: they were cads, louts, yet again they were treating the Health Service disrespectfully, they were lucky he was in a hurry, the Minister of Civilian Police would certainly be hearing all about this . . . When they vanished inside the house, he could still be heard uttering imprecations. Sausson forestalled Margont's question.

'They're policemen like me, but we're not from the same force. Oh, no! I take care of criminal investigations, they look after political matters and I've no idea where you fit in . . . They work for Joseph I, I work for the people of Paris, and that's not the same thing at all. This one murder has set off a triple investigation. And to think that when a washerwoman is stabbed, my superiors complain I spend too much time looking for the culprit! All those fellows arrived with Monsieur Palenier. And all because I mentioned the name Kevlokine. They're grabbing everyone who tries to come in to the Gunans' house. But there are so many visitors that by the end of the day they will have arrested the whole of Paris.'

'Very clever. The real royalists will be lost in the crowd; it will be hard to separate them out. Every one of them must have taken care to concoct his cover.'

Jean-Quenin arrived in a fury, scarlet-faced, his case in hand, his uniform hidden under a light-coloured overcoat. He opened his mouth to speak but his friend gestured that he should stay silent.

'This is Inspector Sausson, and he must not know anything about me,' Margont explained. 'Perhaps he will leave us . . .'

He would pay for saying that. Sausson tensed. His lips folded and disappeared with the words he swallowed down. He turned abruptly and left the room, banging the door.

Jean-Quenin stared at the victim. 'What wasps' nest have you stirred up now, Quentin?' His weary, despairing expression spoke volumes.

'Could you examine the body, please, Jean-Quenin? I won't tell you anything about it so as not to influence you.'

As the medical officer did so, Margont went over to the fireplace. Here the smell of charred flesh was almost unbearable. Grease spots stained the stones of the hearth and there were shreds of burnt clothing. The count must have fallen asleep while the fire was still burning. Had the murderer killed him as he slept and then dragged the body over to the hearth?

Jean-Quenin undressed the corpse.

'I don't understand this. Here again the man was burnt after having been killed. But I can't see how he was killed! It's the first time I've come across a crime like this. Perhaps he was poisoned . . . by a slow-acting poison, which he swallowed at dinner, or drank in a tisane before going to sleep, and which took effect while he slept. But that doesn't really make sense . . . That would mean that the poisoner would have had to come in at least twice: once to pour out the poison, then to mutilate the body, and he would have had to hide himself for hours in the house. As you know, I'm interested in criminal cases and I owe my interest to you. I can tell you that, very often, murderers who use poison choose it so that they don't have to touch their victims, because they find them repulsive!'

Margont was puzzled. 'Can we really be certain that this man was murdered by the same person as Colonel Berle?' he wondered. 'Now I think so, now I think not . . . There are manifest similarities between the murders, but also differences.'

'Wait, I mentioned poison, but let's not be too hasty! It's only a theory, because that's the only weapon I know that can kill a man whilst leaving the body apparently unscathed. But it's also possible that this person was awoken by a noise, that he noticed an intruder in his room, and that his heart, weakened by age and excess, was not strong enough to withstand the sudden shock. Or perhaps his heart gave out with the pain of the first burns, but the murderer went on inflicting them.'

'But the expression on his face is tranquil – doesn't that mean that he was also mutilated after being killed, like Berle? Perhaps he was even killed as he slept; he seems so peaceful with his eyes closed. Then the murderer could have gagged him and bound his hands, to make it look as if the burns were inflicted before death.'

'It's true that the man's relaxed expression does argue in favour of your hypothesis. But that's all it is – a hypothesis; we can't prove it. It doesn't eliminate the second theory that I suggested, which at least explains how the man might have died. A brief intense terror would not necessarily make its mark on the man's face, because death would be very sudden.'

'Would you be able to do an autopsy?'

'If the cause of death were obvious, as in the case of Colonel Berle, I would have refused, because we're so busy dealing with the wounded every day. But this case is different. A doctor should never leave the cause of death unexplained. Otherwise, one of these days, he will miss the signs of that unexplained cause . . .'

'Thank you! I will undertake to get agreement from Inspector Sausson.'

'And from that band of harpies who set on me earlier . . .'

Cause of death unknown . . . Jean-Quenin was, most unaccustomedly, agitated. He would not let himself be beaten! He was going to discuss the mystery with colleagues. Every time he was checked in his battle against death, far from leading him to concede defeat, it just reinforced his determination to continue fighting, on and on. He would sometimes refer to patients ten years after their deaths, as if they had died just the other day.

Margont told him the little he knew about Count Kevlokine, and where Lefine was staying, so that he would be able to pass on his conclusions. Then he called Sausson back and made his request. Jean-Quenin added that he would have to have the body taken to his hospital, as soon as possible.

'On the express condition that I can be present at the autopsy. That way, I'll be sure that you don't conceal the results from me.'

As Sausson was organising the removal of the remains, Jean-Quenin collected anything that might have contained food or drink: a glass and pitcher from the bedroom, plates and three dirty cups from the kitchen . . .

Margont questioned Keberk privately. He described the members of the Swords of the King to him, to see whether any of them had been seen at the house. But Keberk shook his head at each description, and it was impossible to tell whether he had never in fact seen any of them, or whether he was lying to protect his employers. In any case, he seemed so overcome that his answers could not be trusted.

Finally Margont went to see where the intruder had broken in. As with Berle, the shutters had been shattered, probably with a crowbar, and a windowpane had been broken to open the window.

As Margont was about to leave, Sausson called out to him: 'Do you know what the little royalist emblem signifies?'

'Goodbye, Inspector . . .'

CHAPTER 26

THAT very evening Jean-Quenin Brémond let Margont know, via Lefine, that he had to see him as soon as possible. Margont was slightly irritated by this, but he complied. He left the print shop and, taking all necessary precautions, went to the meeting place Jean-Quenin had specified, in front of the Église Saint-Gervais. The medical officer was in civilian clothes, which was rare. Margont was grateful for his prudence.

'What's going on, Jean-Quenin?'

The doctor was agitated, excited. It was the first time that Margont had seen him in such a state. Jean-Quenin – who normally kept a tight check on his emotions, even when he was amputating on the battlefield – seemed to be in the grip of a feverish disturbance that was making his blood boil.

'Quentin, I know what killed Count Kevlokine. During the autopsy, I pretended not to understand anything, to hide my discovery from Inspector Sausson, because I know you want to keep him away from your investigation. I found no trace of poison in the food remains, or in the glasses or cups I found at the Gunans' house, so the policeman suspected nothing. It's . . . it's . . .'

Margont was proud of his ability to keep his cool, but he considered that normally Jean-Quenin was even better at it. Now as he looked at his friend in such a state, he had the impression he was looking at a mountain trembling.

'Quentin, Count Kevlokine was asphyxiated. But he wasn't strangled: there were no marks on his neck and his larynx was not damaged. That's not because of the gag either: he would have bitten down on the material and I would have found fibres in his mouth, his face would have shown suffering and terror . . . His heart was in perfect condition. It wasn't apoplexy. There were no blisters on the arms or in the mouth, and the trachea was healthy and unaltered, so in this murder also, the burns were definitely inflicted post-mortem. I hid that as well from Inspector Sausson, who knows nothing about medicine. So, in short, it was a complete mystery! I thought I was going mad. I was like a mathematician who discovers an addition where one plus one does not equal two. Do you see what I mean?'

'I think so . . .'

'In these situations when I'm at a loss, I have a system. I go back over everything from the very beginning; I go back to the basics. So I started the autopsy over again, although the abdomen and the thoracic cavity were already open, and I had removed the heart, the liver—'

'Thanks, Jean-Quenin! I'd rather you spared me the details, unless they're absolutely essential for me to understand what you are about to explain.'

'All right, briefly, you start an autopsy by observing the corpse. As you might imagine, overwork often means that doctors skip that stage. So I begin to examine the body. And that's when I discover a prick in the neck. Not caused by an insect; there was no local inflammation, no bump. No, just a dot of blood. The prick of a needle. Apparently inexplicable asphyxia, so sudden that the victim did not have time to suffer –

judging by his serene expression – no visible lesions, a needle prick: death by curare poisoning!'

'What? I've never heard of curare. And what does it have to do with the needle prick?'

'It's a poison found in South America. Amazonian Indians use it for hunting.'

'Amazonian Indians?'

'Listen to what I'm telling you! There are many variations of the poison. Each Amazonian tribe has its own recipe and they use dozens of different ingredients: plants, caterpillars, insects, snakes, poisonous toads, various other kinds of poison . . . So really one should refer to curares. Not much is known about them. But you have to understand that a single drop is sufficient to kill in a few seconds. All you have to do is dip a needle in curare and inject yourself, and that will be the end of you! There are no antidotes: death is inevitable. The poison paralyses the muscles – we don't know how – and death results from asphyxiation, because the respiratory muscles are paralysed.'

'A poison that acts through the blood?'

Margont was passionate about history and had read several accounts by *conquistadores* and Portuguese soldiers describing the deaths of their men, sometimes in a few moments, following often tiny wounds from arrows or darts from blowpipes. But this was Paris, not the Amazon.

'How do you know all this, Jean-Quenin? Are you sure? If you're mistaken—'

'I'm certain! I've always wanted to do medical research so I keep myself well informed. At the moment, because of the war, I'm devoting myself to the wounded and to helping my friends.

But when there's finally peace, I will spend my time on research! You see, Quentin, you often talk about the newspaper you want to found. Well, this is my dream: to continue to care for people by researching new cures. It just so happens that France is one of the most advanced countries in pharmacology, a new science that studies the properties of chemical substances with the aim of discovering new remedies, and of better understanding how the human body functions. Perhaps you've heard of Magendie? He's a master in the field, even better than the English, who are also making great strides in this sphere! I have the privilege of knowing him – French medical research is a small world. It was he who told me about curare a few years ago. Magendie favours experimental research: starting not from some hypothetical stance, but from concrete experience. Curare has such a spectacular effect on the human body that anyone who finds out how it works will certainly have made a major discovery. Parisian doctors pay fortunes to get hold of the stuff! Fortunes!'

Jean-Quenin put his hands on Margont's shoulders, though he was not normally demonstrative. Not only did curare cause paralysis, it also drove researchers mad . . .

'Quentin, you often ask me to help you, and I've never asked for anything in exchange. But today, I'm asking for something! I'm asking you, if you ever lay your hands on this curare, to give it to me.'

'Well, I actually want to lay my hands on whoever made use of the curare. I agree though. If I succeed—'

Jean-Quenin shook his hand vigorously. 'Thank you, Quentin!'

'Wait . . . How did the curare get to Paris?'

'I'm not sure. Apparently it doesn't last more than a few months. The problem is that Brazil is a viceroyalty of Portugal, and we've been at war with them for several years. With all these conflicts, exotic substances are hard to come by. English researchers are ahead of the French in this respect because they're allied to Portugal, which allows them to get hold of curare more easily than we can.'

What a simplistic way of representing the war! Jean-Quenin, although normally so philanthropic, was displaying breathtaking egotism.

Margont wondered out loud whether members of a Parisian royalist group would have been able to get hold of curare through the Allies. If they had the right contacts and enough money, it was quite possible.

He added: 'It must have taken them months to get it! They would have had to contact an Allied agent, get him to agree to undertake to find it, then convince the Portuguese to send one of their ships to Brazil – although that is happening all the time: in 1807, Portugal's prince regent fled from the French armies and installed his court in Rio de Janeiro – to bring back curare, which would have to be obtained from an Amazonian tribe . . .'

If Jean-Quenin was right, the Swords of the King had been preparing their action for much longer than Margont had imagined. And it was also unlikely that the murderer was operating on his own. It would take the support of an organisation to mount such an operation.

'Hang on, the murderer must be a doctor!' exclaimed Margont.

Jean-Quenin took a moment to react, then he reddened. That had not crossed his mind. 'Very probably. A doctor or a traveller who's been to South America.'

'Or else a French aristocrat who fled to Portugal, then followed the court to Rio. Have you told me everything?'

'Yes.'

Margont thanked him and left his friend. Jean-Quenin wandered around Paris for a while, trying to calm himself down. But he could not stop thinking about his plans for greatness and his imagination ran riot. Margont had not understood at all . . . He didn't want to make a great discovery for reasons of self-aggrandisement! All his life he had had the feeling that he had not done enough for his patients. Today he had felt that it really would be possible for him to take a giant leap forward for medicine. There were so many people he had not been able to save and their ghosts accompanied him everywhere – yes, everywhere! – forming a monstrous cohort that was growing with the years. If he succeeded in discovering the secret of curare, then he would be able to appease those tormented souls. Like every doctor he dreamt of being able to say one day, 'Yes, I have done more good than harm in my life.'

CHAPTER 27

O N 27 March, Paris was in turmoil. Until then Napoleon and his army had formed a barrier between the Parisians and the bad news, shielding them from the worst of it. But now that the Emperor had moved away to threaten the rear of the Allied armies, the citizens were exposed to the flow of bad tidings that accompanied the haggard streams of refugees, wounded, deserters, and soldiers that were converging on Paris from all over the country.

Margont had difficulty making his way through the crowds, skirting round chaotic groups only to find himself enmeshed in further rabble. Wagons were piling up, heaps of furniture and trunks stuffed to overflowing were falling over, adding to the uproar, and the guards of honour were getting impatient with the crowds. Those who wanted to leave were no more able to move than those who were arriving; the columns of soldiers were collecting new conscripts, known as Marie-Louises, in their wake (in 1813 the Empress Marie-Louise had signed the decrees, in the absence of her husband). All this humanity formed a sort of glue that stuck to the passers-by, forcing them to elbow their way through.

Somewhere near his printing works, Margont went into a packed cabaret. He had asked Lefine to meet him there and found him seated in a corner, drinking beer. He was savouring the drink as if it might be his last.

'It's the end of the world, our world anyway,' he declared, putting his glass down on the table.

'Don't be so defeatist!'

'No, of course not. You're going to set me right.'

Margont drew closer and spoke into his ear. 'Now people are beginning to realise what's happening, their reactions are going to be unpredictable. Who knows how a panicked crowd will react if a group of determined royalists promises them the sun, the moon and the stars? Paris is becoming a powder keg and our friends are about to throw torches into its midst.'

He indicated that he and Lefine should leave. He needed air, although he was not sure he would be able to breathe any more easily outside.

'I've had an idea. Follow me, you'll understand in a minute where we're going. But first, we'll get our bearings.'

Margont was not normally mysterious like this, at least not with his close friends. But Lefine was not put out. He went with Margont in all confidence, without wasting time wondering where he was being taken.

Lefine gave Margont back the button found in Notre-Dame. Unfortunately the friend who worked in the commissariat had not been able to identify it and had reached the conclusion that it was not a French army button. Despite his best efforts, Lefine had been unable to find out anything new about their suspects either. Catherine de Saltonges had not left her house, and she had not received any visitors.

Margont told Lefine about his second meeting with Joseph and Talleyrand, and how he had been given a new objective, about his examination of Count Kevlokine's body and what

Jean-Quenin had discovered. He had also obtained copies of two reports from Mathurin Jelent, which he had read and then immediately destroyed. Lefine reproached him for not observing the security precautions they had agreed on, but again Margont objected that time was pressing.

The first report had been written by Inspector Sausson for his superiors. He was making no progress with his investigation, which he found incomprehensible. Not being a man to mince his words, he had written: 'I am almost coming to suspect that someone (why and under whose orders I cannot yet say) is hiding clues from the official and only legitimate investigators, in order to conduct a parallel investigation.' No doubt those words had sent Joseph into a rage.

The second had been produced by the section of Joseph's secret police that had arrested the people visiting the Gunans. It was an incomplete, censored copy. And it didn't say who the author of the report was. All names had been omitted; some paragraphs simply fizzled out, since their endings had been scored through. Certain sentences were limping because parts of them had been amputated. This half-report revealed that so far twenty visitors had been interrogated, but that it had not been possible to tell which were genuine royalist agitators.

'But why murder the Tsar's envoy?' said Lefine.

They were walking past the Botanical Gardens. Napoleon had had it transformed into a zoological park.

'I don't know, Fernand. I'm not even sure that Colonel Berle and Count Kevlokine were murdered by the same person. Joseph and Talleyrand were counting on the latter to help them negotiate a separate peace with the Russians. Perhaps our assassin had found that out, or guessed, and that was the motive for the murder. The extremists kill the moderates, the moderates end up killing the extremists, even though that's what they themselves have become. Isn't that one of the bloody lessons the Revolution taught us?'

'But why leave the emblem of the Swords of the King?'

Margont had developed a sort of tic, a grimace. Leading investigations made him adopt the expressions of a hunting dog scenting the odour of its prey.

'That's a very good question! Either, there's one murderer who's sending a signal to others in the group that he's prepared to execute them if they don't start to take action! That would be proof that he didn't care about being rewarded for his acts since, if the monarchy is restored, Louis XVIII will immediately imprison the man who killed the Tsar's friend, even if that same man has done him a great service by preventing a compromise from being reached between Napoleon and Alexander I. Or else, we are looking at two murderers, and the second one is trying to pass his crime off as being committed by the first, by using the symbol and by mutilating the body with burns.'

'In the first case, it only makes sense if the Swords of the King find out that their symbol was pinned to Count Kevlokine's body.'

'You're right. But the Swords of the King know all sorts of things they don't tell me! I was completely unaware that some of them were in contact with Kevlokine; it's possible that the police keep them informed. Honoré de Nolant must have kept in contact with his old colleagues who're still serving the Empire. We can't assume they don't know about the symbol –

they're very well connected. If they don't know already, they'll find out sooner or later.'

'Are we sure it's the same symbol?'

'Yes. Mathurin Jelent told me that Joseph's agents compared the two emblems – Monsieur Palenier removed the second one from the body, right under the nose of Sausson . . . They're identical. But we still know nothing about the symbols.'

Margont slowed down. They were almost there. 'Or there's a third possibility. Maybe the assassin isn't genuinely royalist. Perhaps he's killing for personal motives and leaving the emblem to make them look like politically motivated crimes.'

'What makes you think that?'

'The burns. We need to probe the significance of fire for the murderer.'

'How do you propose we do that?'

'By coming here.'

Margont pointed out a majestic gateway with two pillars bearing a massive pediment surmounted by a rounded arch. The Salpêtrière hospice welcomed – or more often imprisoned – the capital's old women who could no longer fend for themselves, invalids, the handicapped, indigents, beggars, orphaned or abandoned girls, prisoners of conscience and lunatics.

CHAPTER 28

LEFINE was scarlet with fear and anger. Of all things, madness frightened him the most. He had a long-standing and obscure dread – it must have its roots deep in his psyche – that if he ever set foot in an asylum, he would be locked up there indefinitely. He even wondered if this was what Margont had in mind. He was somewhat reassured by the fact the Salpêtrière was only for women, but what if this was a ruse, and he was later carted off to Bicêtre or Charenton? Margont, who was aware of his friend's fears, tried to be as reassuring as possible.

'Stop battling your demons! We've only come to interview Dr Pinel.'

Pinel, Pinel . . . Lefine had heard of the famous doctor. It was pride that forced him on – he would not flee from his chimeras. But he felt as oppressed, as if all the buildings of the Salpêtrière were closing in on him.

Margont gave the doorkeeper a few coins and he let them through. The place was vast. There were rows of little houses, courtyards, gated yards, gardens filled with trees (walking in the shady fresh air was part of the treatment), streets, a chapel . . . It was a city inside a city, a little Paris inside a big one. Margont felt uncomfortable in the closed environment cut off from the rest of the world.

'It's like a prison in here! Or a fortress, Castle Madness . . .'

Women were strolling along the lime-tree-lined paths. Some

of them were on their own; some were with keepers or nuns (the Empire had recalled the nuns sent away during the Revolution). As soon as any of them looked at Lefine, he felt his fears getting the better of him. Although the vast majority of the inmates were not lunatics, Lefine saw mad people everywhere, in their thousands; they were circling him and Margont, and were about to leap on them, and beat them and suffocate them and crush them under their weight. The more he told himself his fears were ridiculous the more his imagination inflated them.

'Why are we here?'

Margont pointed out the Saint-Louis Chapel, the little masterpiece built by Libéral Bruant, who was better known as the designer of the Hôtel des Invalides.

'I disapprove of it. Ostensibly it allows the inmates to pray in a consecrated place. But I think it's much more about preventing them from going out. Supposing an inmate wants to go for a walk in the Botanical Gardens nearby? Well, she can't; she'll be told to walk in the Salpêtrière gardens. She wants to go to church? She can go to the Salpêtrière chapel. Go for a swim? In the Salpêtrière. Get married? In the Salpêtrière. The Salpêtrière! The Salpêtrière! The Salpêtrière! All this here has been built so that the inmates never have to go out! All of life takes place within these walls. Nothing exists outside these walls. It's like being in a sort of secular abbey for lunatics and old women!'

He remembered the years he had spent in the Abbey of Saint-Guilhem-le-Désert and dizziness clouded his vision. One of the wings of the Salpêtrière exploded in front of his eyes. Stones and mortar were scattered by twelve-pound cannonballs and Austrian artillery shells. It was his fury that had set off the imaginary explosion. The walls were hurled into the air where they broke up like papers torn up in rage; they were pulverised; their debris rained down like the drops of a violent spring storm; clouds of dust blended together forming an ochre fog . . . The battle moved past, receding into the distance. Calm descended. And the lunatics and paupers, much to their astonishment, found themselves free to come out from their shelter, climb through the gaping holes in the walls and wander off, at liberty, into Paris . . .

The warden who was guiding Margont and Lefine indicated a building, telling them that they should go up to the first floor, and then went back to his post.

'Why are we here?' repeated Lefine.

'We're going to ask Dr Pinel about burns inflicted after death.'

Lefine thought that was . . . was . . . how should he put it? There were no words strong enough to express what he thought it was. Absurd, stupid, irrelevant, idiotic, ridiculous, laughable, capricious, grotesque, mad, dangerous, unreasonable! All that and much more besides!

'A doctor of the mind will have a different perspective from ours. Perhaps he will already have encountered a deranged criminal who burns his victims after they're dead,' said Margont.

'Why choose Pinel? I vaguely recognise his name.'

'He was the one who freed the lunatics. In 1793, when he'd just taken up his post at the hospice of Bicêtre, he decided to free the madmen from their chains. To the horror of the wardens.

Their argument was that some of the patients were deranged, raving lunatics whom it was necessary to keep in chains day and night, but Pinel's point was that it was the restraint that caused them to be violent. He decided to begin by freeing twelve of them.'

'Oh, yes, I remember! One of the men freed was Chevingé, a simple soldier who thought he was a general and was giving orders to all and sundry. I was told about it when we were bivouacking and it made a big impression on me. Because I've always secretly wondered if Irénée will end up like Chevingé. When he was a lieutenant he behaved like a colonel and now that he's pretty much a colonel, he thinks he's already a marshal. He's been put in charge of a legion so he thinks he's Julius Caesar. If he gets promoted any further he's going to want to overthrow the Emperor . . . or Louis XVIII.'

Margont did not react to the reference to monarchy.

'I'm not sure if it's myth, but apparently some of the patients he liberated were instantly cured and none of them was violent any more. It sounds too good to be entirely true. But I hope that Pinel was not the only doctor to unchain mad people . . . In any case, he did it and how do you think he was rewarded? He was transferred to the Salpêtrière less than two years later, where he also freed the mad people!'

Margont was excited but nervous. He was gearing himself up to meet one of the people he most admired – a veritable living legend! – and was fearful that the reality would not live up to his expectations.

They went inside the building and were greeted by shouting. A young woman was being forcibly restrained by wardens under torrents of cold water. She was yelling, and struggling, soaked to the skin, her hair plastered to her head, her lips blue. The staff were struggling to control her, water spurted on all sides and Margont was splattered. Lefine, who kept behind Margont, received only a drop on his hand. But he whitened as if all the heat of his body had been absorbed by this one little drop as cold as a snowflake.

'Watch out!' fumed Margont. The meeting was terribly important to him and here he was with wet coat and trousers. 'What are you doing? That water is freezing!'

He rarely made use of his authority in that way, but he had spoken to the men in the tone of a lieutenant-colonel reprimanding his soldiers, even though he was not wearing uniform.

Lefine muttered to him in a conciliatory tone, 'We're in civilian clothes, watch out – they might think you're another Chevingé . . .'

One of the wardens looked Margont up and down.

'It's to refresh her. Dr Pinel says it helps relax someone who is having bad thoughts. A good cold shower abruptly interrupts the flow of those thoughts.'

'What does that mean? Bad thoughts?'

'The poor creature imagines that God is talking to her, that she's a saint!'

'And besides, she's being punished,' countered another warden. 'Because she refuses to eat. She'll be sprayed until she agrees to feed herself.'

Not knowing much about illnesses of the mind and their treatment, Margont dared not interfere any further. But he was consumed with doubt as he turned away to go upstairs.

The hallway on the first floor was very crowded. Several of the residents were waiting to see Dr Pinel. One of them had her arms immobilised in a strait-jacket and was surrounded by three keepers. Although unable to move, her eyes expressed unbounded fury. Was her rage the cause of her immobilisation or the consequence of it? Margont wondered if he would have dared free her had he had the power to do so.

'There are too many people,' remarked Lefine. 'Instead of wasting time, let's come back tomorrow. Or another day . . . or never . . .'

Margont didn't answer. A strange little episode was unfolding. An old man was walking towards him, to the consternation of the staff. Three keepers and two municipal guards were following him, while two other guards took up position at the top of the stairs to block the way down. The man looked about eighty, but could have been younger and aged by what he had suffered. His manner and bearing were aristocratic. He was probably a nobleman of the *ancien régime*. A man of the past therefore and now, perhaps, a man of the future. He was dishevelled, in grubby clothes with an ill-adjusted cravat and a crumpled black ribbon on the ponytail of his tousled wig. He appeared relaxed, warmly welcoming and unruffled, at ease in his shrunken universe.

He accosted Margont with an affable 'Ah, Monsieur! I see you are an ardent supporter of liberty!'

Margont felt as if he had been seen through, as if, under the old man's regard, his body had turned to glass and his innermost thoughts were on display like coloured fluids in a crystal container. What clairvoyance! How had the man been able to read him so clearly? Was it a coincidence? Or was it just that some people's insanity was actually just a different way of seeing things? The fallen aristocrat – Margont was pretty sure that's what he was – saw that he was perplexed.

'It's simply that I observe that the lack of liberty here shocks you, whereas it reassures your friend. Do you know that liberty harbours a paradox? Everyone says they want it, but at the same time they're afraid of it!'

The remark touched a chord with Margont.

'Everyone wants it!' the man said again. 'But when we have it, we hurry to throw it off again. We had kings and once we had overthrown them, we replaced them with an emperor!'

Margont thought he could guess the reason for those guards. The man was probably a republican who had plotted to overthrow Napoleon. A noble republican, by all appearances. He must be a political prisoner. But what was he doing outside Pinel's office? Did he also have an illness of the mind? He seemed very lucid. And the Salpêtrière was only for women. Whatever the case, the man was brave to criticise the Emperor openly.

'Let's take another example. The Revolution demolished religious power. So what do men and women do? Do they take the chance to live freely? No, they marry each other and swear undying loyalty. They bask in monogamy! You, however, seem to cherish freedom for what it really is.'

He laid his hand on Margont's arm as he said this, to emphasise the sincerity of what he was saying. However, the gesture felt a little like a caress. Margont pulled his arm away, more sharply than he intended.

The old man then said regretfully, 'Oh . . . oh, what a shame . . . You're just like all the others, after all. Freedom only appeals to you in the abstract, and not as something to be fully savoured. You want to spend your life seeking it, but only on condition that you never find it . . .'

'That's not true at all! You're mixing everything up!'

'Whilst you, on the other hand, separate everything out! You separate the various liberties and rank them, accepting some and forbidding others. Isn't that just a way of killing off freedom? Isn't freedom all or nothing? How can one be half free?'

At that point, one of the municipal guards intervened: 'Monsieur le Marquis, be quiet!'

To Margont's discomfort, the man performed a deep pantomime bow, exaggerating the movement of his arms, then straightened up and patted into place the disordered hair of his powdered wig.

'I am Comte Donatien Alphonse François de Sade, better known by the name of Marquis de Sade. Whom do I have the honour of addressing?'

'Unfortunately I cannot tell you. However, I can tell you that I have read *Justine ou Les Malheurs de la vertu*. It was very . . . um . . . original.'

The Marquis de Sade was overjoyed. 'A reader! I have fewer of those than I have lovers!'

'You're embellishing your role, Monsieur le Marquis . . .'

'Ah, but that's all that's left to me now: my role! Since the real de Sade was imprisoned by the monarchy, then imprisoned by the Revolution, then imprisoned by the Consulate, who then sent him to the madhouse; and the Empire keeps him locked up . . . The entire world is against me! When I was incarcerated in Sainte-Pélagie – me amongst the saints, the judicial authorities must have a sense of humour! – I was accused of seducing the prisoners. It was true but the conclusion drawn from it was that I was a lunatic and I was sent to Bicêtre! Now I'm at Charenton. The great Pinel wants to see me and that will be a pleasure because apparently he's a little more enlightened than his colleagues. Unfortunately, if he concludes that I am of sane mind, I will have to leave Charenton . . . and I will immediately be sent to prison! So it's in my interests to appear insane and I plan to indulge my "role", as you call it, to the full. That's what society today forces me into. And they say it's me who's mad.'

He leant towards Margont and whispered in his ear, 'If one fine day you finally decide to avail yourself fully of all the freedom nature has to offer, you know my address: hospice de Charenton . . .'

Pinel's office door opened and a woman and a guardian came out. Margont marched shamelessly over, pushing in front of everyone, saying he was sorry, but his problem could not wait. As he crossed the corridor, gesturing to those trying to go in in front of him to let him through, the Marquis de Sade shouted to him, 'Do you know what my greatest regret is, Monsieur? In 1789, I was still imprisoned in the Bastille! I had been there for six years and I stayed until 4 July 1789. Until 4 July 1789! Had the Revolution broken out just ten days earlier, the King would have been overthrown and de Sade freed, and I guarantee you that France today would have been nothing like it is now. I would have shown all those revolutionaries the true face of liberty! France failed its revolution. By just ten days!'

CHAPTER 29

MARGONT went into the office belonging to the medical director of the Salpêtrière. He had been planning to explain everything to Pinel but found himself face to face with a crowd of young doctors and guardians. Exhausted – that was the first word that came to mind on seeing Pinel. Too many people making too many demands of him. And he was nearly seventy. Margont's entrance annoyed him.

'Go back outside and wait your turn, Monsieur! I don't doubt that your problem is genuine, I imagine you have come to seek help for one of your relatives, but those in front of you are also in need.'

Already two men had risen. One had his hands on his hips, the other his arms crossed, encouraging Margont to leave of his own accord. Margont undid his belt and fiddled with the buckle until it opened, revealing a small compartment. He took a piece of paper from this strange hiding place, and unfolded it again and again, finally handing Pinel a letter. The latter glanced at it and his eye fell on Joseph Bonaparte's signature. He looked up, hesitating, unsure whether he was dealing with a madman or with a genuine imperial agent.

'I would request everyone to leave us,' ordered Margont.

To everyone's astonishment, Pinel agreed and they all obeyed without asking any questions. Margont explained the reason for his visit, emphasising how important it was to keep what he said secret. The doctor was immediately interested; his eyes blazed like two little suns above the dark clouds of the circles beneath.

'You want to use my knowledge of insanity to help unmask a criminal? What a novel but tempting idea! Please sit down. So you think the criminal you're hunting might have a mental illness?'

'It's just a thought. But the burns inflicted after death . . .'

'An insane criminal hiding in the ranks of mentally healthy criminals – if such a concept makes sense. In the eyes of his accomplices he would appear quite normal . . .'

'Have you ever come across such a case?'

'I must admit I haven't.' Pinel looked thoughtful. 'Do you know why I was appointed to Bicêtre in 1793? It was because they wanted me to categorise patients. People were being guillotined left, right and centre, France had gone mad – that doesn't just happen to individuals, it can happen to societies, to countries as well. The Committee of Public Safety was convinced that royalists and foreign agents were concealing themselves amongst the lunatics. When I treated a nobleman or a cleric I had to certify that he was genuinely ill. If I were to say that he was of sound mind, he would be sent to the guillotine! Happily I always came to the conclusion that they were insane. Today I can admit that sometimes I lied. All that is just to say how much your question troubles me. In 1793 they wanted me to unmask the sane hiding amongst the insane, so that they could execute them; twenty years on, you would like me to help you find a madman in the midst of healthy people so that he can be sent to prison. Your request is like a mirror image of what I was asked to do in 1793. I don't really understand why everyone is determined to find a line so that the insane can be put on one side of it and the sane on the other side. Such a line does not exist. They are us, we are them. You appear to me to be perfectly reasonable today, but you might just as easily appear to have lost your mind in a year's time. Whilst the insane might well have recovered their reason. And that's without taking into account those whom today we consider insane, but whom we will later come to understand just had a different way of looking at the world, a way that we didn't understand at the time. I'm thinking for example of the Marquis de Sade, whom you must have seen in the corridor . . .'

Anxious to bring the conversation back to his inquiry, Margont voiced one of his thoughts. 'I thought of all the things that fire symbolises in the Bible. The suspects are all aristocratic, so religion for them—'

'Fire? But it's not fire that is the most striking thing in what you have told me. It's the *repetition* of fire. He burnt someone, then he burnt someone *else*.'

'I think I follow, more or less . . . So might it be someone who was himself burnt?'

'More than that! He's still burning today.'

'You think this man is in some way haunted by fire? He has been the victim of fire in one way or another. He thinks about it constantly . . .'

Margont vaguely understood that. He had participated in several battles and they regularly came back to him as night-mares. The same went for his childhood memories of being shut up in the Abbey of Saint-Guilhem-le-Désert, although these days, those memories were not as strong.

'Unlike some of my colleagues,' emphasised Pinel, 'I think that mental illnesses have a cause, that they result from shocks to the mind, which themselves stem from violent emotions that the subject was unable to control. The man you're looking for has probably suffered a traumatic experience to do with fire, which has disturbed the working of his mind.'

'So if we find the original inferno, we will be able to identify the man . . .' said Margont thoughtfully.

Pinel was delighted. 'Bravo! You should become a doctor and treat the insane, like I do!'

'Pardon?'

'I'm serious! Everyone is interested in the mind but no one wants to work with the insane! Do you know what most of my colleagues do when confronted with madness? They bleed the patient! What an aberration! They're so worried by anything abstract that they want to do something practical, although it has be said that bleeding is the opposite of practical! The profession would appeal to you and I think you would have a gift for it. If you were interested, and you started your medical studies, I would willingly accept you as a pupil.'

Margont was struck dumb and the doctor went joyously on, 'Have you never thought what you will do when the war is over?'

Lefine sniggered. 'Will it ever be over?'

'I think about it all the time,' replied Margont. 'I'd like to launch a newspaper—' He caught himself. He had said too much!

'Do both!' suggested Pinel. 'The study of madness would give you plenty of material for your articles, believe you me! There would be enough to fill ten newspapers on the subject of the ill treatment of the insane. When I decreed they should be freed from their chains, I was almost locked up with them!'

'I'll think about your proposition. But going back to our investigation . . . The fire . . .'

'You're hiding behind the fire so that you don't have to answer my offer. That's understandable. But it still stands. Take all the time you need to think about it.'

'Do you think the murderer is unstable?'

'No. It's not someone who was operating in a blind fury otherwise they would have destroyed everything in the room, making an unbelievable uproar, which would have had the police come running. I don't think either that they hear voices, because the poor souls who suffer from that plague are so deranged by it that when they go to commit a crime, they are easily found out. Because their thoughts are so disturbed, they're incapable of scheming and carrying through a coherent plan. Besides, their illness is evident in their behaviour and their speech . . .'

'I haven't noticed anything like that in any of my suspects.'

'This man is in full possession of his intellectual faculties. But he has been profoundly affected by fire and is trying to free himself from the grip of its memory. There are many kinds of debilitating or oppressive feelings: grief, hate, regret, fear, remorse, envy, jealousy . . . But they don't degenerate into madness unless they reach great intensity, often after a shock.'

Margont clasped his hands together. It was an instinctive

gesture, as if his ideas were floating in front of him like a cloud of midges, and he was trying to gather them together. It was also like the strange prayer of a believer, who was so exasperated by religion that he thought himself an atheist.

'He's hiding in a group of monarchists. Might he be dividing his thoughts between his obsessive fear and his political ideals? No, everything is linked to the fire. In one way or another, even his royalist loyalty must relate to fire.'

Pinel nodded. 'I think so too. He seems to have a real monomania about fire. It's an obsession, his only one. Even if there is something else that interests him, which initially has nothing to do with fire, fire will spread in his mind and burn it up.'

'Something else or someone else that interests him. And he will be obsessed until he succeeds in extinguishing the blaze – assuming that's his aim. How will he be able to do that?'

Pinel gave an apologetic smile. 'I think you know how . . .'

In a sense, Margont did. He had been haunted by his own 'fire': being sent away to the Abbey Saint-Guilhem-le-Désert. Unfortunately by the time that fire had in effect been reduced to embers, a new fire had been ignited in him by the war. 'He has to settle the score with his past . . .'

'Isn't that what we all do, all through our lives?'

'Why are the burns in different places on the two victims? The face, then the arms. Is that significant?'

'Yes, it will be significant, but I'm not sure how. You mustn't ignore that question. Because fire is at the heart of this criminal's monomania. All his thoughts converge sooner or later on fire. So nothing he does with fire is without meaning.'

Pinel could offer no help on the question of curare. Margont shook the doctor's hand warmly. He was physically exhausted – as if the conversation had been a race several hours long – but his spirit had been completely revived. 'I can never thank you enough!'

'Good luck. And think about my proposition.'

CHAPTER 30

O N 28 March, now that the Allies' real plan had been discovered, Napoleon held a new council of war at Saint-Dizier. The day before, they had learnt of the destruction of General Pacthod's division and the retreat of Marshals Marmont and Mortier to Paris. Only Marshal Macdonald was in favour of abandoning the capital and battering the rear of the enemy lines with all their fire power. All the other officers wanted to try to save Paris. The Emperor came to a decision. The French army would hurry towards the capital to rescue it – if they could get there in time. A race against the Allies began.

CHAPTER 31

MARGONT was waiting under the arcades of Rue de Rivoli. In 1801, Napoleon Bonaparte had decided to run a long, large avenue east to west along the Seine. This one went past, amongst other things, the Louvre and the Tuileries Palace. It was part of a grand scheme of urbanisation: fine residences were to be built with steeply pitched roofs, a sewer system, paving of the streets. And so Rue de Rivoli was born. But no one wanted a home in the new buildings, which were all identical and lined up like stone soldiers awaiting imperial review. It was very humiliating for Napoleon to realise that Parisians wanted nothing to do with his magnificent Rue de Rivoli. To encourage people, now the Imperial Government was offering a thirty-year exemption from taxes to each buyer. But it was not working. Rue de Rivoli remained resolutely empty . . . Lefine had tried to convince Margont that they should pool their meagre resources to buy lodgings because he was sure that one day they would be very valuable. Margont had, of course, refused. Frankly, who would want to leave their children a measly apartment on Rue de Rivoli?

He spotted Charles de Varencourt, whom he had asked a woman begging in the street to go and find, and waved to him. He looked distraught, resembling a ship in distress. He was almost unrecognisable. He kept wiping his face, which continually filmed again with sweat.

He glared at Margont. 'Are you trying to get us killed? Why have you summoned me? I should never have come. You have five minutes.'

'That's for me to decide, not you. If you hadn't come I would have gone myself to knock on your door until you opened up!'

Varencourt was breathing heavily like a hunted deer that hears the baying and the blowing of horns coming nearer. 'Oh, so that's why they chose you for this! It's because you have no awareness of danger! You don't know it, but you're the walking dead.'

He led Margont off to the side, all the while talking in low tones, although there were few people about. 'The Allies are marching on Paris! So there's no knowing to what lengths the royalists will go. They're all going to be outdoing each other in daring. They're like caged animals about to burst out of their prisons.'

Margont looked at him. He spoke sarcastically: 'The situation has been critical for a while now. So there must be another reason for your panic.'

Varencourt paled further. He looked like a snowman melting in the sun.

'It's a good thing after all that you're not a card player. Because you don't know when you're beaten. When I have a bad hand I withdraw from the game. At the moment I'm drawing worse and worse cards and you're forcing me to up the betting. When I approached the police with information, I thought the Emperor would crush the Allies as he'd always done before. I never for a moment thought they would reach here. I bet on spades but what turned up was an avalanche of diamonds and hearts. If the Allies win, they will go through the millions of documents the Empire has accumulated: dossiers, reports, accounts . . . There has never in the whole of our history been such a monstrous, meddling bureaucracy. They will study everything and we will be unmasked. Instead of talking to you, I should be trying to get myself onto the first ship.'

'A great player like you would never let yourself become flustered like this. You're hiding something from me.'

'How do you know that I like playing with these odds?'

'You're avoiding my question.'

'The committee is meeting tonight. I don't know where. They will probably come and get you. Don't go. Disappear – that's the best advice I can give you.'

'Well, the best advice I can give you is not to disappear. Because if you do, the police will soon make you reappear. Did you know that the Swords of the King were in contact with Count Kevlokine?'

'With who?' Varencourt frowned. Margont would have liked to grab him by the collar and shake him vigorously.

'Stop treating me like an imbecile! You know very well who I'm referring to.'

'You still don't get it, do you? We bet on the losing side!'

Margont was not even talking the same language as Varencourt. What was worse, their minds did not work in the same way at all: his was abstract, intangible, made up of ideas, whereas Charles de Varencourt's, all cogs and wheels, was more like Pascal's calculating machine.

'Let me rephrase the question,' Margont said. 'Why did you not tell me about Kevlokine?'

'Because some subjects are off limits!'

Varencourt's face had changed. He now looked less fearful and more resolute.

'That was a very important subject with the group. They were always talking about the necessity of getting in touch with the Tsar's agent. They talked about it so much because they did not know how to go about it. Then suddenly, a few weeks before you were admitted, they stopped talking about it at all!'

He clapped his hands like a fairground clown. 'But at the same time Vicomte de Leaume also acquired what I can only describe as an air of invincibility. Our group were "spearheading the fight against the tyrant", we were going to "take the enemy in a pincer movement" . . . I thought that he had probably succeeded in contacting Kevlokine. It felt as if an important milestone had been reached and I realised bitterly that they were concealing the good news from me. I might be a traitor but I still have feelings. So one evening – about ten days before we met – I said, casually, "I know that we're being of great service to the Restoration. What a pity our efforts will never come to the attention of His Majesty!" '

He clenched his teeth. 'You should have seen the looks they gave each other! They still told me nothing, though. They'll pay for that! There are days when being a traitor and stabbing people in the back brings you more than just financial satisfaction. I think everyone knew except me! It was Baron de Nolant who was caught out by me. He hadn't noticed the looks the others were giving and launched in gaily with, "The Tsar will tell His Majesty." Jean-Baptiste de Châtel cut him off: "Where are we with finding more people to help us?" and afterwards the conversation turned to that subject. A bit too speedily and in a rather haphazard manner.'

'Why did you not tell me any of this?'

'Because it was too dangerous a subject! They must have been planning something with Kevlokine!'

Margont forced himself to stay calm. Listening to Varencourt was like reading *Le Moniteur* or *Le Journal de Paris*: truth and lies were intertwined. It was quite hard to work out what to dismiss and what might be partly true. But by listening carefully, Margont managed to pick out the contradictions and ignore what was palpably untrue. He was able to gather little snippets, and start to put them together.

'So,' he told Varencourt, 'you told us about everything except the most important things.'

Varencourt raised a finger, advocate for his own lost cause. 'Not exactly. I would say that everything is linked. The posters, Count Kevlokine, the rebellion, the assassination of Colonel Berle . . . I have no idea who killed the Tsar's agent. What I can tell you is that since his murder, they've changed—'

Varencourt broke off abruptly, aware that he had said too much.

'So you did know! How did the group find out that Kevlokine had been murdered?' Margont pressed him.

'Honoré de Nolant knows people. He has informers . . . I don't know who . . . But Leaume told me this morning that the count had been murdered. He didn't tell me any more than that.'

'Did he come to your house?'

'No. I was playing cards at an inn I'm fond of. Vicomte de Leaume arrived out of the blue and invited me for a "walk". He was asking me all about you. He asked me again where we met, and when, who we met through, and why. Luckily I was well prepared for his questions. And he does seem to have begun to accept you recently. Then he announced that Kevlokine was dead. That's what's changed my hand. That and the arrival of the Allies.'

They had walked a little further along and stopped by the Tuileries Gardens, which were separated from Rue de Rivoli by elegant railings. Joyful chatter could be heard from the gardens, where soldiers and beautiful girls were strolling in couples, laughing and swearing undying love to each other; luxurious little carriages were passing, drawn at the trot. The Spanish dragoons, newly arrived in Paris, were the heroes of the hour. These élite soldiers were feared even by the Spanish guerrillas who nicknamed them '*cabeʒas de oro*' – gold heads – because of their gold-coloured copper helmets. People who still believed Napoleon could win were milling about under the windows of the Tuileries Palace, or were besieging the imperial palace, sneering at the 'cowards' and flaunting their convictions. It was a strange spectacle, as if time had stopped. It was the end of March 1814 everywhere else but here in the Tuileries, where the sunny days of Austerlitz still shone.

Margont said nothing. He did not know if Louis de Leaume was aware that they had found the emblem of the Swords of the King on Count Kevlokine's body. And he did not want to give anything away by asking Varencourt.

'Go on!' he said instead.

'There isn't anything else! Really, I swear!'

'Does he suspect one of the members of the group?'

'What makes you say that? It would make no sense . . . one doesn't fire on one's own side!'

'Well, you do!'

Varencourt bristled at that. 'I really think you should disappear,' he advised Margont. 'But not till after tonight's meeting! If you flee now, by the end of the afternoon they'll realise you're gone. And all their suspicions will ricochet onto me, because I'm the one who introduced you. But if you go after the meeting – and I'll go too – they'll take longer to notice and we'll be able to put some distance between them and us. Yes, now I think about it properly, that's what we should do . . .'

He almost took Margont by the arm, but thought better of it. 'Do as you like, you obstinate blighter. I only ask one thing: that when you do decide to disappear, you'll let me know! Or else you'll have my death on your conscience. And I know you have a conscience, very much so. Just swear that you will let me know when you're withdrawing from the game!'

'If such a thing were to happen, I'd do my best to let you know.'

Varencourt did not look very reassured. Something had happened to make him nervous. He was an experienced and talented manipulator. The explanations he had given did not seem enough to justify the state he was in. And there was something slightly theatrical about his fear: the way he had almost taken Margont's arm, and sometimes mumbled his answers, his entreaties. Was he really as afraid as he was making out? Or was he acting fearful to mask his real state of mind? The more

Margont had opened up to him, the more Varencourt had seemed to respond with lies.

'Where were you the night Châtel, Leaume and Nolant turned up unannounced at my lodgings to force me to use my printing press?'

'I don't know anything about that.'

'Someone searched my room the same day that I met the committee.'

'That's hardly surprising. Although it's a pretty useless precaution to take. Who would be stupid enough to leave anything compromising at home? We're all searched, followed, watched . . . By others and by other members of the group! You learn to live with it . . .'

'Who is Catherine de Saltonges's lover?'

Varencourt reddened. He opened his mouth but found himself incapable of replying. He seemed to be suffocating, like a fish yanked out of the water by a hook and dropped on the riverbank. 'I don't . . . involve myself in such things . . .'

He looked very uncomfortable indeed. Was he in love with the woman?

'Let's leave her out of this,' he finally managed. 'She's already lived through enough crises, don't you think?'

He pulled himself together and looked Margont straight in the eye. 'As we're taking the gloves off, let's take them all the way off. You must already know that Jean-Baptiste de Châtel was summoned to appear before the tribunal of the Spanish Inquisition. Well, it wasn't only because of his heresy and violations of Roman Catholic dogma. He was also accused of acts of sodomy. I learnt that from Louis de Leaume one day when Châtel had yet again contradicted him and acted as if he were the leader of the group. Leaume exclaimed, "You're supposed to love me. Although not too much, of course. Didn't the Inquisition succeed in putting you off such things?" Later, when I asked him about it, Vicomte de Leaume told me that Châtel had had an affair with one of the monks at the Abbey d'Aljanfe. In December 1812, Châtel tried to join the Knights of the Faith. But one of their committee members had emigrated to Madrid in the past and had heard about Châtel. The man revealed what he knew and Châtel was turned down. When Châtel wanted to join the Swords of the King, the Knights of the Faith informed Vicomte de Leaume. But he accepted Châtel nevertheless. And in the beginning they got on extremely well, even though today you would find that hard to believe. However, since the Vicomte's allusion to Châtel's habits, they've hated each other. Now you know all that, is your investigation any further advanced?'

Oh, yes! thought Margont. He had already suspected that there was something else between Leaume and Châtel besides a mere power struggle. The assured, arrogant stare Jean-Baptiste de Châtel gave Louis de Leaume . . . Perhaps Leaume was right and Châtel was attracted to him. His fury with Leaume might be the result of unrequited love. Margont also noted how Charles de Varencourt had eluded his question about Catherine de Saltonges. Varencourt had brandished the new information just as Margont had him in a tight corner. Like the Mongols in the Middle Ages, Varencourt took care never to empty his quiver. So when he was threatened, he always had some arrows to fire off. Margont decided to move in still closer.

'So you don't know who is the father of the baby Mademoiselle de Saltonges was carrying?'

'A baby? And why *was* carrying?'

He turned his head away; he had obviously guessed the answer to the second question. When he spoke again, he was on the verge of tears.

'You are a very skilled investigator. I had counted on always being one step ahead of you. But you have outstripped me without me even being aware of it.'

He was again trying to steer the conversation away from Mademoiselle de Saltonges – the only subject that rendered him speechless. He was silent and looked off into the distance. He must be in love with her. Margont repeated his questions. In vain. When he took Varencourt's sleeve to pull him out of his torpor, Varencourt looked at him in surprise, as if it was a stranger who had tugged at him.

'Do whatever you want,' he murmured.

'Armed rebellion, a campaign of murders . . . Now tell me about the third plan.'

Varencourt again looked him in the eye. He had dropped his mask of fear and now his eyes were full of suffering. 'Ah, yes, the third plan. You have guessed that as well. Joseph wasn't so stupid after all when he took you on as investigator. Yes, the third plan . . . They do have one. But I don't know what it is and, frankly, now I don't care! No doubt you will find out what it is eventually. You discover everything whilst I'm just a poor blind man!'

His eyes were swimming with tears. But underneath the salty lakes, an angry, desperate light continued to blaze. Margont was seeing another side to Charles de Varencourt, who said, 'I think we've talked enough today.'

All the same, as Margont turned to leave, Varencourt called him back. 'I'd like to ask you a question. You owe me that. Suppose the Allies win, and Paris falls into their hands. Then imagine that you finally unmask Colonel Berle's killer. Will you take the risk of going to the royal police to reveal what you've discovered?'

'Of course!'

Varencourt had expected Margont to say that, but he still didn't understand.

'But why? Why not keep a low profile? Why risk going to prison?'

Perhaps Margont would not have replied in other circumstances. But he felt sorry for Varencourt.

'You can't understand, because we're so different. I value justice more than my own life. It comes from my philanthropy, which is a quality that's hard to bear, I can assure you. But that's the way it is. The Revolution changed my life, and gave me my love of liberty. And you can't have liberty without justice. It's difficult to explain. I can't really find the words to explain my determination, but I do beg you to believe that it is unfailing. So yes, I will go on to the end of my investigation, even though I have personally nothing to gain from it and even if the sky falls in before then.'

Varencourt thought about his words. 'Thank you for the sincerity of your reply.'

'Since we are sharing confidences, and I have never understood card players, I also have a question. Why do you enjoy it so much? What does it bring you?'

'It makes me feel alive! Goodbye, "Chevalier".'

They separated. As he walked Margont reflected that he had upset Varencourt so badly that he might try to exact his revenge by denouncing him. When you push someone to the brink, all he has to do is grab you and spin around and you will be the one tumbling into the abyss in his place . . .

CHAPTER 32

EVERYTHING was ready! At least that was what Mathurin Jelent had assured Margont, who was hard at work in the printing shop. Outside, Joseph's agents were keeping watch. He had never met them, and did not try to spot them. He hadn't noticed them when he had gone out that morning to meet Varencourt in Rue de Rivoli – his life now depended on people he had never met. And he felt that it was absurd that at a time when two hundred thousand invaders were marching towards Paris, and when he might well lose his life in a shoot-out that very evening, he was engaged in printing fripperies! He brandished a proof, the ink still wet and shining.

'What on earth is the point of this? "Madame la Baronne de Bijonsert has the pleasure of inviting you to her Spring Ball to be held at her house on 29 March." And she wants five hundred invitations! She might as well have asked for two hundred thousand, because with all the Allies on the way, she could have a fine Spring Ball!'

'She's imperial nobility . . .' explained Mathurin Jelent.

'And so?'

'And so she's squandering her money, throwing it out of the window. She's doing everything she can to spend a million in a week. Because if Louis XVIII comes to the throne, Baronne de Bijonsert will have to hand her large house over to Baron something or other – Baron *Ancien Régime*, that is – who lived there before the Revolution, and perhaps he'll take some of her worldly goods as well. When you are about to lose everything, or almost everything, you might as well treat yourself to a lovely last evening of fun. No one can make you hand over your memories.'

Margont was furious but pretended to be delighted. He told himself if he continued to live with these double thoughts he would really start to lose his mind. He noticed that he had absent-mindedly screwed up the invitation card into a ball.

'Spoilt proof. It'll have to be redone.'

Lefine was also there, installed in front of an empty workbench, inert in the midst of all the activity, like the queen bee, dozing in the midst of the worker bees. After Margont had revealed what Varencourt had said, Lefine decided he'd better stay with his friend at all times. He had that catlike quality of being able to swing instantly from activity to complete rest and vice versa. Whilst every evening Margont needed an hour of reading to calm his thoughts – if his thoughts were ever really calm – Lefine would plunge effortlessly into a state of beatific repose, enjoying the present without thinking about the dark clouds on the horizon. At the moment he was thinking what a fine thing it would be to be a printer. Baronne de Bijonsert wanted five hundred invitations? You'd just print five hundred and one and then you would be off to the ball! A free banquet, dancing with pretty girls. You'd just have to arrive late, when the Baronne had stopped greeting people at the door, and mingle with the crowd. His fingers slid over another proof that had fallen – quite by chance! – into his pocket.

Margont was kicking himself for having allowed Lefine to be

seen by the Swords of the King. Yet again he had failed to think through the consequences of his ideas.

The shadows were lengthening in the streets, like dark plants extending tendrils of night. The door opened; a gust of icy air filled the room. Margont recognised their visitor. He was one of the men who had come to his lodgings with Vicomte de Leaume.

'Monsieur Lami and I have some business to attend to,' Margont announced to his staff.

Lefine and he went outside, following the visitor, who said not a word.

CHAPTER 33

CROWDS moved with difficulty through the streets. The poor lighting – old oil lanterns swinging in the wind at the end of their cords like hanged men – increased the impression of chaos. Margont and Lefine had to exert themselves to keep up with their guide. He was walking rapidly, pushing past refugees looking for somewhere to install their families, who were perched on the top of overloaded carts. Margont wondered if Joseph's agents were managing to follow. How many were there? Mathurin Jelent had not been able to tell him.

One thing was worrying Margont. Their guide never turned round. He should have done, to make sure that no one was following them. Why was he not taking that most basic of precautions?

The Seine appeared. They took Pont de la Tournelle, crossed Île Saint-Louis, the quietest district in Paris even though it was in the heart of the capital, known for its elegant houses built in the reigns of Louis XIII and Louis XIV, and rejoined the other bank by Pont Marie. They immediately turned right and followed the Seine. Margont called to their guide, 'Slow down, or we'll lose you.'

The man set off across Pont d'Austerlitz, taking them back to the left bank that they had just left. It was crowded with refugees heading for the miserable Faubourg Saint-Marcel in the hope of finding cheap accommodation. People were jostling each other and cursing. Margont was waving his arms like a man drowning in a human sea. They were almost back on the other bank again. Margont and Lefine had just passed a forage cart when two men surged up behind them and forced them to speed up again, by pushing them onwards.

'Faster, Monsieur de Langès, faster.'

Margont recognised one of them; he had also been there when Vicomte de Leaume had made his impromptu visit. The boy guiding the cart pulled on the horse's bit to drag him out of the way, and the cart blocked the bridge. 'Careful! Careful! Hey, calm down! Gently!' he cried, although he was agitating the horse by pulling his head this way and that.

Meanwhile the three men dragged Margont and Lefine along the little streets of the Faubourg Saint-Marcel.

CHAPTER 34

MARGONT tried to slow the pace. But the two men behind him were hurrying them harder than ever. They turned off down a little street, then took another, then a third. A drunkard wandering in a labyrinth would not have taken a more circuitous route. Margont was not familiar with the area, which was visibly seedy. The men were doing all they could to mislead him and, in any case, he did not have a very good sense of direction. His only hope of knowing where they were lay with Lefine. They snaked through a passage between two houses so narrow that they had to pass in single file. The man bringing up the rear stopped in the middle of the cut-throat little alley and started to chew tobacco, while the rest of the group moved on. If Joseph's agents were still following, the man would block their route . . .

They arrived in a dingy courtyard choked by the buildings surrounding it. Their guide took them into an old house and indicated the stairs.

'They're waiting for you up there.'

The guide waited downstairs, sharing guard duty with his accomplice.

A bizarre sight greeted Margont and Lefine when they got upstairs. The closed shutters and drawn curtains transformed the large room into a sort of cocoon illuminated inside by lamps. The five committee members of the Swords of the King sat amongst an array of sumptuous objects: marquetry Regency chests of drawers, Dutch dressers, high-backed Louis XIII chairs, Louis XIV and Louis XV armchairs, card tables, dainty writing tables with little hiding places for secreting compromising letters, alcove sofas . . . The room was an Ali Baba's cave hidden in the midst of the houses of the Forty Thieves.

Vicomte de Leaume invited them to sit down.

'Coming here is always a pleasure. It's our treasure-trove,' he explained. 'So many of us had to emigrate to all the capitals of Europe. And often had to abandon our larger pieces of furniture. But rather than leave them to the revolutionaries, we sometimes managed to stow them in hiding places like this. Our refugee friends in London have entrusted us with the task of keeping this place safe. In exchange, we are allowed to sell some of the pieces. As long as we use the proceeds for the cause, of course.'

Margont sat down in a comfortable flowered armchair.

'A Louis XVI armchair: the chair of the beheaded,' joked Honoré de Nolant.

The tasteless joke should have attracted the ire of his companions, but they didn't seem to have heard him. Lefine chose a seat as different as possible from his friend's. Leaume was relaxed and happy.

'I see you have brought Monsieur Plami—'

' "Lami": L, A, M, I, Monsieur le Vicomte,' corrected Lefine.

'It's of no importance. Whatever his name is, just this once I will allow him to attend our meeting. You'll understand why in a minute.'

Margont was thinking about all the different elements of the situation at once. He was watching the committee members, studying their demeanour, thinking about Joseph's agents – perhaps the ones following Varencourt or Catherine de Saltonges had not been shaken off; he was concentrating on playing his role to the best of his ability. He was also taking in every detail of the house. During his campaigns he had learnt to evaluate distances and to note the smallest details, as a matter of survival. When he was leading his soldiers into the open on a battlefield, it was essential to have thought already that shots could come from that wood over there, three hundred paces to the north-west, that, running, they would only need thirty seconds to reach that sunken road that stretched from east to west and would be an excellent defensive position, that there would surely be water – water! – in that verdant green copse tucked off to the east, because he had spied weeping willows there, and those trees were usually found near streams and ponds . . . So, without appearing to do so, he was counting the yards separating him from the door and the windows.

He noticed that everyone was nervous except Charles de Varencourt, who had found his equilibrium again. Margont would have been more reassured to see him as pale as he had been earlier that day. What had happened to soothe him? And Catherine de Saltonges, although tense, showed no sign of the drama she had lived through a week earlier.

Louis de Leaume gloated, 'This place is the jewel in our crown. We come here when our morale is flagging, when we have suffered a reverse, and it always cheers us up! But today, we've come for the opposite reason. The news is not just good, it's excellent! Miraculous! And I've chosen this place for us to celebrate in. The Allies are at the gates of the capital! They will attack at any minute. And it's important that they take Paris as rapidly as possible. So they need us more than ever at this moment.'

'All the Parisian monarchist groups have just seen their worth increase tenfold,' explained Honoré de Nolant.

It was not like Nolant to keep interrupting in that way. Moreover, his humour was dark and cynical. So he was also acting out of character.

'The more we help our allies,' Louis de Leaume went on, 'the harder it will be for them not to return the throne to its only legitimate claimant: His Majesty Louis XVIII. So now's the time to swing into action.'

'Right away,' added Honoré de Nolant, producing a pistol, which he pointed at Margont.

Guns appeared on all sides. Louis de Leaume also aimed at Margont. Varencourt and Jean-Baptiste de Châtel had Lefine covered. Only Catherine de Saltonges's hands were empty.

'What's this for?' asked Margont.

Louis de Leaume laughed heartily.

'Even looking down the barrel of a gun, you still refuse to give up? My opinion of you has gone up a little. But it won't work. We know you are both traitors.'

'You sold us out!' Margont shouted at Charles de Varencourt, who laughed.

'Not at all! You still don't understand, do you?'

Vicomte de Leaume could not resist showing off the extent of his triumph. 'We knew all along, even before our first meeting.'

That was a sledgehammer blow to Margont. But his survival instinct and tenacity allowed him to conceal his shock. His thoughts raced, analysing everything at astonishing speed. His only aim was to escape from this alive, along with Lefine, of course. So first, he tried to stall for time. Joseph's secret police might still be on their trail, or Varencourt's or Catherine de Saltonges's . . . They would have to hold tight until they were found!

Catherine de Saltonges did not seem to be enjoying the situation. She wouldn't look at the prisoners.

Vicomte de Leaume declared: 'We're going to lock you in a cellar until the Allies liberate Paris, which won't be long now. When that happens you will be transferred to prison, until the King's judicial service has time to consider your case. However, I'm pretty sure you don't have to worry too much. His Majesty will be intent on obtaining the support of all his subjects, royalists, republicans and Bonapartists. Since you haven't harmed our cause in any way, I'm sure you will soon be freed.'

Catherine de Saltonges rose. 'I have to go home. I have a prior arrangement . . .'

'Go ahead, my dear. Roland will go with you,' Louis de Leaume replied.

She hurried off. 'Roland' must be one of the two men keeping watch downstairs. At least that's what Margont hoped.

There was something odd about Leaume reassuring them about their fate. And now Catherine de Saltonges was leaving the room, just as she had stayed out of the way the night Honoré de Nolant had held a knife to Margont's throat. The situation that night could easily have escalated and she didn't like to witness violence . . . And another thing, Vicomte de Leaume had just revealed too much, when he was normally obsessively secretive . . . Putting it all together, it was obvious to Margont that the group were going to murder them both. That's why they had chosen to have them brought here: it was the place that would give the group the necessary fortitude to kill two unarmed men in cold blood. Unless he thought of a way out, Margont had only a few more minutes to live . . .

'So,' he said to Lefine, 'we should have listened to Galouche's advice! When we tell him this . . .'

Their friend Galouche was reposing at the bottom of a communal grave on the Moscow battlefield . . . Lefine nodded. He had understood the message.

Leaume made Margont stand up and started to frisk him. 'Where is it?' His gestures were quick and precise. His left hand was searching everywhere. His right continued to point the pistol at Margont's heart. 'The letter! Where is it?'

'What letter?'

'Oh, no you don't, Monsieur, no . . . I think I've proved that you're the fool here, not me. I want the letter that your bosses gave you.'

If he were to fire, Margont rated his chances of survival as . . . nil.

Varencourt intervened: 'He's trying to play for time. Of course he's in possession of an official document attesting that he's working for the Emperor.'

So that's what they were after, thought Margont. The whole set-up, the faked betrayal by Charles de Varencourt, Margont's pretend admission to the Swords of the King: all that effort and risk was for the letter. So it must be necessary for the execution of their plan.

'It's at home,' said Margont.

'No it's not!' replied Honoré de Nolant. 'I searched your room myself and I'm certain it's not there!'

Leaume was pulling so hard on Margont's shirt that it tore.

'We'll strip you if we have to, but we will find it. Perhaps we'll have to torture your friend as you watch, until you tell us where it is! The police must have told you my life story. I escaped from a mass grave . . .'

Jean-Baptiste de Châtel added, 'The Angel of Death held him in its arms and even though he escaped, the Angel had time to consume his soul . . .'

To protect Lefine, Margont replied, 'It's in the buckle of my belt.'

Leaume extracted the hidden paper and moved back with his find. He unfolded the letter, his gun still trained on Margont.

'This is it!' He was triumphant. 'So you're not a spy, you're a soldier. A lieutenant-colonel, no less! That's why your informants couldn't identify him, Honoré. Lieutenant-Colonel Quentin Margont. It's signed by Joseph I, King of Spain!'

Margont was trying to work out when would be the best moment to fling himself at them – they would be two against four. It was useless to wait for them to make a mistake. He would have to provoke an error and rush into the breach. Who was the weak link in the group? Varencourt! He was the one who had carried out the trickiest part of their plan and was in the most delicate situation. That afternoon, he had been on edge because he was worried that Margont would not come to the meeting, or would discover that he was being manipulated. So Varencourt had tried to persuade him to come, with the argument that afterwards he could more completely disappear. Nevertheless he had not been sure that his scheme would work. Had the other members of the group noticed his tension? There it was! That was the chink Margont was looking for! He would play on their suspicion and fears.

'We're going to tie you up and gag you. We have everything we need now,' concluded Louis de Leaume.

'So do I. I have succeeded in my mission!' announced Margont.

'Oh, really?' Jean-Baptiste de Châtel challenged him, his index finger caressing the trigger of his pistol.

'The posters and the assassination of Colonel Berle were just diversions. You needed me for your third plan, the most spectacular one, the one that would have the most impact, your masterstroke!'

Louis de Leaume's face creased in surprise. 'How did you hear about that?'

'He's cunning,' warned Varencourt. 'But he doesn't know anything more.'

Margont threw his last card on the table: it was just an idea, speculation, an ill-formed hypothesis. But if he said nothing, they would kill him and Lefine, so what did he have to lose?

'On the contrary, I know everything. You're going to assassinate Napoleon.'

The group froze in consternation. It was strange to see them still pointing their weapons but looking worried. Louis de Leaume was dismayed. No, he really had not imagined things turning out like this. He was experiencing the disappointment of the player who announces with a smirk: 'Checkmate' only to have his opponent reply: 'If you will allow me . . .' and move one of his pieces to continue the game! His error of judgement had tarnished his joy like a spot of grease come to stain the glittering costume of his triumph.

Varencourt was worried by their leader's anxiety. 'He's just saying whatever comes into his head, making it up as he goes along. It's just coincidence that he's hit on the right thing!'

Margont looked supremely calm. It was just an act but he was putting his soul into it. Noticing this, Lefine followed suit, his serenity echoing his friend's magnificently. They both acted as if everything was going exactly as they had hoped.

'Charles de Varencourt told me everything,' announced Margont.

'That's not true!' Varencourt fumed.

'I don't believe you,' said Vicomte de Leaume. But it was precisely because he was wondering if it could be true that he rejected it out loud.

'Do you want more proof?' asked Margont. 'Charles explained that you wanted to kill the Emperor with a needle soaked in a rare poison with astonishing properties. It acts through the bloodstream and a single drop is enough to finish a man off. It's called curare and is used by the Indian tribes of the Amazon. It paralyses the muscles and the victim dies of suff—'

'But I didn't tell him anything!' Charles de Varencourt insisted. He wondered who could have revealed these things to Margont.

The latter was triumphant. His enemies were giving each

other worried glances, not sure how to react to this unforeseen development.

Margont spoke to Varencourt: 'Come on, don't worry, Charles, you can stop pretending now. The police are surrounding the house. We've won! You're going to be able to realise your dream of spending the rest of your life losing the twenty thousand francs Joseph promised you, playing cards.'

Varencourt lost his temper. He was about to fire at Margont, but Louis de Leaume grabbed his arm, obliging him to lower his weapon.

'Now!' yelled Margont, lunging at Honoré de Nolant, who had turned to look at Leaume and Varencourt.

Lefine, accustomed to hand-to-hand conflict, pounced on Jean-Baptiste de Châtel with the speed of a cat. Châtel fired, but too late: Lefine had already pushed the gun out of the way and the bullet sped off to murder a chest of drawers. Louis de Leaume would have been able to finish off Margont, who had turned his back on him to beat up Honoré de Nolant. But as he believed Charles de Varencourt was guilty of giving their plan away, it was him he floored first with a pistol-whip to the jaw. Varencourt subsided groaning, dropping his pistol, and in the time it took Leaume to pick it up, Margont and Lefine had already reached the door. During their tussle Margont had forced Honoré de Nolant to drop his weapon, but had not managed to get hold of it. Nolant recovered it and, in concert with the Vicomte and Châtel, who took a small-calibre pistol from his pocket, went in hot pursuit of the two fugitives. Margont was taking the stairs several at a time. He could see the man who had guided them here waiting at the bottom holding a pistol. As Margont was unarmed he transformed himself into a projectile, launching himself at the man from the fifth step up. He struck the man at full speed, hurling him against the door. The door handle slammed violently into the man's back and he collapsed howling. Lefine grabbed the man's dropped gun and whirled round, pointing it at the top of the stairs, while Margont undid the bolts of the door. The other man who had stayed downstairs was nowhere to be seen – perhaps he had accompanied Catherine de Saltonges, or else he was stationed outside. Lefine took aim at a silhouette. All he could see of his pursuer was his outline against the light, but he guessed that the man was aiming at him too. He did not allow anything to disturb his concentration. He did not let fear or pity muddy his intention. He was not thinking about his own situation, was not worrying about what would happen to him if he were to miss his target. No, all he saw was an imaginary line, a straight line running from the barrel of his gun to his adversary, who had had more time to adjust his aim but who had manifestly failed to conquer his fears. He delayed and Lefine fired. The silhouette collapsed and instinctively the two men behind fell back to take cover.

Margont and Lefine ran outside and charged across the courtyard. The man charged with blocking the narrow passage appeared, pistol at the ready. He was barring their way.

Lefine prepared to attack him but Margont shouted: 'Police! Police!'

And their opponent fled, melting into the surrounding alleys. The obsession with secrecy that was second nature to the Swords of the King, and had served them so well until now, was being turned against them. Vicomte de Leaume had not warned the man that Margont and Lefine were spies, for fear of spreading alarm. Shutters creaked open and a shot rang out. The bullet shattered against a wall just as the two fugitives disappeared in their turn into the streets. Lefine led the way and, after several detours, eventually succeeded in finding Pont d'Austerlitz.

'Help!' yelled Margont to a line of Marie-Louises.

The young conscripts brandished their weapons in all directions. Some wanted to protect the poor frightened blighter running towards them; others prepared to fire at him to protect Lefine, whom they took to be his victim; still others copied their brothers in arms without having decided yet who they should fire on; the appalled crowd scattered, fearing a shoot-out; several men who could have been taken simply for passers-by pulled pistols from their overcoats; National Guardsmen appeared, rifles at the ready . . . Everyone was prepared to kill everyone else. Gradually calm was restored. One of the armed civilians came over to Margont, his weapon lowered to avoid any misunderstanding.

'I'm delighted to see you safe! I'm Monsieur Palenier. As arranged, we were following you, but we lost you on the bridge because of that damned haycart! Where are the men we need to arrest?'

'Imbeciles! Incompetent imbeciles!' was all that Margont could manage to splutter in response.

CHAPTER 35

MARGONT recounted the happenings to Palenier, who in turn relayed them to Joseph. When the latter heard that the Swords of the King had been planning to assassinate his brother, he flew into a terrible rage. But it was obvious that his shouting and recriminations were partly to camouflage his fear. He immediately mobilised all available forces but to little avail.

His personal police burst into various houses where they thought members of the Swords of the King were hiding and arrested some suspects. They went back to the 'treasure-trove' and picked up the man Margont had wounded. But as Leaume, with his mania for secrecy, had not told him anything, he could provide no new information. The man Lefine had shot had escaped with the others. There were drops of blood on the stairs, but the telltale trail ended abruptly in the courtyard – he must have taken care to stem the bleeding with a handkerchief. Lefine thought they would find him not far from Charles de Varencourt's body, but that was not the case. Margont voiced the theory that it had taken so long for Joseph's agents to surround the house – because Lefine had had trouble finding the building again – that Charles de Varencout had been able to prove his innocence to the others. Or else he had profited from the general panic and had managed to escape.

The only committee member they arrested was Catherine de Saltonges, and that was perfectly straightforward. She had gone home, thinking she had several hours before Margont and Lefine's bosses realised they were missing, and was gathering her belongings, preparing to leave Paris, when Joseph's police burst in. So it was the least culpable member, the one who had not wanted to be present at a double murder, that was arrested. She had been taken to Temple prison where Palenier interrogated her, but did not mistreat her, Margont having made him swear on his honour not to.

Margont was also going to question her. But first, exhausted by the events of the past few days, he returned with Lefine to their barracks, to calm his rage and fears, and work out a tactic to make Catherine de Saltonges talk. For he was absolutely certain that she would give nothing away to Joseph's agents.

CHAPTER 36

T HE companies of the 2nd Legion were training in the courtyard, sullying the night with the din of their orders and discordant rhythmical steps. The voice of Colonel Saber could be heard at regular intervals bellowing a command, 'In column formation!' Then there would be the clatter of running steps, whisperings, the metallic clanking of a bayonet dropping to the ground, confused noises, hesitations, exasperated reprimands from the NCOs. Nothing ever went quite right and Saber would make them start all over again from the beginning. There he was, sitting straight up on his black horse, in full regalia, the Légion d'Honneur on his chest, pointing at wrongdoers with his sabre, for all the world like the god Odin trying to resurrect the Wild Hunt. But the heroic soldiers killed in battle would never get up again to defend Paris . . .

Margont was recuperating his strength, stretched out on his bed – a real bed, not a louse-ridden palliasse. He was turning the button in his fingers and it gleamed in the moonlight. The distortions and the patterns caught the light in various ways, creating a changing mosaic of shadows and golden points. He felt as if he were handling a box of secrets that he would only be able to open once he had worked out the subtle mechanism. He applied his usual method of approaching the problem from several different angles, hoping that inspiration would strike, allowing him to see the button in a new way. And it did! To

such an extent that he wondered if it was the same button . . .
Those symbols . . . There was a sort of À, or a sort of ´A, or π
. . . An À with a strange accent, horizontal, and attached to the
letter and rolled back on itself . . . A bizarre 'A' surmounted by
something . . . Margont sat up suddenly. So suddenly that the
button dropped from his fingers and fell on the floor. He could
not quite take in the implications of what he had realised.
His heart was thumping as if he were in danger; his muscles
tensed – he was ready to attack; cold sweat trickled down his
back . . . His body seemed to have understood before his mind
. . . Margont wondered why he had not leapt up already to
retrieve the button and examine it again. He rose and picked it
up cautiously, as if it were one of those old hand grenades,
which no army ever used any more because of their tendency to
explode in the hands of the grenadiers supposed to toss them at
the enemy. He held it in front of his eyes, closer and closer, to
try to see it more clearly.

The strange consecutive marks he had mistaken for damage
to the button were in fact the astonishing outline of symbols. It
was not that the letter was very badly worn away, it was
actually only a little damaged. What had misled him was that it
was represented in a very unusual way. An 'A' styled in the
Cyrillic way and topped by a cross with triangular arms: the
monogram of Tsar Alexander and the cross of the Opolchenie,
the Russian militia. The button came from a Russian army
uniform. Margont's mind was immediately filled with
unwelcome memories. How vivid they were! An expanse of
grass spread itself rapidly across the floor: the immense
Moscow plain unfurled in front of him, pushing back the walls

of the bedroom as if they were mere straw. Lines and lines of French soldiers advanced elbow to elbow; Margont was marching with them, Lefine at his side. Cannonballs rained on them, mowing men down, dismembering them, throwing up unbelievable sprays of blood. 'Close ranks! Close ranks!' yelled Margont. The Russians were converging on them, dark-green multitudes slicing through the vivid green of the hills. They were shouting 'Hurrah! Hurrah!' seemingly contemptuous of the missiles raining down on them as well. They were everywhere, on all sides, terrible hordes hurtling down the slopes towards them. Margont was covered in blood, but it wasn't his, or perhaps it was and he was well and truly injured; he no longer knew . . . The lines collided, skewering themselves on the thousands of bayonets. A Russian infantryman charged Margont, his eyes blazing, his mouth stretched wide in a yell of rage, like one of the three Furies. A French soldier intercepted him, brandishing a bayonet, and the Russian, carried away in a trance by his ardour, was impaled on the point. He used his last seconds of life to fire point-blank at his adversary's stomach. The two soldiers collapsed at Margont's feet. They seemed to be arm in arm, their lips touching in a bloody parody of a kiss. Margont was wreathed in gun smoke. All around him, figures were massacring each other, making an absurd Chinese shadow theatre. The plain was gradually filling with a reddish light.

Then another memory. It was hot. Something was burning. *Everything* was burning. Moscow was in flames. Margont found himself running through the streets, dressed any old how, and still only half awake. Lefine, Saber and

Piquebois were dragging him in their wake. Buildings were falling down, spitting out millions of burning fragments, which filled the night, twirling in the wind like swarms of fireflies, then falling to the ground further away. It was like being caught in the rain, but the drops were incandescent. The very night seemed to be turning red as if it were about to burst into flames itself. Then somewhere on the road back to France, snow began to fall. Flakes swirled in a thick fog. Margont shivered inside his many layers of clothing, walking on a carpet of white, seeing nothing but white, swallowing it, even. White on white. The world seemed to have been erased. During the last hours of the Grande Armée's retreat from Moscow, Margont felt he was the last person alive. The snowflakes were covering him over little by little, obliterating him too. And then a fissure appeared in the ground, growing wider. No, not a fissure, it was the river whose black waters were carrying along blocks of ice and corpses. The Berezina. Margont went over to the riverbank. He was so tired. The retreat had been going on for weeks. Marching, always marching under attack from the Cossacks, the partisans or the regular army. He was so desperate he thought of submerging himself in the water. Yes, how tempting to sink into an inky sleep . . . A point of light appeared in the depths of the current. It was a little gold object apparently rising to the surface. The button . . . Its feeble golden glimmer was shining in his palm . . .

Margont came back to reality. He was here in his officer's room in his barracks. He was in Paris, Moscow was over. He repeated that obvious truth to himself.

He closed his hand around the button, willing it to disappear. But it was too late, he could not now close the Pandora's box. A second flood of memories washed over him and he sank again into chaotic reminiscences of snowstorms and massacres.

CHAPTER 37

'Attention!'

Lefine froze. Unluckily a captain had spotted him in a corridor and ordered him into uniform to rejoin his company. His protestations and explanations had proved fruitless. He therefore found himself on Place Vendôme, the mustering place of the 2nd Legion – one thousand three hundred soldiers, two four-pound cannons and two eight-pound cannons.

The National Guard were at the end of their tether. Some were swaying gently back and forth. Two had already collapsed in exhaustion. No one dared look up for fear of catching the eye of the colonel. So instead, everyone was staring at his horse, Beau Coureur, or Beelzebub, as he was commonly known. Saber was mad with rage.

'I appear to be commanding a legion of scarecrows. Unfortunately our opponents are not sparrows!'

Beelzebub came spontaneously over to stand by Lefine, putting his muzzle close to Lefine's face. The horse was said to have supernatural powers, like thinking up insults for his master to use.

'At ease!' thundered Saber. 'Sergeant Lefine! Now you are an experienced combatant! How do you explain the lamentable state of your soldiers' uniforms?'

Lefine was despairing. To think they had once been friends!

Saber had certainly changed. Was that what was meant by power corrupting?

'The men are exhausted, Colonel!' he cried.

'When we are tired, so are the enemy! It's the first side to yield that loses! On my command: in attack columns!'

The result was pathetic. The National Guard were staggering; they no longer knew left from right. Watching them was like seeing mosquitoes swarming about, attracted by pools of light.

Margont, who had seen that the barracks were almost empty of soldiers, had guessed what had happened when he had discovered that Lefine was nowhere to be found. To make things easier he had had two horses saddled. He rode one and led the other beast by the bridle. Beelzebub immediately turned his head in their direction. Margont spotted Lefine and waved him over. Was he so absorbed in the investigation that he did not notice all the men exercising? Or was he openly rebelling against his colonel? Lefine felt like a piece of meat being fought over by two furious dogs.

'I've discovered something new. We have to act immediately!' insisted Margont.

Lefine saluted his colonel, gave his rifle to a guardsman who didn't have one – there weren't enough to go round – and joined Margont. Saber watched them leaving. He pointed at Margont with his sword.

'Thank heavens there's someone other than me in this legion who's doing something! Continue with your manoeuvre!'

He waited until the attack column was finally formed. He saw the men struggling, knocking into each other, jostling to get into the correct positions. They didn't look happy. Well then, how would they look when he gave the order to move from attack line to battle line?

Margont and Lefine hurried off into the freezing streets.

It was almost midnight, but Paris was still very busy. In the rich quarters conversations and music escaped from the lighted houses. The rich were going to eat, talk, dance and gamble until two in the morning, when tea would be served – not English, of course, lapsang souchong! – and green tea punch and sweetmeats. As incredible as it might seem, many Parisians still did not believe that Paris was threatened. They assumed that Napoleon would sort it all out. In the poorer areas too, people were still about, making merry in the cabarets. In winter cabarets were supposed to close at ten o'clock in the evening, but regulars paid no heed to that and continued to have fun. The commissioner of each arrondissement was supposed to go round enforcing the closing hours, accompanied by an officer of the peace, three inspectors and half a dozen soldiers from the municipal guard, but this inevitably deteriorated into fisticuffs.

Lefine besieged Margont with questions, but did not receive much response. Lefine was accustomed to his friend's ways and knew he had to wait for him to order his thoughts.

Margont handed their horses to a sentry and Joseph's men admitted them to the Temple prison.

A warder led them through dark corridors running with humidity. They ended up in a room dimly lit by a single malodorous oil lamp that did not give out much light.

'I'll let Monsieur Palenier know you're here,' said the warder as he withdrew.

Margont knew next to nothing about Palenier. But he was annoyed with him and the feeling was mutual. Palenier considered that it was Margont's fault that the arrest of the committee members of the Swords of the King had failed, and he was trying to persuade Joseph of that fact.

'I would like to know where we stand,' Lefine stated for the fourth time.

Finally Margont was listening. 'Yes, of course. Everything is brutally clear now.'

'I'm not sure about clear, but I can certainly believe the brutally part!'

'Taking everything in the right order . . . It's when they stole Joseph's letter from me that I realised that Leaume and his colleagues were going to try to assassinate the Emperor. Then there's the curare and the fact that we know the man who used it is definitely a member of the Swords of the King. They must have gone to a lot of trouble to obtain such a rare substance. If you want to poison someone in France there are lots of other types of poison available. What was to stop them using arsenic? Or cyanide? Then I realised that imperial bigwigs all have tasters and trusted servants to oversee the preparation of their food. I also understood that the Swords of the King must be aiming at someone extremely important or else the Allies wouldn't have agreed to help them procure the curare. Even though it's possible that it was merely a business transaction, and the Swords of the King paid intermediaries, our royalists must have had the co-operation of the Portuguese and perhaps also the English, who have had special links with Portugal ever since they transferred their court to Brazil.'

He passed his hands through his hair, a familiar mannerism of his.

'Here's what I think. First, Charles de Varencourt becomes a police informer, but he's playing a double game, and acting with the knowledge of the committee members. Secondly, one of them, I don't know which yet, murders Colonel Berle and leaves the group's emblem on the body. Their aim is to trigger an inquiry, which they hope will be led by a secret police agent, as is often the case when a murder has political and military implications. Varencourt will, of course, be questioned by the investigator. They hadn't envisaged that I would insist that Varencourt should arrange for me to become a committee member, but they adapt their plan accordingly. They agree to take risks to allay my suspicions: they meet me – all the committee members are obliged to introduce themselves to me, since I had forced them to admit me to the heart of their com- mittee – they go to my printing press . . . At our next meeting Varencourt has to try to assess whether I am going to advise Joseph to try to arrest everyone or not. He's forced to give me accurate information about the main committee members because if he feeds me nonsense Joseph's agents will notice that his information does not tally with what they already know. And the aim of all that was just to get their hands on the letter Joseph had given me! It's not easy to get close to Napoleon. But if someone passes themselves off as one of Joseph's secret police, if he obviously has detailed knowledge of the investi- gation he is talking about and if he presents a letter signed by Joseph I, the Emperor's own brother, then he would be allowed to speak to Napoleon after being searched. And what guard would notice a needle slipped into a pocket? Jean-Quenin assures me that one simple injection of curare is fatal in a few seconds.'

Lefine was gradually grasping the idea.

'So one of them really was going to try to assassinate the Emperor . . .'

'No! *I* was going to try to assassinate the Emperor! It's my name written on that letter: Lieutenant-Colonel Quentin Margont!'

He was so furious he seemed on the point of tearing up everything around him, since he could not tear up the damned letter. Lefine was not yet convinced, like a St Thomas demanding further proof. 'But why the burns? Why kill the Tsar's envoy?'

Margont brandished the damaged button.

'The answers are all here! Come with me. I'm going to question Catherine de Saltonges. I'm going to force her to tell me who her lover is. And that, my friend, is our killer.'

CHAPTER 38

PALENIER appeared, with one of his men. They were both scarlet with rage.

'The whore! She's given us nothing!' Palenier fumed.

'Do I have to go on interrogating her, Monsieur?' asked his subordinate.

Margont noted that the man had not said 'inspector' or 'superintendent'. In the civilian police there were many subdivisions, and there was sometimes rivalry between them. There was the general police division, then each of the Foreign, Business, Finance and War Ministries had their own police; Fouché had run his own police force, as Savary and Joseph did now, and Napoleon himself had several police forces that reported only to him. Almost all the great figures of the Empire had set up their own police, so as not to have to depend on the informers of their rivals and to ensure their rapid rise through the imperial hierarchy by trying to be the best informed. And of course there were countless double and triple agents and it was impossible to tell who was obeying whom and why.

'I will go and interrogate her,' announced Margont.

He fully expected Palenier to refuse, but the latter merely gestured graciously for him to go ahead. 'By all means . . . We will wait outside. But no violence! Some interrogators employ violence, but we do not subscribe to such practices.'

'Nor do I.'

Margont set off down a different corridor, barred by an iron door, which the warder opened for him. Lefine, Palenier and his subordinate followed him. They stopped in front of a heavy door with a spyhole. Margont drew back the bolts and went into the cell alone.

Catherine de Saltonges gave a shriek when she saw him come in. She put her fist in her mouth and bit down on it to calm herself. She had thought he was dead.

'Good evening, Mademoiselle,' said Margont ironically. 'Are you being well treated?'

She pulled herself together, took a breath and replied acidly, 'Of course! Who would be foolish enough to mistreat a royalist three days before the return of the King?'

Margont was hurt by that remark. He saw the interview as a duel. He had barely saluted her with his blade, and she had already delivered a blow and scored a direct hit!

'Yes, I have even been served chicken,' she added. 'It was delicious!'

'I'm not here to discuss chicken. We have more important things to talk about.'

'I won't tell you anything!'

'But, Mademoiselle, you don't have to tell me anything; I know all there is to know.'

Catherine de Saltonges frowned at that. She did not believe him, of course. Nevertheless, having just endured almost an hour of questions from Palenier and his subaltern, she was thrown by Margont's appearance.

'So what was it you thought you might be able to tell me, Mademoiselle?' asked Margont, smiling. 'That you planned to assassinate the Emperor? By poisoning him with a needle soaked in curare? That the murderer is going to pass himself off as me – Lieutenant-Colonel Quentin Margont, to give you my real name – thanks to the intrepid Charles de Varencourt, the fake traitor?'

Catherine de Saltonges was finding it hard to breathe. The 'secrets' she had been prepared to defend unto death – that she had easily hidden from that halfwit Palenier – were now being thrown in her face by Margont like so many empty oyster shells.

Margont burst out laughing. 'Do you think there is a single thing you know that I don't, Mademoiselle? In fact you're the one who should be asking me questions!'

'How long have you known?'

'That's not important. Several of your committee members have been arrested.'

He was marching to and fro in the cell. She followed him with her eyes. 'Several', so some were still free . . .

'You're wondering which we have in custody and which are free, aren't you?'

She almost asked a question, but held herself back, and smiled in her turn.

'No. And you can't know everything. There must be something missing, or you wouldn't be going to all this trouble.'

It must have required astonishing self-control to continue to reason clearly when her world had just collapsed around her ears. She counterattacked immediately.

'You speak with a great deal of assurance, Monsieur. But beware! I am less a prisoner than you are! In three days, at the very latest, the Allies will free me from this cell, but they will lock you up for thirty years!'

The idea of being locked up was unbearable to Margont. And the fear of it was enough to blow his thoughts off course, like a gust of wind blowing through a game of patience about to be brilliantly completed.

'If I were you, Monsieur, I would be exerting all my energy in wiping clean some of my debts. You have harmed us. But there's still time to convince me to speak in your favour when you appear before the King's court.'

Margont was saying furiously to himself, she's the one in prison, I should have the upper hand here.

Catherine de Saltonges went on with her attack. 'It would still be possible to say that you were forced into accepting the mission!'

'Which is actually the case . . .' Margont could not prevent himself from saying.

'It doesn't matter whether it's true or not; it just has to be believable! I will testify for you, and I'll say that you treated me well. In victory, one can afford to be lenient. But no more of your questions now. If you go on tormenting me, you will be treated like an imperialist! And you will pay dearly for that!'

Questions! Margont seized on the word. 'My questions? But I have no questions. I know everything. It's the other way round. I'm amazed that you don't want to know what happened to your friend? I'm talking, of course, about the friend you're so close to. You know what I mean, don't you?'

She reddened. 'No, I don't know what you mean . . .'

'I mean your lover, the father of that child you were not able to keep . . .'

Catherine de Saltonges's eyes filled with tears and she could not look at Margont so did not see how disgusted he was with himself for having stirred up her grief and intruded into her private life. But this investigation had become personal for him. He had almost been murdered, and because of him, so had Lefine. The royalists had tried to steal his name. And a murderer was preparing to kill using his identity – when he, Quentin Margont, had so often struggled to prevent crimes.

'I do understand why you decided it was better that the child should not be born . . . What sort of life could it have had? With a father consumed by fire . . .'

She looked at him as if he were a supernatural, an angel who could read her thoughts. And since he could not be an angel of God, he must be an angel of the devil, a fallen angel, evil . . .

Margont continued. 'Yes, the fire that burns in him day and night, which eats him from the inside; the inferno that was ignited by the Russian campaign and was never extinguished. Even your love is not enough to put out the flames.'

Had it really been a duel she would have laid down her sword at that point. But Margont had to follow through the sequence he had started. He had not completed his moves, and the killer blow would come at the end.

She murmured: 'How do you know this? He spoke to you about Moscow? How is that possible? I took a year to find out, but you know already?' Her voice was barely audible.

'Of course, it's all completely understandable,' continued Margont. 'He's already lost so many of his family . . .'

Margont was replaying Catherine de Saltonges's own words to her. She could hardly tell the difference now between her own thoughts and what Margont was saying.

She sat down on the floor for fear of falling. She started hitting the ground with her fist as hard as she could and the pain blotted out her thoughts. She was taking refuge in physical suffering. Margont caught her fist to force her to stop.

'The assassination plan is suicidal, and you know that full well. Whether it succeeds or fails, the perpetrator is bound to be killed by one of the Emperor's guards or captured, tried and sentenced to death. And since the plan is common knowledge now, it has almost no chance of succeeding. But you know him even better than I do. If he's free, he will still try, against all odds and even though it's pure madness. On the other hand, if we have arrested him, he'll be safe. Ask me the question and I'll tell you which it is.'

'Is . . .?'

She was seeing his face again. Even in their most intimate moments, even as she was dressing again, still feeling the warmth of his body against hers, he was pensive, mentally checking for the nth time whether his plan was properly thought through.

'Is Charles still alive? Have you arrested him?' she whispered.

'He's at liberty. He's going to try to carry through his plan.'

CHAPTER 39

As soon as he left the cell, Margont called a guard over. 'Keep the spyhole open at all times. She may well try to take her life, but she won't be able to if you keep an eye on her. If anything happens to her, you will have me to reckon with. She'll be all right in a little while. At least, that's what I'm assuming. She's certainly a woman of great strength of character.'

He moved off with Lefine. Palenier followed, complimenting him, whilst at the same time resolving that he would write in his report for Joseph that it had been he who had conducted the successful interview, and that Margont had done not a bad job of assisting him.

'I still don't quite follow,' said Lefine.

'I think Mademoiselle de Saltonges told the truth. For a start, she wasn't in a state to be able to come up with a defensive strategy, and secondly, why would she have lied when she thought I already knew? So Charles de Varencourt is the culprit. This is what must have happened. Varencourt was born in 1773. He lived happily in the France of Louis XVI but the Revolution brought his comfortable life to an abrupt end. Even though we don't know the exact details, we have a rough idea of what he went through. The insurgents arrived, he was subjected to violence and all sorts of extortion, then his wordly goods were officially confiscated. Members of his family must have perished. Catherine de Saltonges said about him, "He has already lost so many of his family." He decided to escape by emigrating. In 1792 he went to England. But later he moved to Russia, to Moscow – Catherine has just confirmed that!'

He looked serious. Even though he detested Charles de Varencourt, he could not help being moved by the tragedies he had suffered.

'Most French aristocrats who emigrated chose cities that were close – if not geographically then culturally. London, Berlin, Hamburg, Vienna or Madrid. I think Charles de Varencourt really suffered from the horrors of the Revolution. I may be a republican, but I don't forget the blood and dark times of the Revolution. That's why he went to the other side of the world. He must have said to himself: "At least there, I won't have to hear about revolutionary France!" What a horrid trick history played on him. At first, of course, Charles must have congratulated himself on his choice. Our armies were in Vienna, Berlin, Madrid. Even after Trafalgar, when the Royal Navy destroyed most of our fleet, people were still focused on invading England. Through a tunnel under the Channel. There was an engineer called Albert Mathieu-Favier, who had drawings for the project and who recommended using aeration chimneys that would just be long enough to reach up out of the sea. No one thought Napoleon would try to reach Moscow . . . Varencourt needed to have a profession to support himself. I'm pretty certain he studied medicine. I can't prove it, but there are three arguments that support my theory.'

Margont spoke with authority, emphasising his arguments with gestures.

'First, Colonel Berle was killed by a knife blow that was struck with precision, indicating that the murderer is either a hardened combatant, a butcher or a doctor. Secondly, curare is a little-known poison. The only people who've heard of it are doctors, explorers interested in the Amazon and, perhaps, some Portuguese who've taken refuge in Brazil. Thirdly, the button! I'll come to that in a moment.'

'Medical studies in Russian?' said Palenier incredulously.

'No, in Latin and French. Many medical texts are in Latin, which Charles de Varencourt would certainly have learnt. In France, some medical courses are still in Latin and it's the same in other countries, and probably in Russia. It's an old European idiosyncrasy. I even had the option of taking my theological studies in Latin, but that's another story . . . And you know that the Russian aristocracy speak our language fluently. Before the Revolution, and the Russian campaign, our culture was revered. French was considered a noble language, and Russian the common people's language. Refined people spoke French during meals, went to Marivaux plays and read Voltaire and Rousseau in the original. Varencourt would have been able to ask questions of his teachers in his native language and he would quite easily have been able to get hold of medical treatises in French.'

'I can confirm that the Russian nobility speak French,' said Lefine. 'We, Monsieur, took part in the Russian campaign!'

Palenier did not believe him. Survivors of the Russian campaign? Of course they were! Everyone knew that, apart from the Emperor and his marshals, everyone died out there.

'Where would he have found the money?'

'He must have managed to save some of his things and take them with him. He made a new life for himself there. He made friends, married. I would guess his family-in-law were nobility or rich bourgeoisie who helped finance his studies, then establish his practice.'

'How can you . . . ?'

'I'm coming to that! So Varencourt managed somehow to establish himself. His first life had been smashed to bits, but he had had the strength to make another one. And then in 1812, when the Grande Armée launched its attack on Russia, his world was overturned once again. It's not hard to imagine Charles de Varencourt's state of mind. The Revolution that had destroyed his first life was now threatening him again, this time under the guise of the "Republican Empire"! The Russian campaign was like no other. As my friend said, we were there.'

'The 84th of the Line!' added Lefine. 'And we were there in the Great Redoubt of Moscow! Yes, Monsieur!'

'When we arrived in Moscow, the city was not entirely empty. Almost all the Russian inhabitants had fled and some of the foreigners had been expelled beforehand by Count Rostopchin, the Governor-General, but there were still, amongst others, Italians, Russians of French origin, some French . . . They told us that the Russians were suspicious of them and considered they were all spies and traitors. Several had received threats or insults or had been attacked. That's what must have happened to Varencourt. He would have felt more Russian than French, since he hated imperial France. But that would not have prevented him from being mistreated. His friends would have stopped talking to him, people would have stopped coming for consultations . . . The more our armies advanced the more virulent the anti-French demonstrations became. So what would you have done to prove your Russian patriotism? What steps would you have taken to calm the populace before it broke down your door to destroy your house, brutalise your family and yourself, or worse?'

To Palenier the answer was obvious. 'I would have joined the army and gone in uniform to see all my friends and neighbours.'

Margont displayed the button. 'And that's exactly what he did. This is a Russian uniform button with the emblem of the Moscow militia on it.'

Lefine took the button out of his hand, beating Palenier to it. Yes, now he knew, it was obvious what it was.

'How can you be sure it's the Moscow militia?' queried Palenier.

'Because we would recognise that symbol anywhere – we were fired on by the militia continually!' retorted Lefine. 'All through the retreat and at the Battle of Berezina. That emblem was on the militia's toques, their felt hats, their helmets and their shakos. We told you, we took part in the Russian campaign!'

'It's this button that proves that Charles de Varencourt is indeed a doctor,' explained Margont. 'It's not regulation. The uniform it's from was certainly magnificent and so inevitably belonged to an officer. The lower ranks of the militia wore civilian clothes – pelisses or grey, green or beige greatcoats. The only sign that they were soldiers was the emblem on their headgear, their haversacks and their weapons – when they had any. The officers, on the other hand, did wear uniform. Varencourt had a sumptuous non-regulation uniform made for himself. That was tolerated in all armies, who were always happy to see their soldiers clothed at their own expense, especially militiamen, the outcasts of the military system. He wanted his uniform to be flashy – "Look at me! Now I'm an officer in the Moscow Opolchenie! So you see, I *am* loyal to Russia." In Austria and in France it's exactly the same – the militiamen who equip themselves are better regarded. No one really has any confidence in the French National Guard, although they do their best, but everyone reveres the guards of honour. The only difference between the two is that the latter are very well equipped, from their own pocket, and they wear showy uniforms like the hussars. So they have the right to all the honours and the Emperor has even included them in the Imperial Guard. I do accept that they have shown themselves to be full of courage.'

Palenier shook his head.

'In view of what you've told us, it's impossible that a Frenchman, established in Moscow for only a few years, would be promoted to officer rank, even for the purposes of fighting the French. A soldier, yes, but an officer . . .'

'Only an officer has the right to a stylish uniform. No army would put up with their simple soldiers being better dressed than their superiors. There's a reason that when Charles de Varencourt enrolled in the militia, the Russians would have been *obliged* to make him an officer. And the reason is, he's a doctor! All European armies give doctors officer rank. There are no regulations that envisage 'doctor soldiers'. And armies have terrible need of doctors. They would have been glad to have him, especially as he would have been a non-combatant.'

Margont paused. He reflected that he had something in common with Varencourt. He was combative! Once more Varencourt had not given up in the face of adversity; he had not lamented his fate. He had confronted it head-on.

'Varencourt thought he had found the perfect solution. Imagine him walking about Moscow, in his fabulous uniform, Russian solders coming to attention and saluting him as he passed . . . It put him beyond reproach! I agree with you, Monsieur Palenier, I would also have gone to the neighbours who had insulted me and spat in their faces. And as I was enjoying the look on their pale features, I would have asked them when they were going to join the militia! Varencourt had become more Russian than the Russians! You have to remember the prevailing mood at that time. The Russians were convinced they were going to crush the Grande Armée and that the French would never succeed in reaching Moscow. We were already weakened by the long march, by fighting and by the constant harassment of the Cossacks, whilst our enemies had been strengthened by drawing together all the troops from all over their enormous country, as big as a continent. Varencourt went with the army, as he was obliged to do from then on. He would certainly have been present at the Battle of Borodino, since Moscow sent a good number of militiamen to swell the ranks of the Russian army just before that important encounter.'

Margont again paused. So Charles de Varencourt had already crossed his path. On 7 September 1812, in the thick of the battle, they might have been only yards apart, and those yards would have been strewn with corpses.

'We won and the Russian army received the order to retreat. Later, the prisoners told us that when they heard the order, the Russian soldiers almost mutinied. They wanted to continue fighting; they were refusing to abandon Moscow. Varencourt would assuredly have agreed with that view. But the withdrawal was imposed on them. The Russian army withdrew back through Moscow. When the population saw what they were doing, people understood that the city was being abandoned to its fate. Rostopchin ordered an evacuation of the city, and all those who had not already done so hastily fled. The soldiers were given very strict instructions: anyone leaving the ranks faced the death penalty. A short truce had been concluded, on condition that the Russian army crossed Moscow "without stopping for an instant", to use the Emperor's exact words. And in any case, Kutusov, the commander-in-chief of the Russian army, did not want half his soldiers disappearing in Moscow to find their families. Perhaps that's what Varencourt would have wanted to do. But he followed the army. He didn't know that Moscow was going to be burnt, and that his wife could not leave the city because she was pregnant.'

'How do you know she was?' demanded Lefine.

'When I spoke to the abortionist, she repeated what Catherine de Saltonges had told her. Apparently she had said, just before her abortion, "Fate is conspiring to kill his children before they are born." Charles de Varencourt's wife must have been close to giving birth, so would not have been able to walk or to be transported for several days in a cart. Either Varencourt

267

was unaware of his wife's condition, or he wanted to desert but didn't succeed and escaped the firing squad because doctors were so much in demand.'

Palenier knew that he was missing some pieces of the puzzle, but he wanted to interrupt Margont as little as possible. For once he had stumbled on an investigator who did not persist in keeping all his discoveries to himself. If Margont continued to divulge information at this rate, they would both receive a nice promotion! When someone is climbing, hold tight to their coat-tails; when someone is falling, let go of them as quickly as possible. That was Palenier's philosophy.

Margont went on with his explanations. The tragedies of Charles de Varencourt's life seemed to cast a shadow over his own face.

'Moscow burnt, and his wife and unborn child died in the fire. That's the wife that Varencourt has never left, to quote Catherine de Saltonges. It's also possible that other members of his family-in-law stayed with his wife – her parents, for example – and so also perished. Now we can begin to understand Varencourt a little better. We can see how he would think constantly about fire. Moscow tipped him over the edge. For the second time his universe was wiped out, pulverised, literally reduced to cinders. Except this time he didn't try to make a third life. He decided to seek vengeance. He came back to France and got himself admitted to the Swords of the King. He proposed a ridiculously daring and immoderate plan: to assassinate Napoleon. Just that. The Swords of the King must have laughed at him, taken him for a madman. But he developed his idea. Precisely and methodically. Fernand, you know the rest. The plan convinced the group's committee who were, for the most part, fanatics. They were so enthusiastic, in fact, that they admitted Varencourt to their circle. The Swords of the King were following several courses of action and it made sense to have Charles de Varencourt take charge of the assassination plan. He played the role of the traitor who was willing to sell out his friends. That was how he would get to know the investigator assigned by Joseph, whose identity he planned to steal. It was also he who assassinated Colonel Berle. The burns give him away. The committee had agreed that he should kill Berle, but he could not resist mutilating the body with fire. That proves he was alone when he committed the crime. An accomplice would never have let him do such a thing and would have told Vicomte de Leaume about his behaviour. The group knew that Charles de Varencourt killed Berle and that he had left their symbol as agreed. But the Swords of the King most certainly did not know about the mutilations.'

'So that's why he killed Count Kevlokine!' exclaimed Palenier. 'How could he avenge the Moscow fire unless he found a way of harming the Russians? After all, the Russians were to blame for the whole thing!'

What was striking about Palenier was his ability to sustain a lie with such conviction that it was almost believable. The Russians blamed the French totally for the destruction of Moscow, but the French – Palenier, for example – blamed the Russians. In fact they were both equally to blame. Obviously if the French had not attacked Russia, the ancient capital would not have been destroyed. But Napoleon would certainly never have given an order to burn the city because he wanted to make peace with the Tsar, and also because he needed the city intact so that the Grande Armée could rest and recuperate there.

Margont had been in Moscow when the fire broke out. In common with other soldiers he had seen the arsonists at work: Russian police in civilian clothes and prisoners and enemy aliens freed specially to help. But fire engines? All taken away by order of Rostopchin, the Governor-General of Moscow. And fire barges? Sabotaged and burnt. Rostopchin seemed to have acted on his own initiative, not on the orders of Alexander I, who adored the city and never stopped lamenting its destruction. Rostopchin had decided to pursue the scorched-earth policy that had worked so well for the Russians up until then, but he pushed it to the extreme. The fire of Moscow caused such a hue and cry that Rostopchin denied what he had done. He swore that the French and some Russian thieves and other criminals were responsible, that the soldiers of the Grande Armée had pillaged the houses and set them alight, either from drunken high spirits or by accidentally knocking over candles. Such things had happened, but he refused to admit that hundreds of fires had been started by Russians and that the water pumps had been deliberately suppressed. Only he had the necessary authority to give those orders and make sure they were carried out effectively. Margont knew a great deal about it. He had almost been burnt alive in Moscow, along with Lefine, Saber, Piquebois and Jean-Quenin! So he had taken care to find out everything after the event.

The causes of the fire of Moscow were the talk of the salons throughout Europe. Everyone had an opinion, according to whether they supported the French or the Russians. Ironically, Margont found himself in the same boat as Charles de Varencourt; they were both surviving victims. Of course, Margont hadn't lost nearly as much as the man he was after. But he could appreciate the profound effect the fire had had on him. Russians, French, allies of the French (most of whom were now allies of Russia): they were all to blame.

'To avenge the fire of Moscow he would have to find a way of harming the French and the Russians,' corrected Margont, giving Palenier a furious look. Varencourt had made common cause with the royalists. But Varencourt was acting for personal, not political reasons. To such an extent that he was quite prepared to betray his allies by using them to find out where Count Kevlokine lived so that he could murder him. Count Kevlokine had been murdered for the sins of Count Rostopchin – they were both friends of the Tsar, close friends. Now Napoleon was going to pay for the sins of . . . Napoleon.

He pictured the Moscow fire. Burning for four days. And then the aftermath. Four-fifths of the city destroyed, twenty thousand dead. Those thousands and thousands of flames had left behind a spark that still burnt today, eighteen months later, fanned by Charles de Varencourt. It had travelled across one thousand five hundred miles to reach Paris with one sole ambition: to burn up Napoleon. The flames' return . . .

It might seem hopeless: one man against an emperor and the thousands of people who guard him. But the flame from a single candle can burn down an entire forest . . .

Margont turned to leave, then thought better of it and went to see Catherine de Saltonges. She was sitting despondently on her bed, staring unseeingly in front of her. He put the button down beside her.

'That belongs to you,' he murmured.

She looked at the object, picked it up and gently closed her hands round it, as if she were cradling the last star to shine in her universe.

CHAPTER 40

MARGONT, Lefine, Palenier and his subordinate went to Varencourt's house. The surrounding streets, muddy and malodorous, evoked a swamp in which rows of run-down houses were planted. The address Charles had given the police was just a garret, 'a pigeon house', as Lefine had called it. Under other circumstances it would have been comical to see the men crammed into the small space, bumping into each other and knocking their heads on the ceiling as they searched. Four policemen were already there when they arrived and declared they had found nothing of interest.

'What do you think about that?' Palenier asked Margont casually.

'I must admit I'm vexed. The group had confidently expected to do away with my friend and me. Happily, they had counted without your being on hand to save us!'

Palenier coloured, but continued to look at Margont, not wanting to lose face in front of his men.

'True, we've arrested only Catherine de Saltonges and a lookout,' Margont went on, 'but Charles de Varencourt would not have had time to come back here. And it would have been too risky. I had hoped that we would have found some clues . . . He must have at least two places he stays. This one – where the "Varencourt who sells his secrets to the Empire" lives – and another where he must be now. And that's also where he stored the poison and everything he needed to carry out his plan. Here, there would always have been the risk that the police would lose confidence in him and storm in to search everything from top to bottom.'

'His mistress would surely know the other address.'

'I very much doubt it. Look at Colonel Berle's murder, the complexity of their plan, the double game he's playing. Charles de Varencourt is careful; he's meticulous. I don't think he would have made an error like that. Especially as, thanks to Louis de Leaume, he must have access to many different houses. And then, the other address is probably a little hovel like this. Can you imagine making love amidst the flasks of poison you are going to use to murder someone? Perhaps they would meet at her house, but I don't think so, because Catherine de Saltonges has servants: it wouldn't have been safe. I expect they met in hotels, passing themselves off as a couple on their travels. In any case, there's no point in deluding ourselves, she's not going to tell us anything more.'

He went over to the mattress where the police had lined up the objects they had found. A meagre haul. He picked up a Bible and opened it where there was a bookmark. Although the Bible was obviously fairly new – the binding was in good condition and the edges of the pages were still white – the two pages marked were dirty, crumpled and worn. Sentences had been crossed out, angrily, with a pen, sometimes tearing the paper, leaving only one verse, as if to signify that God did not exist, that one should not love one's neighbour, and that all the words in the Bible were worthless except these remaining lines. Margont was disappointed, because the verse was not one of the passages he had thought of.

He read: 'Deuteronomy, chapter 19, verse 21: "And thine eye shall not pity; but life shall go for life, eye for eye, tooth for tooth, hand for hand, foot for foot."'

'The law of retaliation . . .' commented Palenier. 'We know exactly what he wanted to retaliate for . . .'

Margont turned his attention to the bookmark, gave a start and dropped the Bible, which crashed onto the floor.

'Don't touch anything!' shouted Palenier, who was worried by the story of the deadly poison and thought that perhaps Varencourt had booby-trapped his apartment with needles soaked in curare.

Margont retrieved the Bible, then the bookmark, which was actually a little paper pocket. Inside there was a lock of very light blonde hair. It had not come from Catherine de Saltonges. Charles de Varencourt's Muscovite wife must have given it to him before he joined the Russian army. That was presumably all that remained of the woman now.

The other objects were all everyday items: a comb, a ewer, clothes . . . Nothing that had anything to do with Charles de Varencourt's Russian past or with his current plans.

They did not discover anything interesting either in Catherine de Saltonges's house in Faubourg Saint-Germain. The police had read the letters they found in her writing desk, but none of them had been written by Charles de Varencourt; the books on the shelves were not noteworthy; the servants confirmed that Varencourt had never visited.

When Margont took his leave, Palenier shook his hand, saying, 'Let us know if you find out anything new!'

'I tell you everything, but I never receive any information in return.'

'That's not true!'

'I counted six policemen at Mademoiselle de Saltonges's house, four at Varencourt's. Including the policemen who came with you, and you yourself, that makes twelve people. A whole army of you! And I imagine that's just the visible part of a much larger operation.'

'But the Emperor's security is at stake! It turns out that unfortunately it's going to be impossible to warn the Emperor about the danger to his life, with all our enemies between us and the army.'

Margont left, staggering with exhaustion, accompanied by Lefine.

Day was breaking timidly. A few golden rays of sunshine ventured between the clouds. It was already 29 March. Margont mounted his horse, but Lefine did not follow suit.

'I have a request,' he said. 'Our inquiry isn't making any progress. We'll just have to await developments . . . I'd like to be excused from returning to the barracks immediately. Don't worry, I'll be back in time for the great battle. But bearing in mind that we might both be killed tomorrow, I don't want to spend my last hours practising manoeuvres and being sworn at by our colonel and one-time friend. I'd much rather spend them with someone charming and dear to my heart.'

Margont took a piece of paper and wrote out a free pass. He signed it and added his rank and number and the fact that he and Lefine were taking part in a mission under the personal orders of Joseph I. 'You have until midnight. I can't let you have longer.'

Lefine grabbed his safe-conduct joyously, bounded into his saddle and trotted off. Margont had been thinking that he would go back to his legion. But his friend was right. How should he spend what might be his second-last day alive? Alas, he did not have someone dear to his heart. All right then! He would give himself until midday. Midday! Afterwards he would sleep for a while, then go and join his soldiers. Just a few hours for himself. He had earned it. He felt invigorated as he pointed his horse in the direction of the Louvre.

CHAPTER 41

THE former palace of the kings of France had been transformed into a place of such unimaginable wonder that it appeared unreal, mythical. It had been turned into 'the perfect museum'. Hundreds of masterpieces from all countries had been gathered together in one grandiose place accessible to the public.

The museum was born of the scandalous pillaging of artworks from the countries vanquished by the republican and imperial armies, but nevertheless the result was fabulous. It was based on two principles. The first was the republican idea that art must be available for the public to see. The message was that the possessions of the aristocracy were being redistributed to the people, not physically, for that would have been to cause further inequalities, but visually, in public museums. In 1801 the Directory had created them all over the country and others had appeared later. The second principle was that art should be used as propaganda. Napoleon was adept at this – he liked to exhibit 'trophies' taken from the enemy. And he had renamed the French Museum or Central Museum of the Republic, the Napoleon Museum.

It made Margont smile to think that Napoleon's religious marriage to Marie-Louise of Austria had taken place not in Notre-Dame but in the Louvre, in the large square hall, which had been transformed for the occasion into a chapel. In republican and imperial France, museums were the new cathedrals.

He went past the Arc de Triomphe du Carrousel, which adorned the square between the Tuileries Palace and the Louvre. It had been erected to commemorate the signing of the peace treaty between France and England at Amiens in 1802. Alas, in the years following the treaty the English and French fought more often than ever. They confronted each other all over the world: in Europe, in the colonies, on the seas . . . They would even have fought under the seas, had someone succeeded in realising the crazy plan of the tunnel under the Channel. The only real product of the treaty of Amiens, as it turned out, was the impressive Arc de Triomphe du Carrousel.

The museum was not open, but Margont slipped one of the attendants a good tip to open it for him. Again, Margont was stupefied to see that Paris continued to live almost normally.

He began to walk through galleries of indescribable opulence. He wandered slowly, sometimes hurrying towards a work, then turning back to see another one. He was immersing himself in the labyrinth of art, freeing his mind of rigorous classifications and didactic organisation and allowing his subjectivity to direct him like Ariadne's thread. Around him satyrs chased nymphs; he was disconcerted by the beauty of a Venus, aroused by the erotic pose of another; Eros sat astride a centaur; Diana received the allegiance of stags and does in a clearing; gladiators slaughtered each other; the draping of togas and robes was so realistic he fully expected to see their stone folds stirring in the breeze; a marble Cupid gently gathered up a butterfly; the paintings were exuberant with here an azure sky filled with cherubs, there a ferocious evocation of a medieval battle; there were the subtle contrasts of chiaroscuros and the seductive charms of Mademoiselle Caroline Rivière painted by Ingres; the flamboyant depictions of Ancient Rome, bright with colour and movement, contrasted with the calm intimacy of the Three Graces, naked and taken by surprise by the unwelcome spectator. Margont was surrounded by Raphael, Rembrandt, Michelangelo, Rubens, Correggio, Veronese, Poussin, David, the Van Eyck brothers. He was drunk on beauty. Then he arrived in front of the Mona Lisa. Yes, if the world were about to be destroyed, he would be quite content to die contemplating that smile.

As he was roaming about in that fashion, he was struck by one particular work, an ancient mosaic imported from Italy. He had never heard of it, and its position in the museum, stuck in the corner of one of the galleries, indicated that Dominique Vivant Denon, the director of the museum and the mastermind behind this 'Louvre of all the conquests', knew little more. But what emotion! Margont was overcome by vertigo. The large mosaic fragment represented the face of a woman. Why did he find her so haunting? Her beauty upset him. He reflected that at that very moment, his friend Fernand was in the arms of his lover, whilst here he was with a two-thousand-year-old beauty made of pieces of coloured stone . . . His thoughts darkened further. A Prussian cannonball might very well blow him to smithereens in a few hours, turning him into a mosaic of flesh . . .

He still could not tear himself away from that face. He stretched out a hand and brushed her cheek; he was enraptured. The woman seemed to be trying to tell him something.

His gaze moved from tessera to tessera, taking in the whole picture, then focusing on a single detail. Sometimes he saw a Roman beauty, sometimes all he saw were little fragments of colour. He was reminded of the investigation. Each clue and each of his deductions was like one of those tesserae. And piecing them together in the right order would reveal the whole picture in all its clarity. He had understood everything! Everything fitted, everything made sense! He kept repeating that to himself, but the woman seemed to be murmuring, 'Not exactly . . .'

He decided to embark on a sort of exercise. He would go once more through all the elements of the inquiry, treating each like a piece of mosaic and building a complete solution.

As he did this, he was able to clear up a few little mysteries without it altering the overall picture. Varencourt had stolen documents about the defence of Paris from Colonel Berle's house to confuse investigators about the motives for the murder. He hadn't used curare to kill Berle, because he didn't yet have any. He had procured it later, thanks to the contacts of the secret society and used it to kill Count Kevlokine in a sort of run-through before attempting to murder the Emperor with it. Varencourt had not imagined that the investigator would call on a doctor for help, still less that the doctor in question would be brilliant enough to be able to discover the true cause of death. People were supposed to assume that Kevlokine's heart had not been able to stand the pain of the burns. Varencourt was extremely intelligent, but he did sometimes underestimate his enemies. None of this changed Margont's initial conclusions.

But there were two little mysteries that did not fit. First, why did Charles de Varencourt not burn Count Kevlokine's face as he had burnt Colonel Berle's? And secondly, why had he left the Swords of the King emblem on the second corpse, if his motivation was vengeance for the fire of Moscow? Margont was annoyed. The two details were like tesserae left over after he had completed the mosaic! He had been so happy, so proud that he had been able to unmask his adversaries. But now there were these two annoying grains of sand. He would almost have liked to sweep them under the carpet . . .

A memory came to him. He loved to talk medicine with Jean-Quenin. One day he had asked him what, in his opinion, was the hardest thing to learn in his field. Margont had been prepared for anything – complicated anatomical drawings bristling with Latin terms, or exotic illness, pharmacology – except for the response he received. Jean-Quenin had said, 'The hardest thing is having the modesty and courage to reconsider a diagnosis.' Now Margont finally understood what his friend had meant.

He remembered that Pinel had confirmed that the question of which part of the body had been burnt should not be overlooked.

He mentally swept away the old mosaic and started again with the two surplus tesserae, which he placed in the middle of the new picture. But he was incapable of fitting the other elements round them.

The Roman lady continued to smile at him, relishing her unalterable beauty. Meanwhile, Margont now felt more fragmented than she was.

CHAPTER 42

O N 29 March, Napoleon rose at two in the morning. The French army set off on a frenzied march.

But it was not fast enough to worry the Allies, so the Emperor decided he needed to take more dramatic risks. He sent an advance guard of only a thousand cavalry commanded by General Guyot. The rest of the army would follow as quickly as possible. It was important for the French to show themselves, to appear with a great fanfare behind the enemy. Their only hope was to play on the fear that Napoleon inspired and to fool the enemy into thinking that he would suddenly materialise with all his troops.

That day Parisians were alarmed to watch Empress Marie-Louise and her son, the King of Rome, leaving Paris for Blois, escorted by two thousand soldiers.

The evening before, Joseph Bonaparte had convened the regency council to decide whether the Empress should leave or stay. Talleyrand had proposed that the Empress and her son remain in Paris, and most of the council agreed. Marie-Louise herself wanted to stay. But Joseph produced a letter from Napoleon dated 6 March in which he ordered that his wife and son should be helped to leave Paris if the city were menaced. The order was intended to ensure that they would not fall into the hands of the enemy. Everyone agreed to obey Napoleon's injunction, which also included a number of dignitaries, ministers and members of the Senate.

Joseph hoped to lessen the impact of the Empress's departure by having a proclamation posted all over Paris stating that he would be staying. But all that did was give rise to a little ditty:

> *Great King Joseph wan and pale*
> *Stayed behind to save us all*
> *But if this plan of his should fail*
> *Rest assured he'll save himself!*

Marshals Marmont and Mortier arrived on the outskirts of the capital and immediately positioned their twelve thousand men to protect the city.

The Allies, on their side, were organising their multitudes of combatants. Troops were dispatched to occupy various strategic points, others were held back to support the troops in front or to await Napoleon's arrival. The attack on Paris was to be led by thirty-five thousand men split into three giant columns, which would descend on Paris like three Titans. The Allies expected little resistance, but they were nevertheless going to throw all their available resources into the battle. They wanted to conquer Paris as quickly as possible.

The Allied regiments rejoiced as they arrived in sight of the capital. Thousands of voices could be heard crying, 'Paris! Paris!' as the soldiers brandished rifles and sabres.

CHAPTER 43

On the morning of 30 March the call to arms went out across the faubourgs of Paris. The semi-circular French front extended across ten miles, constituting the external line of defence on the outskirts of the capital. It was organised in two sections with Marshal Mortier commanding the left flank to the west and Marshal Marmont the right flank to the east. Joseph Bonaparte positioned himself in the centre.

They had rallied as many troops as humanly possible: regular soldiers, trainee soldiers, National Guardsmen, policemen, students, firemen from Paris, firemen from the Imperial Guard, volunteers in civilian clothes, invalided soldiers, old veterans . . . There were forty-five thousand combatants in all. But a great number of them had never fought. Only twenty-one thousand were deployed on the defensive exterior line. The others were garrisoned in Paris.

Their only chance of winning was to hold firm until Napoleon exploded behind the Allies, sowing chaos and horror. When that happened the monumental coalition would find itself trapped between the devil and the deep blue sea and would hopefully suffer a cataclysmic defeat.

The Allies had fully understood that and had decided to launch their assault even before they were properly deployed.

At six in the morning, from the heights of la Villette, Marshal

Mortier gave the order to fire the first cannon shot. The Battle of Paris was launched.

Joseph Bonaparte had established his headquarters at the top of Montmartre. He was confident simply because he was not aware of the enormity of their situation. He had been told on the 26th that Napoleon had won a victory at Saint-Dizier and so had deduced that the Allies' act of daring was nothing but a flash in the pan. He believed that his brother was forcing the enemy to retreat and that only a few isolated army corps would appear at the gates of Paris. He could hear cannon fire from the right, where Marmont was stationed. But no one was threatening Montmartre for the moment.

The hill had been well fortified with ditches, palisades and earth bulwarks, and was equipped with seven cannons operated by sixty artillerymen. The infantry force defending these entrenchments was made up of two hundred and fifty firemen of the Imperial Guard.

Some troops had been positioned in front of them, including some of the 2nd Legion of the National Guard. Saber was there in his grand 'commanding colonel of the legion' uniform. He was furious because he had only been able to bring with him some of his troops. Only six thousand soldiers of the National Guard had been allocated to the exterior defence of Paris. The others had stayed inside Paris, to maintain order there and to bolster the interior defence at the barriers (which were just palisades in front of the gates of Paris, used to prevent people from evading the payment of border taxes). Saber deployed his soldiers as skirmishers in the vineyards, the meadows and the gardens.

'We're protecting a key position!' he repeated. 'No one can seize Paris without first taking Montmartre. If you retreat, Paris will be lost! If you stand firm until the Emperor gets here, Paris will be saved! It's quite simple – Paris is depending on you!'

He assumed an air of great assurance. 'Make each tree, each hole, a bastion!'

He marched past his own positions, and began to inspect the line next to his. Margont, embarrassed, covered his face with his hand. How like Irénée! He had been a colonel for less than three months and here he was behaving like the general in charge of the whole battlefield. But there were so few experienced officers about that even soldiers not under his command listened to him, saluted him and exclaimed, 'Long live Colonel Saber!'

Lefine and Piquebois organised their own entrenchment. They had felled a poplar and pruned its branches. Their men imitated them and trees were falling all around them.

'This should have been done two weeks ago!' fumed Lefine.

Margont looked to the right. The din of the fighting over there was getting louder and louder . . .

On the right flank, an hour before sunrise, Marshal Marmont launched an audacious attack on the enemy. He wanted to take back the plateau of Romainville, which had been evacuated the night before. To this end he had led part of his troops to assault the plain. He had grossly underestimated the number of enemy forces but fortunately the enemy had also grossly overestimated the strength of his and had withdrawn into the village. So paradoxically, in this sector the fighting began with a spectacular French victory.

But the Allies had continued with their deployment and, having mobilised reinforcements, now attacked the French right flank from all sides.

On the left flank, the Allies were already a little behind with their battle plan, since it was incredibly complex to organise such a vast quantity of troops. But they now prepared to launch a blistering attack on the heights of la Villette.

By ten o'clock the battle was intensifying everywhere. From the top of Montmartre the enemy troops could be seen arriving from the north, still quite far away, level with Bourget. The mass of soldiers swelled bigger and bigger as they drew nearer. It looked like one division – no, it was a few divisions . . . One army corps. No, perhaps it was two . . . No, it wasn't, it was several corps . . .

Joseph finally grasped the appalling reality. Wherever he pointed his telescope, he saw the enemy. The town of Saint-Denis was surrounded and thousands of skirmishers were invading the plain in front of him like swarms of grasshoppers. Joseph became increasingly anxious. A messenger brought him a note from the Tsar inviting him, somewhat menacingly, to negotiate. He decided to return to Paris with some of his closest advisers.

'Where's he going?' asked Margont.

'Perhaps where the situation is critical?' hazarded Piquebois.

Saber snorted. 'There's only one place Joseph should be and that's at the top of Montmartre, which is the cornerstone of our centre. And that's why he's fled. So there we have it. The defence of Paris has just been made leaderless right in front of our eyes. Now we'll all have to manage as best we can.'

At Château des Brouillards Joseph had a brief consultation with his defence council, which included General Clarke, Minister for War, and General Hulin, Governor of Paris. He showed them the Tsar's letter. The council decided to call a halt to the fighting. Joseph sent a message to Marshal Marmont to inform him that he was authorised to enter into talks with the Allies.

Marmont received the missive. But it did not order him to cease battle, it merely allowed him to do so should he and Mortier no longer be able to hold their positions. So Marmont, who was managing to contain the enemy attacks, felt he could continue to fight and possibly hold out until Napoleon came. He immediately sent Colonel Fabvier to inform Joseph of his point of view, in the hope of changing his mind.

Fabvier went to the top of Montmartre in search of Joseph. When he could not be found there, Fabvier turned round and set off to look for him, but he failed, because Joseph was already galloping off to Saint-Cloud.

Marshal Marmont decided to go on fighting.

The hours passed and the French continued to resist doggedly. The situation was, however, deteriorating for them.

The right flank was being steadily pushed back.

The defence of the village of Montreuil had collapsed under the combined bombardment of the Russian Guard, the Prussian Guard and the Baden Guard.

The village of Pantin had been taken and was still in the hands of the Russians and the Prussians, despite the frenzied attacks of General Curial, who was trying to take it back.

The Russians and Prussians had also taken over the gardens of Romainville and had immediately stationed a battery there, which bombarded the French to keep them back. General Raevski, the hero of the defence of the Great Redoubt during the Battle of Borodino, had sent a division of grenadiers to meet Marshal Marmont, who was leading a counterattack in the hope of retaking the plain, and managed to force him back.

Marmont had fallen back to Le Pré-Saint-Gervais and alternated between counterattacking and defending.

Wurtemberger and Austrian troops reinforced by Russian cavalry were pressing round to the south-east to see whether they could get round the French line. The Château of Vincennes, firmly held by General Daumesnil and well served by large-calibre cannons, represented a significant obstacle. But they skirted round it and gained control of Saint-Maur, Charenton and Bercy. Pahlen's Russian cavalry – hussars, uhlans, dragoons and Cossacks – tried to get past Marshal Marmont but were stopped by twenty-eight cannons, manned by students, backed up by National Guardsmen, a few policemen, dragoons and cuirassiers.

Allied reinforcements continued to flow in from all sides, like bees coming to cluster around each French position.

The French left wing was also severely buffeted.

After violent fighting, the village of Aubervilliers was taken by the Russians under General Langeron, a French aristocrat who had joined the Russian army shortly after the Revolution.

The villages of la Villette and la Chapelle had resisted for hours, under a deluge of artillery fire. But they had finally succumbed to the incessant attacks of Generals Kleist, Yorck and Woronzow.

Cossacks, sent out as scouts, reached the Bois de Boulogne looking for the breach that would allow the Allies to get round Marshal Mortier and attack him from behind.

General Langeron had been slowed down for hours, partly because of the unforeseen and energetic resistance of Savarin and his eight hundred men in the town of Saint-Denis. Six thousand Russians had been held in check and their general, Kapzevich, had finally informed Langeron that it would be impossible for him to take Saint-Denis. Langeron had to come to terms with this unexpected problem. And now that the previous points of resistance of Aubervilliers, la Villette and la Chapelle had been annihilated, he could focus all his attention on the principal objective: Montmartre.

Leaume had asked all his members to a meeting. But only fifteen of them had turned up. Out of forty! They would all willingly show up to talk and quibble, to squabble and criticise. But now that it was time to take action . . .

Vicomte de Leaume and the members who had responded to his call set about trying to alarm the Parisians. They went to the gates of the city where volunteers in civilian clothes asked the National Guard to provide them with arms. They mingled with the volunteers as if they were on their side and tried to demoralise them by harping on the dangers. 'We're going to have to get a move on; it's ten of them for every one of us. If we delay any longer, all will be lost!' 'What, no rifles for us? How are we going to fight? We might as well open the gates to the Prussians straight away!' 'Hear that din? That's the Allies coming to get us!' After a while the others started to look at them suspiciously. Time to slip away, saying that they would try to find arms elsewhere . . . Royalists from other groups were operating the same tactics at other gates.

Honoré de Nolant was satisfied with their strategy. Varencourt – who had regained the confidence of the group when it was discovered, as they fled, that the police were not surrounding the treasure-trove – had removed the bullet that Margont's sidekick had lodged in his arm. Nolant, however, was still in pain and felt that he had already taken his fair share of gunfire.

But Leaume and Châtel wanted to do far more. They abandoned Honoré de Nolant, who complained that he was weakened by his wound and that he couldn't walk any further, and took the rest of the men and armed them with pistols and swords from one of their secret caches. When they went out onto the streets again, they were all sporting the cockades, white scarves and emblems of the Swords of the King.

Vicomte de Leaume led the little troop towards the Montmartre gate. It was the perfect place, because a little further north Joseph Bonaparte had established his headquarters on the top of the hill of Montmartre. If Leaume and his men caused trouble inside the gate, the French constituting the external defence would panic. They would think that some of the enemy had managed to slip round them and into the city. The royalists were taking a huge risk, but if they succeeded they would be spectacularly rewarded! Should Joseph lose his nerve – and that would be just like him – if he were to gallop down the hill to take refuge in Paris for fear of being killed or captured, everyone around him would abandon their posts in panic and flee with him. And then it would have been he, Vicomte de Leaume, who, by a daring coup, would have allowed the Allies to take the deserted hill of Montmartre. What a triumph that would be! A masterstroke! A kingly stroke!

But his hopes were dashed when he saw the Montmartre gate. There were far more guards posted there than he had imagined. He could see at least a hundred National Guardsmen, invalid soldiers pressed back into service, volunteers keen to get their hands on rifles . . . Yet normally the gate was one of the least used. The group stopped, undecided.

Leaume had assumed that because the Allies had so many more troops at their disposal, the French would post almost all their defenders on the exterior line. That's why he had chosen somewhere he thought would be poorly defended for his point of attack. But that part of his planning had backfired. In Leaume's opinion, the interior defence had been overmanned at the expense of the exterior line. Then he thought again. Was this not proof that royalist groups had succeeded in well and truly frightening Joseph?

'We should turn back,' advised Jean-Baptiste de Châtel.

'No! There are wounded everywhere – they must have removed them from the front to pile them up here. Look at that confusion! The guards are demoralised. Let's incite them to abandon their posts!' Leaume gestured to the others to advance.

The soldiers watched the arrival of the royalists in stupefaction. What were these apparitions? The Vicomte's men began to distribute flyers, printed thanks to Margont. When the soldiers did not take them, they laid them on the ground for all to read.

'Long live the King! Long live Louis XVIII! Long live the Bourbons!' chanted Châtel, and the others followed suit.

A detonation rang out and one of the royalists fell to the ground – a National Guardsman had opened fire. Then gunfire came from all sides. Several members of the Swords of the King were old hands and were not about to give up so easily. Leaume wanted to charge the Montmartre gate. That would show everyone! But Jean-Baptiste de Châtel took his arm to hold him back. Another National Guardsman took aim at the Vicomte, whom he discerned was the leader of the band. He was only a few feet from his target. Châtel saw the danger and placed himself deliberately between Louis de Leaume and the shooter as he fired. The bullet struck him full in the chest and he was killed instantly. Leaume and the others fled.

That little battle had lasted barely a minute.

General Langeron organised all his troops in two columns. The eight thousand men of St-Priest's VIII Corps on one side and the five thousand of Kapzevich's X Corps on the other. Then he launched them straight at Montmartre and its handful of defenders.

The French at the front of the defence were firing and firing . . . The Russians fell on all sides but were not firing much so as not to slow their progress. Those who did not bolt in the face of the Russian advance were skewered by bayonets and then trampled over. The last cavalry of Belliard – the cavalry brigade of Dautencourt's Imperial Guard, which was made up of chasseurs, lancers and General Sparre's dragoons – charged the enemy in the hope of pushing them back. Any cavalrymen who managed to get through the Russian dragoons blocking them found themselves surrounded by assorted hordes slashing and skewering; they were engulfed and disappeared.

Saber, who was everywhere at once, gesticulated with his sword. 'Fire away!'

Lefine had grabbed a rifle from one of the dead – there were not enough to go round and the NCOs of the National Guard had not been given any – and adjusted his sights onto Russian officers, easily recognisable by their bicornes or plumed shakos.

Margont shouted orders. But he could not take his eyes from the tidal wave that was sweeping towards them, engulfing everything in its way. As the Russians charged he felt the earth tremble beneath his feet.

The defenders were rammed by the masses of attacking forces. The guardsmen were riddled with balls at point-blank range; blows from rifle butts and bayonets rained down on those at the front. Margont found himself on the slope of Montmartre – he ran forward and took cover behind a palisade. The Russians were mad with fervour. They had been waiting for this day for so long! They were trampling the corpses of their comrades that were filling the ditches. They were trying to scale the parapets, digging under the stakes to try to destabilise them. Margont noticed Lefine and Piquebois, who were defending the entrance of an entrenchment along with firemen from the Imperial Guard, National Guardsmen and soldiers of the line. There was smoke everywhere. The cannons of Montmartre thundered, propelling a volley of cannonballs over the Russians, tearing through their lines and disrupting the waves of attackers. Chasseurs, riflemen, musketeers, grenadiers, drummers, officers, horses and aides-de-camp were flattened. Not far from Margont there were guttural shouts of 'Hurrah! Hurrah! Hurrah!' It was the war cry of the Russians! The enemy attackers had breached the first line of defence. They burst into the entrenchment, slashing everything. Soldiers fled, knocking into Margont and dragging him along with them. He tried to join the second line, which was backing up the first. The French, panicked, were falling into the ditches they had themselves dug a little earlier. Margont raised his head. He wished that the hill were much higher. Already they had lost the base of it; the sky was much nearer. They would have to do everything they could to slow the Russians down, because once the French reached the summit they would find themselves trapped there like rats. Margont could see the officers up there amongst the windmills. Windmills! What a joke! He was going to die at the foot of a windmill. A quixotic death.

The Russians were falling, slipping, tripping over one another and killing each other. Their corpses littered the slope. But they were persevering. Their sappers were attacking the palisades with axes, their infantry giving their comrades a leg up over the sides. All that separated them from Margont were some posts and earth bulwarks. He could not believe his eyes. The enemy were blithely approaching the mouths of the French cannons pointing out of the portholes. How could they do that, knowing the batteries were about to fire? They took aim at the artillerymen, picked off one here, wounded another there . . . Finally the cannons fired, belching forth a hail of cannonballs that massacred everyone. There was a moment of hesitation as the smoke cleared, revealing a gaping hole in the Russian ranks. Then the enemy converged anew, closing up the gaps and resumed felling the sides of the palisades. Some Russian riflemen succeeded in heaving themselves onto the top of the palisades, but were cut down immediately. Margont called over a group of firemen and guardsmen, only to see them torn apart in front of his eyes. Some other Russians had got hold of one of the French cannons and turned it on their enemy, even though in doing so they sprayed as many of their compatriots with fire as they did French soldiers. The cannon was already being reloaded by the Russians. Margont threw himself forward to reclaim it. He thought the soldiers that went with him were helping him, but in fact they were fleeing another breach, unaware that they were throwing themselves at further danger. There were only a handful of Russians manoeuvring the cannon. They continued to load the cannon instead of defending themselves; they let themselves be massacred. There were only two of them left. One of them protected his companion by standing in front of him, and was mown down by three musket balls. The other fired off a shot before collapsing, mortally wounded. Margont threw himself to the ground just in time, sheltering behind the corpses. A hail of shot pulverised everyone around him. When the smoke had cleared it seemed as if the entire world had perished, as if he were the only survivor.

He spotted Saber addressing his soldiers. There were Lefine and Piquebois too. He hurried towards his friend. 'We'll have to fall back . . . But where to?' he demanded.

Saber looked at him, not seeming to recognise him, and retorted: 'I will never give up! If there's only one man left standing it will be me! I will be the last Parisian!'

He brandished his sabre in the direction of Paris.

'Counterattack with bayonets!'

'You're mad, Irénée! We're surrounded! We've lost! Look around you! There is no one left, everyone is dead!'

'The dead are coming with me!' he yelled.

And he dashed forward, straight at the Russians, who were cutting off their escape route. He ran down the slope towards Paris, followed by about forty defenders, charging with their bayonets at the ready. Piquebois was amongst them, brandishing his sabre that seemed to promise death to anyone who tried to stand in his way.

'Counterattack!' yelled Margont in his turn, throwing himself into the turmoil, followed by Lefine. It was impossible to stay still; either they had to move up the hill or go down and Margont had just had a kind of premonition. Up there at the foot of one of the Montmartre windmills – maybe even at the same spot where he had lain daydreaming the other day – his tomb awaited him. He preferred to throw himself into the jaws of death rather than to wait for it to catch him.

The rank and file had no idea what to do in the midst of the collapse. Whenever they saw a colonel, a lieutenant-colonel, a captain or other foot soldiers attacking the Russians they imitated them, hoping that those officers would guide them to their salvation.

Up until that point, the Russians had been the assailants, and they were very surprised to see the French charging desperately down the slope straight at them and slicing down anyone in their path. The Russians behind those felled in this way were flung backwards. They retreated, not because they wanted to, but because they were being shoved back by this group of mad Frenchmen, who were swept along on a wave of incredible determination. They were slipping and losing their footing, stumbling and rolling over, but nevertheless these men knocked into the enemy, destabilising them in their turn. The slope was so steep it was very difficult to stay upright. This was not so much a counterattack as the frenetic flinging of a pack of French dogs into a Russian game of skittles. The French, encouraged by the miraculous success of their efforts, rampaged through the Russians, pressing them ever further back. The French combatants were mad with fury. They felt invincible, immortal. Although they were being cut down by bullets and bayonet thrusts, they succeeded in crossing through the enemy lines, which immediately closed up behind them.

Margont, Piquebois and Lefine were among those who escaped and made for Paris. At the very top of the hill, meanwhile, the Russians were massacring the last remaining gunners. Margont was crying: Saber was not with them.

*

One of Marmont's aides-de-camp had tried to reach the summit of Montmartre to find out if Joseph had left someone in command of its defence.

He was unable to fulfil his mission because Langeron had launched his attack. But he was there during the last few minutes of the resistance of Montmartre and Saber's charge. He returned to present his report to Marshal Marmont.

'That's extraordinary!' Marmont exclaimed. 'King Joseph is supposed to be in command of us all, but he's left! And it's a colonel who's distinguishing himself instead! What's the name of this colonel?'

'He's Colonel Saber of the 2nd Legion, Your Excellency.'

'I want the Emperor notified that I would respectfully ask that this colonel be promoted to the rank of general. He has succeeded in causing the accursed Langeron a lot of trouble with the help of only a handful of men!'

'But . . . Your Excellency . . . the colonel is dead. I saw him fall with my own eyes.'

The marshal's face hardened. 'That changes nothing. He is to be made a general posthumously.'

The regiments of the Army of Silesia, the Russian Guard and the Prussian Guard finally managed to seize the heights of Chaumont. There were so many Prussians there that all along the slopes and heights their blue forms could be seen like so many ants. It was like a flood submerging the grassy heights, about to spill over and engulf the capital below.

These troops overwhelmed Marshal Marmont's men from

the rear, forcing them to withdraw to Belleville, and then hurried to set up their batteries of cannons and twelve-pounders. When they opened fire their shots battered the city of Paris itself.

The room was tiny, perched right at the top of an old house. Its walls and beams were covered with dozens of paintings, shunted together, their frames touching. There were depictions of naval battles with ships on fire sinking into the waves, the Great Fire of London in 1666, a forest fire, setting suns that seemed to set the sky ablaze . . . It was a display of scarlets, oranges, vibrant yellows and other fiery hues, amidst expanses of sooty black, making it seem as if the room were permanently on fire.

Varencourt was standing facing the only window, watching the distant battle and counting the plumes of smoke. He distinctly saw black shapes crossing the sky and falling on the houses. In most cases, he didn't witness any impact but from time to time a projectile struck the roof of a building at full tilt, spraying up debris, or clipped a corner, sending a wall crashing down, releasing clouds of dust. As he watched, a house burst apart, and another shell knocked a roof into the air. The detonations merged into one another, eventually making one continuous crackling. Now buildings were falling on all sides. A plume of black smoke over there – the first fire! Then somewhere else a building collapsed, burying an entire street. Debris showered over north-west Paris and the columns of smoke accumulated. Varencourt took a flask of vodka that he had bought in the ruins of Moscow after the French had left. He had never tasted it, keeping it instead for this very occasion. He poured himself a glass and drank a toast to the cannonballs destroying Paris. As the spirit slipped down his throat he felt as if he were swallowing the fire of Moscow.

Napoleon was still advancing. He was accompanied now only by those closest to him and about a hundred cavalry. All he wanted now was to reach Paris and take command of the defence of the city.

In the end the entire French front simply folded under the weight of the enemy. The heights were lost and the exterior defences overwhelmed, and still there was no sign of the Emperor. At four o'clock Marshal Marmont, who was wounded in the arm and had narrowly avoided capture, sent three officers to the enemy vanguards to ask for a suspension of hostilities.

The Allies had lost nine thousand men, either injured or killed, and the French, four thousand.

The silence was eerie. The soldiers' ears still rang with the cacophony of combat, as if they could not believe that calm had returned.

The silence spoke to Catherine de Saltonges, huddled in a torpor in the corner of her cell. It was murmuring something to her: the Allies had won. But she herself had lost everything. Almost everything. She still had her pride! In spite of the torment her ex-husband had put her through, in spite of the hardships of the Revolution, of her inability to keep her lover in her arms, the loss of her child, yes, in spite of all that, nothing would ever succeed in breaking her spirit.

She stood up, walked over to the door and began to beat on it with the flat of her hand and called out to her gaolers, 'This is it, Messieurs. It's time for us to change places.'

CHAPTER 44

AFTER several hours of negotiation, the capitulation of Paris was signed.

The regular troops of the French army had been authorised to withdraw and they were to leave Paris by seven o'clock the next morning. The National Guard, on the other hand, was pronounced to be 'in a totally different category from the troops of the line'. The text of the capitulation specified that '. . . it would be maintained, disarmed or discharged, according to the will of the Allies'.

These orders circulated and Margont was alarmed when they reached him. Paris was going to be occupied and he was specifically forbidden to go with the retreating army. He was to wait for the Allies in the capital and report to them. He was worried that he would be thrown in gaol. On the other hand, if he disobeyed orders and followed the French army, he would be arrested anyway.

'We'll just have to discharge ourselves! I'd rather remove myself than wait to be forcibly removed by others,' declared Lefine.

He took Margont and Piquebois round to his lady-friend's house. It was dark. A woman opened the door. Margont was so exhausted and demoralised that he felt completely drained. The only things he took in about the woman were her striking face and the fact that her eyes were red from weeping. She burst into tears as she took Lefine in her arms. Margont stretched himself out on the floor and fell asleep instantly.

On the morning of 31 March, Margont, Lefine and Piquebois took the time to wash thoroughly to remove all traces of the gunpowder they were covered in. Lefine's friend was a widow. They borrowed her husband's clothes in order to pass themselves off as civilians.

'We have to find Varencourt,' Margont stated. 'I'm sure he's still in Paris.'

Lefine knew Margont much too well to be surprised by his proposal. He knew that his friend needed this investigation. But he was torn between his desire to help Margont and his desire to stay and protect his lady-friend, in case any enemy mercenaries should show up. They finally agreed that Piquebois would stay with her and they would barricade themselves in. Piquebois was a formidable swordsman and woe betide anyone who provoked him to unleash his sabre!

Margont and Lefine left. They had stuffed their uniforms into two bags, which they abandoned a few streets away in the heart of the Marais, in a dark corner. They were unarmed, having given their weapons the day before to the retreating regular army. Piquebois, however, had kept his sabre, which he refused to be parted from, and a pistol.

Margont tried to work out what he would do if he were Varencourt. Would he wait in Paris? Would he try to profit from the general chaos to get close to Napoleon? Where would

Napoleon be, and had he been warned about the proposed attempt on his life?

He followed Lefine without noticing where they were going. Other people seemed to be going in the same direction. They reached the Champs-Élysées and found it lined with an astonishing number of Parisians. Some were wearing white cockades or armbands; others were simply waving white handkerchiefs and shouting, 'Long live Louis XVIII!' So this was the grand procession of the Allies. At the head came the Cossacks of the Guard, in scarlet. Next the Tsar, Generalissimo. Schwarzenberg, the King of Prussia and the Prince of Wurtemberg, all accompanied by their sumptously attired general staff. Two regiments of Austrian grenadiers followed them, all dressed in white and wearing bearskins, then Russian grenadiers with shakos topped by long black plumes, and thousands of soldiers of the Prussian Guard and the Russian Guard. Then there was a mass of Russian curassiers, and more and more and more of them. The Chevalier Guard brought up the rear in their white uniforms and black cuirasses. It was these élite cavalrymen who had wounded Piquebois at the Battle of Austerlitz. Lucky that he wasn't here, because the sight of them always reduced him to wild rage.

Margont still couldn't take in what he was seeing. He kept looking from the part-built Arc de Triomphe to the streams of Allied soldiers marching rhythmically past, and back again to the monument.

Lefine muttered to himself, 'So it really is all over . . .'

The Allies were each wearing a white armband or a white scarf, and the Parisians thought they were demonstrating their support for Louis XVIII. In reality, however, the white was merely meant to distinguish them from French soldiers, since the diversity of uniforms on both sides made it hard to distinguish one side from the other.

Margont tried to think about something else. In fact he had something else very important to consider. The Roman lady in the mosaic came back to him. He decided to go through all the clues he had, but starting with the two that did not fit his original hypothesis, namely that Count Kevlokine's face had not been burnt, and that the murderer had left the emblem of the Swords of the King on his corpse.

The crowd was yelling, 'Long live Louis XVIII! Long live the Bourbons!' and some were even falling in behind the Allied procession in the footsteps of the last Chevalier Guards. But Margont neither saw nor heard them.

Varencourt had not been able to resist burning the second victim. But he had spared his victim's face, contenting himself with burning his arms. What would have happened if he had mutilated his face in the same way as Colonel Berle's? Count Kevlokine would not have been identified. Nevertheless, Joseph would probably still have sent Margont to the scene of the crime, because of the Swords of the King symbol. So the two elements came together to give the same result: that Margont would investigate the murder. Margont knew that Varencourt wanted to use Margont's identity but why did he need to become 'the man investigating Count Kevlokine's murder'?

Margont finally worked it out. Yes, this time his hypothesis incorporated those two discordant elements that had previously made no sense. But now the pattern the clues made was not the same. Only a few tesserae had changed places but it was no longer Napoleon's face that the mosaic spelt out. Margont grabbed Lefine's arm.

'Varencourt is going to kill the Tsar. He led the Swords of the King to believe that his plan was to poison Napoleon, because he needed their help. But actually he manipulated them just like he manipulated me. He murdered Count Kevlokine in order to get near Alexander!'

'But—'

'The Tsar knew Count Kevlokine. He will want to know who killed and mutilated his friend so he would probably agree to see anyone who had information about the killing. If Alexander were to be killed by a "French officer", "Lieutenant-Colonel Margont", carrying an instruction from Joseph Bonaparte, the Russian soldiers would think that the Tsar had been executed on Napoleon's orders. They would immediately vent their rage on Paris! They would put everything to fire and the sword! And that's exactly what Charles de Varencourt wants. He wants the Emperor wandering through a Paris reduced to cinders, amidst the rubble of the monuments he's had erected, and the incinerated remains of the people he loves. That's what Varencourt's vengeance is really about. He'd like Napoleon to go through exactly what he himself went through – an eye for an eye, a tooth for a tooth. Paris for Moscow.'

Lefine tried to find an objection, but Margont added: 'The Tsar would be dead and Paris razed to the ground, because the Russians would burn everything. That would be vengeance indeed against the two people responsible for the burning of Moscow. Because even if that's not what Alexander wanted, he was the one who set in train the events that led to that catastrophe. Everything began in Moscow, everything was to finish in Paris. Ever since the disaster of the retreat from Moscow, Charles de Varencourt guessed that, sooner or later, the Empire would collapse. So he came here and worked out his plan while little by little the Tsar and the other crowned heads of Europe closed in on France, dreaming of their triumphal entry into Paris, just as we have paraded through Vienna, Berlin, Madrid, Moscow . . . He progressively adapted his plan to events and opportunities . . . Since his life had been destroyed he was obsessed with fire. Fire and gambling. Gambling was the only thing that could distract him from fire. Thanks to gambling he was able to experience vivid emotions, he told me as much. Gambling temporarily filled the void in his life and kept fire at bay for a few hours . . . Only Catherine de Saltonges might have been able to prevent all this. With her Varencourt almost succeeded in rebuilding his life one more time. One day she found the damaged button and eventually he told her the whole story. But unfortunately she did not succeed in laying the ghost of her lover's past.'

Lefine was speechless.

'Where is the Tsar?' Margont asked him.

'Well, he passed in front of us more than three hours ago . . .'

'If I'm right, Charles de Varencourt will try to put his plan into action now. It's exactly the right moment. All the Allies will still be reeling from yesterday's fighting . . . We have to warn the Tsar!'

CHAPTER 45

VARENCOURT left his cramped living quarters. He had expected the streets to be empty but, on the contary, there were masses of people around. The Parisians wanted to see the Allied soldiers up close. People looked at him in alarm and civilians gave him a wide berth as though his face were ravaged by leprosy. It was because he was wearing the uniform of a lieutenant-colonel in the National Guard and that made him a target. He had obtained the uniform by brazenly bursting into a military outfitter's and showing them the letter from Joseph. He had received what he needed in less than two hours.

He walked with the calm assurance of someone who has nothing left to lose since he would be dead in a short while. He was putting into action the last stage of the plan he had been hatching for months; he was showing his final hand.

He could hear the marching of many boots, and the pounding of hoofs. Obviously a large troop. The Allies were deploying all over Paris.

Varencourt drew attention to himself, raising his arms high, with Joseph's letter in one hand and, in the other, a piece of white material. He was unarmed. In the avenue an impeccable column of Prussian and Russian infantry filed past, and also passing at that moment were some Russian riflemen in their black gaiters, dark-green coats and breeches and black-plumed shakos. The demonstration by the 'French officer' caused incredible confusion. Some of the infantry turned their heads but continued to march, as if they could not believe what they were seeing; others broke ranks to encircle Charles de Varencourt, their weapons trained on him; two captains came over with sabres drawn; their riflemen fanned out into the streets, causing passing Parisians to scatter like pigeons taking flight.

'I'm a messenger! I'm unarmed!' Varencourt explained composedly in Russian.

Had anyone fired, Varencourt would have been killed instantly. But he wasn't worried about that. He was already a dead man – he had nothing to fear from death. Quite the reverse, deep inside he was jubilant, like a mathematician who is finally able to test the equation he has spent months formulating.

But no shot rang out. After all, the Frenchman was brandishing a white flag and did not appear hostile. Besides, he was obviously a high-ranking officer and anyone who shot him would have to answer to his superiors. And he spoke Russian – like a native!

A major from the infantry came to plant his standard in front of Varencourt, who said, still in Russian: 'I am Lieutenant-Colonel Margont. The King of Spain, Joseph I, brother of our Emperor Napoleon I, has charged me with a mission. I must see the Tsar immediately.'

He held out the letter. The major nodded towards a captain, who rode over, plucked the document from Varencourt's hands and proceeded to read it and then translate it for his superior.

'You speak good Russian,' remarked the captain.

'I was part of the Russian campaign. I took advantage of that to learn the rudiments of your language.'

Those words alone, 'the Russian campaign', were enough to infuriate the Russians. And that was what Varencourt was aiming at. These soldiers did not know it, but they were the first little blades of grass that he was setting light to. It was too early for the blaze to take hold, but soon, very soon . . .

'Why do you want to see the Tsar?' demanded the captain.

'My mission is absolutely confidential. Joseph's orders are for me to explain it to the Tsar in person.'

A colonel came over with his regimental chief of staff. What was all this? His entire column was being held up by a single Frenchman? He began to berate the major; the captain was still interrogating Varencourt whilst trying to answer the colonel's questions . . . The more the Russians tried to show that they were in control of the situation, the more obvious it became that they didn't know what to do.

'It doesn't say anywhere in this letter from Joseph that you are to speak to the Tsar,' objected the captain.

'Of course not! How could it?'

The Russian officers frowned. Varencourt was giving them mixed messages and they were not sure if they should take him seriously. Since the Frenchman spoke Russian, the colonel addressed him directly.

'Does your message come from Joseph Bonaparte or from Napoleon himself?'

Varencourt was overjoyed, but he did not let it show. Had they not asked him that question he would somehow have had to lead them to ask it.

'My message comes from our Emperor who passed it on to Joseph, who in turn charged me with communicating it to the

Tsar. But I can't say any more! All that you need to know is that I am acting on the orders of Napoleon I! You can search me to make sure I am unarmed, then take me to the Tsar. I am acting on the written orders of someone who is much more senior than you are. None of you has the necessary authority to prevent me from speaking to His Imperial Majesty Alexander I. Only the Tsar can decide if he will refuse to see me.'

The few months he had served in the Russian army before deserting had educated him in how rigidly Russian soldiers interpreted matters of hierarchy. The colonel nodded and the infantry major gave the order for him.

'Search him!'

Two riflemen did so, then a captain searched him again very carefully. Finally the colonel spoke quite slowly in Russian.

'I'm giving you one last chance. If you admit that you have fooled us, I give you my word as an officer that I will let you go free. On condition that you return to wherever you sprang from.'

'I am on a mission at the order of the Emperor and the King of Spain. I must speak to the Tsar.'

The colonel gave instructions to the major, who led a group of about fifty riflemen to escort Varencourt to Alexander I.

Margont was interrogating the passers-by. 'Do you know where the Tsar is?'

People laughed at him or insulted him – no one knew anything. He hesitated to ask the Allied soldiers, for fear of arousing their suspicions. For want of a better idea, he headed towards the Tuileries Palace. In Moscow, Napoleon had taken up residence in the Kremlin, so Margont hoped that Alexander would follow the same logic.

'Where is the Tsar?' he persisted.

He finally found someone who could tell him. 'He's just installed himself in a magnificent town house on Rue Saint-Florentin, at the home of the greatest traitor of all time, who, of course, welcomed him, bowing and scraping, with open arms: Monsieur de Talleyrand!'

This was so unexpected that Margont thought he had misheard. Even Lefine couldn't believe his ears.

'You're making fun of us, Monsieur . . .'

'No, it's Talleyrand who's made a fool of all of us. All the imperial dignitaries have left Paris – except for him! And has he been thrown in prison, or at least detained under armed guard? Not a bit of it. No, I can assure you, he is at home receiving the Tsar, as we speak! I followed Alexander after his procession down the Champs-Élysées until his soldiers barred my way, and I can definitively tell you that he is at Talleyrand's house. I saw him going in from afar.'

Rue Saint-Florentin crossed Rue de Rivoli. As it happened, it was near the Tuileries. Margont began to run, with Lefine hard on his heels.

Varencourt and his escort first headed towards the Élysée Palace.

But on the way the major hailed one of the Tsar's aides-de-camp just to confirm that the Tsar was actually there. 'He's not,' the aide-de-camp replied. Before the fall of Paris, the Tsar had indeed planned to reside at the Élysée Palace. But as soon as they had entered Paris, the sovereign Allies had been greeted by Talleyrand.

'Talleyrand? Why didn't he flee Paris? Isn't he one of the highest dignitaries of the French Empire?' queried the major in surprise.

'Rats don't leave a ship that's afloat for one that's about to sink!' replied the aide-de-camp, laughing.

The Prince de Bénévent had told Alexander that Napoleon had given the order that the capital must not fall into enemy hands intact. He had warned the Tsar to be extremely careful: it was possible that the sappers of the Imperial Guard had mined the Élysée and the Tsar wouldn't want to take any unnecessary risks . . . And the Tuileries Palace? Probably also mined, Talleyrand shouldn't wonder. He had then added that there was only one place worthy of receiving a tsar, which could be declared categorically safe: his own house. That was how the Tsar ended up residing in Rue Saint-Florentin in the company of Talleyrand himself.

'At Talleyrand's house . . .' repeated the major to make sure he had correctly understood.

Varencourt was horrified: Talleyrand might know the real Margont! He made an effort to stay calm. He had spent months perfecting his plan but he could never have foreseen a problem like this. That Talleyrand! What a turncoat! The devil himself, the real one, would barely have acted with such brass neck. Well, too bad. His plan was a bit risky – like all games of cards

. . . At this very moment Alexander must be completely taken up with savouring his victory. 'Savour all you like, but your pleasure will be short-lived . . .'

Although Varencourt was being closely watched by several riflemen, élite troops, none of them was aware of his agitation. His face remained impassive.

Exhausted and out of breath, Margont was having increasing difficulty running. His lungs and throat were burning. As soon as he noticed enemy soldiers he forced himself to walk – he did not want to draw attention to himself. He tried to catch his breath, watching a regiment of Austrians as they marched by, in their gleaming white, on their way to one of the strategic points in Paris.

The Élysée Palace was surrounded by Allied troops, and they could be seen in even greater number in front of the Tuileries. It was clear to Margont that their most direct route was barred. He looped round towards the Madeleine Church. They were almost there! Almost!

'Messieurs! Messieurs! Stop!' yelled a voice that Margont was determined to ignore.

Lefine, noticing the Prussian soldiers aiming at them, grabbed Margont by the collar to bring him to a stop.

The major spoke to a captain; another captain came over; and then an aide-de-camp. Joseph's letter was passed from hand to hand. The captain in charge of the guard post raised his arm to summon his interpreter because he didn't believe the major's explanations, which annoyed the major. Varencourt betrayed no emotion. He had imagined this scene maybe a thousand times and now, exhilaratingly, it was unfolding exactly as expected! He was being asked all the anticipated questions and giving all his prepared answers. From both sides of Rue de Rivoli, Russian chasseurs were watching the mysterious Frenchman who dared to flaunt his uniform. Exhausted by the fighting, they were sitting in the shade of the arcades, covering the area like a blanket of dark-green ivy. Suddenly those who were watching Varencourt rose and stood to attention, and all the others followed suit, standing up hastily and coming into line, presenting arms. Officers barked orders to hurry them into position. A general from the Russian Guard came striding furiously over, followed closely by a posse of heavily decorated officers. His arrival sowed fear amongst the soldiers. Varencourt pretended to watch him with interest. But really he was looking beyond him to the Prince de Bénévent's house.

'The Tsar's life is in danger! I must speak to the Tsar at once!' Margont was shouting at the top of his voice in German.

The Prussians stared at him contemptuously. A captain asked him, 'And who are you to want to save the Tsar?'

Margont wasn't sure what to say. Should he say he was a lieutenant-colonel? Or would that get him into trouble? He could claim that he also had a letter from Joseph, but they would laugh in his face . . .

'Listen, tell the men guarding the Tsar that someone is trying to assassinate Alexander—'

'His Imperial Majesty Tsar Alexander I!' corrected the officer witheringly.

'The Tsar is about to be assassinated!'

The captain's expression hardened. 'Do you know how many men my battalion lost today? Eighteen. And we've as many injured. So I would advise you to worry about your own safety rather than the Tsar's. We've received strict orders to treat the civilian population respectfully. But you and your friend are of an age to serve in the army. And you don't get a scar of the kind you have on your left cheek by milking cows. I don't think the order to respect civilians extends to soldiers in civilian clothes. So beat it or you might regret it.'

Margont and Lefine melted into the crowd and made their way through the streets to another guard post. This time, however, Margont had chosen a post guarded by Russian soldiers.

The general of the Russian Guard had had the situation explained to him. He read Joseph's letter and immediately tried to get to the bottom of what Varencourt wanted.

'The letter seems to be authentic. But I can't let you pass unless you tell me more about it.'

His French was impeccable, but Charles de Varencourt replied in the guardsman's own language so that as many Russians as possible could understand what he was saying. Every Russian who heard was a little piece of kindling that Varencourt was trying to ignite to become the sparks of his grand inferno. He was shouting angrily, although his anger was just pretence. This was all a game, a hand of cards, his last, his best! And the stake was Paris and every Parisian!

'I've had enough of this! I've repeated myself over and over again! I'm Lieutenant-Colonel Margont and I'm acting on the orders of the Emperor! His Majesty Napoleon I asked his brother Joseph I of Spain to entrust a loyal man with a secret mission. I have the honour of having been chosen for that mission. I will not say any more to a mere general! My orders are to explain myself only to the Tsar himself!'

Russian generals were not used to being spoken to in that disrespectful way. And this one even less than most, to judge by the speed with which all the soldiers around them had jumped to attention and to present arms when he had appeared. Varencourt had noticed that and was making the most of it. He thought he would be more effective if he acted in an arrogant way rather than being servile, courteous and diplomatic. And he had achieved his first objective: the general was furious. He pointed at something off to the side with his white-gloved hand – Varencourt did not even deign to turn to see what it was – and threatened, 'You see that hanging lantern there? I'm going to have it removed and have you strung up by its cord. You will dangle there, your tongue poking from your mouth, under one of the arcades of the beautiful Rue de Rivoli.'

'When your Tsar hears of it, he'll hang you from the next lamppost along.'

It took the general a few seconds to control his rage. Then he gave the order to the sentries: 'Take him to the Tsar!'

The riflemen were not allowed to go with them. Only

soldiers of the Russian or Prussian Guard and aides-de-camp were allowed beyond the guard post.

Margont was refusing to give up; he kept repeating himself to the captain in charge. Sometimes he spoke French, sometimes halting Russian. He wanted someone to go and warn the Tsar and to tell Monsieur Talleyrand that a certain Margont was asking to see him immediately. He raised his voice, he shouted. It was giving the captain a headache. Finally – finally! – after searching him, the officer reached a decision.

'I'm going to see what my major thinks.'

Soldiers and musicians of the Russian and Prussian Guards were lined up on either side of the entrance to Talleyrand's house. This guard of honour pointedly ignored Varencourt as he entered the house. He was so close to achieving his aim . . .

He was parked in a waiting room. The captain ordered ten soldiers of the Guard to watch over him. He was searched one more time. He obediently removed his boots and his coat.

An officer arrived and all the soldiers saluted.

'I am Major Lyzki. I am the one who will decide whether your request will be submitted to the Tsar or not. You're going to have to give me more information. And you'd better not threaten to have me hung from an arcade in Rue de Rivoli . . .'

Although Lyzki had spoken in French, again Varencourt replied in Russian: 'All right. But if you prefer we can speak Russian. I took part in the Russian campaign and I had time to learn a little of your language in Moscow . . .'

Russian campaign. Moscow. Each word was a spark.

'I was at Borodino,' he added confidentially. And immediately he bit his tongue; he should have said 'Moscow', not 'Borodino'! To the French it was 'Moscow', to the Russians, 'Borodino'. He had indeed been at the battle, but as a doctor in the Moscow militia, which was why he was used to saying 'Borodino'. To deflect Lyzki's attention, he went on: 'One of our greatest victories!'

The phrase had its effect. The Russian soldiers were ready to leap on him – they considered it a Russian victory. Or it would have been their victory had they stayed on to fight and not retreated! In their view, and in accordance with Russian propaganda, it was a Russian victory that had been 'spoilt' by the impetuous order to retreat given by staff officers lacking sufficient determination. Lyzki, however, kept his cool.

'So you lived through the retreat from Moscow. Also one of your greatest victories?'

That was a clever response. But in this game of chess, Lyzki had made the wrong move. He had taken a pawn without realising that he could have had checkmate had he not passed over the word 'Borodino'.

Varencourt reiterated once again that he was acting on Napoleon's orders. He then continued, but in French, as though to acknowledge that he felt more at ease in that language.

'A few days ago His Majesty Joseph I charged me with investigating all the royalist organisations in the capital. I was also meant to be looking for Count Kevlokine, a close associate of your Tsar, in fact his principal agent here in Paris.'

Lyzki started to look concerned. 'I know Count Kevlokine well. Continue.'

'The count has been murdered. And what's worse, he was tortured. His hands and arms were burnt.'

'We know that.'

Varencourt had been banking on Alexander knowing this. The Tsar must either have been told about his friend's death by Russian agents, or by informers at the heart of the French police. Or else he had asked people to find out about it, as soon as he had entered Paris.

'Well, it so happens that after a complicated investigation I managed to identify the murderer.'

Major Lyzki had now completely abandoned his nonchalant demeanour.

'What's his name?' he demanded.

'His identity is somewhat problematic. That's why I can speak only to the Tsar himself.'

'I don't understand. You say that you are on a mission for your Emperor, then you speak of an investigation . . .'

'I'm not saying any more! I value my life! Before I reveal anything I want the Tsar's personal assurance that he will protect me.'

Lyzki was very perplexed. What could the man mean? That Napoleon had ordered the murder and torture of Count Kevlokine? Or that Joseph had? Or did he mean, on the contrary, that it was someone close to Louis XVIII who had given the order, which was why the man was so scared and why Napoleon was demanding that the information be passed to the Tsar?

'You certainly seem to be in possession of a good deal of knowledge. But there's one thing I don't understand, Lieutenant-Colonel Margont. Why are you taking all these risks? What's your interest in all this?'

'I value justice above everything else, even my life. It comes from my philanthropy, which is a quality that's hard to bear, I can assure you. But that's the way it is. The Revolution changed my life and gave me my love of liberty. And there can be no liberty without justice. It's hard to explain. I find it difficult to express my determination in words, but I can assure you, it's relentless. I will carry my investigation through to the bitter end, even if there is nothing in it for me and I lose everything because of it.'

That was the reply Margont had given Varencourt the day he asked him whether he would go on with his investigation if Paris fell to the Allies. Varencourt reproduced Margont's sentiment almost word for word, trying to use the same gestures and expression. The card he played at that moment had been lifted directly from Margont's hand . . .

'I'll inform the Tsar of your request,' announced Lyzki as he left the room, holding Joseph's letter.

The major led Margont to his colonel, who was to be found in Place Vendôme. The square was heaving with soldiers – white-clad Austrians, azure Prussian dragoons banded with white belts, blue Prussian infantry, scarlet Cossacks of the Guard . . . A long cord had been attached to the statue of Napoleon dressed as a Roman emperor, which stood atop the column at the centre of the square, and the infantry of ten countries were pulling and pulling to bring it down. Extraordinarily, the statue held firm on its base, a lone figure amidst a horde of adversaries.

The colonel in charge was most displeased to be interrupted. They were spoiling the spectacle! Instead of answering the major, he spoke to one of his captains.

'Find an artillery regiment and tell them to put all the gunpowder they can lay their hands on at the foot of the column!'

The captain was aghast. He had no choice but to obey. But they had all been given orders to be respectful to the Parisians and here was his colonel wanting to blow up the Place Vendôme. With so much gunpowder that the debris would rain down on the Louvre, the Tuileries, the head of the Tsar . . .

'That column's made out of our cannons!' fumed the colonel. 'The cannons we lost at Austerlitz, which they melted down!'

Then he came to his senses and rescinded his order. What? What now? Someone wanted to kill the Tsar? They should go and discuss that with those in charge of protecting His Imperial Majesty. As Margont was rejoicing at this command, finally feeling that it would be possible to get to Rue de Rivoli, the colonel went off towards the column. He was jolly well going to pull on that cord himself, and make his staff officers do the same.

Varencourt was still in the waiting room. Were they keeping him waiting on purpose? Or was Lyzki afraid to disturb the Tsar while he was in the middle of discussing the future of

France and Russia? That was life: you tried to plan what you would be doing in one, two, five or ten years, not knowing that actually you were living your last ten minutes . . .

From Place Vendôme, Margont and Lefine went down Rue de Castiglione and were stopped by some chasseurs of the Russian Guard at the entrance to Rue de Rivoli. Unfortunately this was not the way Varencourt had come, so these soldiers, who only dealt with their street and paid no attention to the continual comings and goings on Rue de Rivoli, knew nothing about any Frenchman asking to see the Tsar.

Margont explained as best he could to a captain sporting a bloodstained bandage on his forehead. Several of his men had also been wounded in the taking of Buttes-Chaumont.

'No one is going to kill the Tsar,' the captain said decisively, once Margont had finished.

Napoleon had renamed the streets running off Rue de Rivoli after his victories, in a bid to make the area more popular. It was at Castiglione, near Mantoue, that Napoleon had beaten the Austrians under Würmser. Three Russian chasseurs were engaged in using their bayonets to try to prise off the stone plaque engraved with the name Castiglione, and the captain was more interested in that activity than in the ramblings of this Frenchman.

Lefine was patting Margont on the back with one hand to calm him, whilst with the other he was restraining him by the sleeve. He knew his friend was perfectly capable of trying to storm through the Russian Guard!

Margont changed tactic. 'Listen, ask Monsieur de Talleyrand to come here. He knows me and will confirm that you should take what I have to say seriously.'

The captain started to lose patience.

Margont added: 'It was only two days ago that Monsieur de Talleyrand was obeying Napoleon and standing shoulder to shoulder with Joseph. He helped organise the defence of Paris. It's partly his fault you're wounded. So it's fair enough to go and disturb him!'

That seemed to appeal to the captain. He had still not come to terms with the fact that Talleyrand, a dignitary of the Empire, had not been thrown in prison. Far from it – the Prince de Bénévent was taking tea with the Tsar!

'All right,' he replied. 'I'll try. Not for you, for my own personal satisfaction. But if you're lying to me I'll have you executed on the spot – your friend too. I have the power to do that. Do you understand me?'

'I understand.'

In the captain's mind, disturbing Talleyrand was the equivalent of removing at one stroke all the street signs in Paris commemorating imperial victories. He gave the order to a lieutenant, who immediately ran off. Margont's Russian was rudimentary. He thought he had grasped what the officer had said but . . . no . . . he must have misunderstood . . . surely . . .

'Could you tell me in French what you just told the lieutenant?' he asked.

The captain looked disgusted as he said, 'I told the lieutenant, "Go and find Monsieur de Talleyrand and tell him that he is requested to present himself at our guard post to deal with a matter of extreme gravity concerning the Tsar. A certain Lieutenant-Colonel Margont is asking to see him. Do your utmost to ensure that the head of the Provisional French Government attends in person." '

'The head of the Provisional French Government?' repeated Margont.

'Yes. Incredible, isn't it?'

Major Lyzki finally reappeared and gave Varencourt back the letter signed by Joseph. He said respectfully, 'Your letter is authentic, we've compared it with other documents we have from Joseph Bonaparte. Now, normally any imperial spokesman would have to be received by representatives of all the Allied countries—'

'There isn't time for that!' exclaimed Varencourt. 'My mission is extremely urgent!'

Lyzki raised his hand to interrupt. 'But in this particular case, we are dealing with a matter personal to the Tsar because he was a close friend of Count Kevlokine. Our Imperial Majesty has therefore agreed to receive you on his own. If you would just follow me . . .'

'You're so right when you say this is personal to the Tsar.'

Margont's heart leapt: Talleyrand was on his way! But when the Prince de Bénévent saw Margont, his face fell. The Russian officer had been most insistent that Talleyrand should go to Rue de Castiglione about 'an extremely grave matter' . . . 'the Tsar'

. . . 'a lieutenant-colonel in civilian clothes' wanted to see him 'in person'. As the officer was merely passing on a message from another officer who had received it from an intermediary, Margont's name and other snippets of information had been lost along the way. Talleyrand had not grasped who wanted to see him or why. He assumed it was some kind of misunderstanding or a madman come to make trouble at the guard post. But since the Russians had insisted that he come, he had agreed, since he felt it was important to maintain good relations with the Tsar's guards.

The Prince de Bénévent had accepted it as another little humiliation inflicted on him by the victors. There were many such indignities. Some of the Allied officers treated him with icy scorn; soldiers stared at him mockingly, as if he were a fairground monkey performing a clever trick; certain of the Tsar's advisers had suggested that he drive Talleyrand from the house – his house! Oh, he had seen it all before. When you operated at his exalted level, it came with the territory. Napoleon had referred to him as 'shit in silk stockings', he had been nicknamed the 'limping devil', the great writer Chateaubriand had said, 'The only time Talleyrand is not conspiring is when he's wheeling and dealing.' It had not occurred to him that the lieutenant-colonel would be Margont. He was completely absorbed in trying to consolidate his highly precarious position and manoeuvring the Allies into reinstating the French monarchy with Louis XVIII as king instead of Bernadotte. He had managed to convince some of the Allies that he spoke for France, and had promised Alexander that tomorrow he would ensure that the Senate confirmed him as president of the Provisional French Government. The Tsar was now closeted in one of Talleyrand's finest salons at the head of a new council of war and Talleyrand was anxious to use every spare moment to win over as many senators as possible to his cause. But now that damned Margont had appeared like a ghost from the past . . .

Talleyrand wore the expression of a prostitute who sees her republican lover of the day before pop up just as she is about to marry the Tsar with great pomp and ceremony.

'Monsieur de Talleyrand, it's not Napoleon Charles de Varencourt is planning to assassinate, it's the Tsar! He wants—'

But the Prince de Bénévent had turned towards the captain in charge of the guard post. 'I've never seen this man before.'

The officer had really wanted to believe that Margont knew Talleyrand, even if he hadn't believed the rest of his story. But Margont had dared to make a fool of him, and he would pay dearly for that! Talleyrand was already leaving.

'You're signing my death warrant!' Margont shouted at him.

Two chasseurs grabbed him roughly and Lefine found himself similarly restrained.

'The Tsar's about to be assassinated!' yelled Margont. 'And he'll be assassinated in *your house*! The Russians will think you're an accomplice!'

Talleyrand turned round. 'Wait a minute! Perhaps I will listen to this man. You never know . . .'

Varencourt followed Major Lyzki across a corridor, through a little sitting room, down another corridor . . . Two soldiers of the Guard came to attention as the major passed. Four infantrymen brought up the rear of the little convoy.

They came to a small room decorated in the imperial style, with many Greco-Roman touches that were more or less authentic. Two grenadiers of the Pavlovski regiment, in mitred caps, guarded double doors at the back of the room. Varencourt calculated his chances. If Talleyrand were with the Tsar, he would fling himself on Alexander, relying on speed and the element of surprise. If Talleyrand were not in the room, he would take time to get as near as possible before making his attack. And he was sure that Talleyrand would not be there! The Tsar believed he was Napoleon's emissary so he would take care to receive him without Talleyrand.

The doors opened. Lyzki let him pass and withdrew.

Varencourt advanced into the room, bowed, then advanced further until a general indicated that he should stop. No sign of Talleyrand!

The Tsar was ensconced in the great hall, the hall of the Eagle, in the company of about twenty men. There was Barclay de Tolly, the commander-in-chief of the Russian army, and generals of the infantry of the line and of the Guard, including the much-decorated Langeron and Raevski. Also present was General Prince Repnine-Volkonski, the Tsar's chief of general staff, who had led the charge of the Chevalier Guard at the Battle of Austerlitz – a charge that even Napoleon had admired. The illustrious company was completed by two Cossack officers of the Guard in scarlet coats, a colonel of the dragoons and one from the cuirassiers, and a few aides-de-camp, one of whom was Colonel Prince Orlov who had negotiated the surrender of Paris.

Varencourt considered all these exalted Russians who were staring at him, and some of whom he knew by reputation. Certainly a tsar of all the Russias could not know each of his subjects individually. What did a tsar care about a certain Ksenia de Varencourt, who had died in September 1812, just before she should have given birth? No! Tsars spoke of colonising Siberia, of wanting to absorb Poland, of Norway, which the Allies had taken from the pro-French Danes to give to the Swedes in order to encourage them to cede Finland to the Russians, of the problem posed by the Austrian Empire . . . Just as astronomers observe planets and galaxies and don't waste their time counting specks of dust . . . And yet a speck of dust could kill a tsar and annihilate Paris and its six hundred thousand inhabitants. All these 'great men' were as straw for his joyous blaze! Yes, he was going to offer his darling wife the most gigantic funeral pyre!

In an armchair a mere ten feet away sat the Tsar, magnificent in his white Chevalier Guard uniform, his chest glittering with medals and decorated with the blue ribbon of the order of Saint-André. He had dressed up for his moment of triumph. In fifty years no one would remember his three predecessors, nor probably his three successors. But everyone would remember Alexander I, the Tsar who had vanquished Napoleon. Varencourt reflected that the most glorious day of the Tsar's life would also be his last.

He began to speak. The Tsar frowned.

An aide-de-camp, who stood beside Alexander, declared: 'Speak up, Lieutenant-Colonel. We can hardly hear you!'

Varencourt took a step forward like someone doing his best to make himself understood. The four soldiers behind him similarly moved forward. He went on with what he was saying, deliberately obfuscating and embellishing his story. But much of what he said was nevertheless true, and his audience, although they were suspicious, did try to untangle the threads of his complicated account involving Joseph, Napoleon, Talleyrand, the Swords of the King, fire . . .

'We can barely make out what you are saying, Lieutenant-Colonel,' said the Tsar irritably.

Varencourt brought his left hand up to his throat while with the right he took hold of the broken brooch he'd found in the ruins of his Muscovite home. It was a card sharp who'd taught him how to distract attention with one hand whilst taking out a card hidden in his sleeve with the other. The officers thought the Frenchman had a neck wound, or had inhaled burning smoke during the fighting, or else was suffering from a sore throat and that was why his voice was so hard to hear. No one saw the jewel, or if they did, they paid it no heed. Varencourt took another step forward.

The aide-de-camp on the Tsar's right reacted sharply and was about to order him to step back, but Varencourt pre-empted him by saying quickly: 'I know the murderer's name but first I want my security guaranteed by Your Imperial Majesty!'

The Tsar frowned. What was going on here? Who was implicated? Was Napoleon the instigator of the crime or was this another of his tricks to divide the coalition by making it look as if one of the Allies were behind the murder of Count Kevlokine? The Frenchman was trying to explain something but he was so hard to follow . . . Varencourt took another step forward, brandishing Joseph's letter in his left hand. He looked worried as he begged the Tsar to promise on his honour, with his staff officers as witnesses, to guarantee his protection if he revealed . . . It seemed to him as if the brooch were beating; he imagined it was his wife's heart he held in his hand . . .

Margont, Lefine and Talleyrand entered the house. Margont was like a madman. He interrogated the infantrymen, who stared at him angrily.

When Major Lyzki came over to deal with this new, noisy intruder, Margont yelled at him, 'You have to warn the Tsar!'

'Don't shout, Monsieur. Who are you?'

'I'm Lieutenant-Colonel Margont. Listen, a man—'

Lyzki gave a nervous laugh. 'Lieutenant-Colonel Margont? But I've just shown him in to see His Imperial Majesty . . .'

Talleyrand panicked. 'I assure you that this is the real Lieutenant-Colonel Margont!'

Lyzki had already spun on his heel and was making for the stairs, shouting in Russian: 'Protect the Tsar!' Soldiers hurried to run after him. Talleyrand, who was not going as fast, was knocked against a wall by a passing grenadier. Upstairs, soldiers took up Lyzki's rallying cry as they began to run. An infantryman grabbed his rifle and used it to bar Margont with all his force against a door to prevent him from going any further.

The din in the corridors reached the great hall. The officers in the hall heard shouts and could make out the odd word: 'Tsar', 'danger', but they assumed the danger was external –

was Napoleon daring to attack Paris to dislodge them? Was there a popular uprising? A second Revolution? An attack by a few desperate imperial soldiers who'd remained in the capital? Only Varencourt understood that he had been found out. It was a little premature, it would have been better if he had been a couple of steps further forward, but too bad! The double doors flew open and he took advantage of the confusion to try to pounce on Alexander. The aide-de-camp's eyes had never left Varencourt and he threw himself forward to bar his passage.

The Tsar didn't understand what was happening. He saw Avilovich grab the Frenchman, who was trying to run towards him. But for some unexplained reason, his aide-de-camp suddenly shuddered and collapsed. A guard who had followed Varencourt managed to seize him by the arm, but was pushed back as the Frenchman toppled backwards as if he were losing consciousness. Some of the generals reacted by unsheathing their sabres, but a quick-witted red-clad Cossack beat them to it and jumped on the assailant, holding him round the waist before he also let go and fell to the ground. Varencourt shouted 'Ksenia!' and flung himself on the Tsar, plunging the pin of the brooch into the monarch's thigh. A bayonet sliced through Varencourt's shoulder and a rifle butt rammed into his neck; guards began to rain kicks on his inert body.

The Tsar, dazed with shock and terror, contemplated the broken brooch, blackened by grime or rather soot, that was protruding from his thigh. He pulled it out angrily as if he were chasing away a wasp that had just stung him. Nothing happened. The needle had exhausted its poison.

EPILOGUE

As soon as Napoleon was informed that Paris had fallen to the enemy, he was all for launching an attack on the capital. He wanted to trap the Allies, taking them by surprise and crushing them between his incoming army and an armed uprising of the Parisians. His marshals dissuaded him from this, however, convincing him that it was all over and that his best course was to abdicate.

Talleyrand succeeded in getting the Senate to confirm officially his role as president of the Provisional French Government. He also used all his wiles to persuade the Allies to restore power to the French monarchy in the person of Louis XVIII. Talleyrand thus entered the service of the King of France.

The Allies occupied Paris. Contrary to the fears of the Parisians, they neither pillaged the city nor maltreated its citizens. They behaved honourably and did not even destroy the buildings that Napoleon had constructed.

Alexander I made Margont a chevalier of the order of Saint-André as a reward for saving his life. Margont was also somewhat surprised to be decorated by . . . the King of France. Louis XVIII himself pinned on the '*décoration du lys*'. As he did so Margont felt a pain in his chest and thought that the King had accidentally pricked him. Later he realised that his impression had been mistaken! Immediately after his decoration he learnt that he was being retired from the army. Napoleon had built France a gigantic army that was no longer needed now that peace had been signed. A hundred infantry regiments and thirty-eight cavalry regiments were suppressed. This had little effect on common soldiers, since with the departure of all conscripts the number of servicemen was already greatly reduced. But thousands of officers had to abandon their commands, to be replaced by royalist officers from before the Revolution or by aristocratic émigrés now returned and keen for a military career. The King took advantage of the suppression of regiments to rid himself of republicans and supporters of Napoleon. To save money, and out of a spirit of vengeance, those officers leaving active service were given only half their pension, which in most cases was not sufficient to live off. Margont, Lefine, Jean-Quenin Brémond and Piquebois all found themselves on half-pension. Saber had survived his injuries and had been taken prisoner by the Russians. As Marshal Marmont's order had been duly transcribed, and as Napoleon would certainly have confirmed the promotion had he had the chance, Saber was, in a way, the 'dead' general of a dead empire. The new authorities remedied the anomaly: he became a retired colonel. On half-pension, of course.

In spite of his requests, Margont did not succeed in persuading the Russians to give him the curare that had been found on Varencourt.

Neither did Margont pursue his old dream of launching a newspaper. He judged that the new regime would not be receptive to free-thinking journalists. And as he wasn't a man who could live without a passion, he found another one! He threw himself into studying medicine, to Jean-Quenin's great joy. He went as often as he could to the Salpêtrière where Pinel welcomed him with open arms.

Varencourt also survived his injuries. The Tsar decided to spare him and had him sent to a prisoner-of-war camp in Siberia where, thanks to his medical knowledge, he was relatively well treated. He was pardoned twenty-two years later by Alexander's successor, Nicholas I. Varencourt stayed in Siberia, where he finally managed to rebuild a satisfactory life.

Vicomte de Leaume and the other survivors of his organisation were not rewarded by Louis XVIII, because the new authorities did not want to be seen to be associated with anyone linked to the man who had murdered an imperial dignitary and who had almost – perhaps involuntarily – caused the death of the Tsar. Disgusted, Louis de Leaume went to try his luck in the New World. By the time he disembarked in Louisiana, he had already formulated ambitious new projects.

Catherine de Saltonges had always been opposed to any of the group's plans involving violence. Louis de Leaume confirmed this and she was allowed to remain in Paris, where she eventually remarried.

In return for Baron Honoré de Nolant's betrayal of Louis XVI, he was gaoled by the King and spent the rest of his days behind bars.

It was Claude Bernard, a French physiologist and pupil of Magendie, who discovered years later that curare caused neuromuscular paralysis by acting on the nerves. This discovery caused a huge leap forward in understanding the functioning of the nervous system. For that discovery and his other scientific research, Claude Bernard became known as one of the greatest scientists of all time.

After extensive discussion the Allies decided to send Napoleon to the island of Elba. He was made sovereign of Elba and was allowed a small court. A very close watch was kept on him, however. The Emperor spent his time walking, gardening, receiving guests, discussing banalities and managing his ridiculous little empire . . . The rest of Europe was persuaded that this was how he would spend the rest of his days. But in reality, he was counting up Louis XVIII's errors. With each fault committed by the French monarch he felt he was a step nearer to returning to Paris . . .

The 2nd Legion of the National Guard of Paris was in reality commanded by Comte Saint-Jean d'Angély, then by Major Odiot.

The exact location of their barracks is unknown.

But it is known that they did assemble in Place Vendôme.

THE OFFICER'S PREY

The Napoleonic Murders

Armand Cabasson

June 1812. Napoleon begins his invasion of Russia leading the largest army Europe has ever seen.

But amongst the troops of the Grande Armée is a savage murderer whose bloodlust is not satisfied in battle.

When an innocent Polish woman is brutally stabbed, Captain Quentin Margont of the 84th Regiment is put in charge of a secret investigation to unmask the perpetrator. Armed with the sole fact that the killer is an officer, Margont knows that he faces a near-impossible task and the greatest challenge to his military career.

'Combines the suspense of a thriller with the compelling narrative of a war epic' *Le Parisien*

'Cabasson skilfully weaves an intriguing mystery into a rich historical background' *Mail on Sunday*

'. . . an enthralling and unromantic account of Napoleonic war seen from a soldier's perspective' *The Morning Star*

'. . . vivid portrayal of the Grande Armée . . .' *Literary Review*

'Cabasson's atmospheric novel makes a splendid war epic . . .' *Sunday Telegraph*

GALLIC BOOKS

978-1-906040-82-6

£7.99

WOLF HUNT

The Napoleonic Murders

Armand Cabasson

May 1809. The forces of Napoleon's Grande Armée are in Austria. For young Lieutenant Lukas Relmyer it is hard to return to the place where he and fellow orphan Franz were kidnapped four years earlier. Franz was brutally murdered and Lukas has vowed to avenge his death.

When the body of another orphan is found on the battlefield, Captain Quentin Margont and Lukas join forces to track down the wolf who is prowling once more in the forests of Aspern . . .

Winner of the Napoleon Foundation's fiction award 2005

GALLIC BOOKS

978-1-906040-83-3

£7.99

CLISSON AND EUGÉNIE

Napoleon Bonaparte

translated by Peter Hicks with an introduction by Armand Cabasson

'Their eyes met . . . and they soon knew that their hearts were made for each other.'

Triumphant on the field of battle, Clisson turns his back on worldly success. He falls in love and marries Eugénie, but how long will their love survive?

The tragic story of Clisson and Eugénie reveals one of history's great leaders also to be an accomplished writer of fiction.

Written in an eloquently Romantic style true to its period, the story offers the reader a fascinating insight into how the young Napoleon viewed love, women and military life.

Aged 26, and having already known success as a soldier, Napoleon was at something of a low ebb both professionally and personally when he began *Clisson and Eugénie*, and there are undoubted parallels between his own life and their story.

Gallic Books

978-1-906040-27-7

£7.99